His Redemption

Nicole Baker

Copyright © 2025 by Nicole Baker

All rights reserved.

No part of this book may be reproduced in any form or by any electronic or mechanical means, including information storage and retrieval systems, without written permission from the author, except for the use of brief quotations in a book review.

Cover Designer: Shanoff Designs

Editor: Jovana Shirley, Unforeseen Editing, www.unforeseenediting.com

Proofreader: Tiffany Hernandez

 Formatted with Vellum

Chapter One

Jessie

"And now downward facing dog," the yoga instructor says calmly. "Raise your right leg into the air and hold it."

Another dozen or so drops of sweat fall from my forehead to the mat, causing my hands to continue to slip.

The room is dark, but I look at everyone around me, and they seem to be handling the temperature just fine. Even Eva—my best friend, who just happened to have a baby a month ago—doesn't seem to be struggling.

"Can you breathe?" I whisper to her as panic begins to build in my body. "I don't think this is a normal amount of sweat that my body is producing."

"Shh," Eva replies quietly. "It's hot yoga. You're supposed to sweat."

There is no way this is normal. I feel like a lobster just placed in a boiling pot. How long has it been? It's a sixty-minute class, but it must have already been ninety minutes.

I bet the instructor has just lost track of time. I should tell her.

"And let's bring our leg down to the mat and move to our child's pose."

Thank fuck. I nearly fall down to my knees as I let my arms relax above my head. This is not what was advertised on the website, where it boasted about opening your pores, detoxifying your body, and promoting overall well-being.

I fail to see how passing out from a heatstroke promotes anything, except for a medical bill after being transported to the emergency room for severe dehydration.

I drank water before this, but I must have sweat out more than I've drunk in the last month.

Eva and I walk outside to the streets of New York City in the sweltering July heat.

"Ah, I feel so refreshed." Eva smiles. "Wasn't that amazing?"

I side-eye her so hard; if it were possible to sprain your eyeball, it would happen. "Eva, that was literal hell on earth."

"Hell on earth? It wasn't that bad. Maybe you pushed yourself too hard your first time. The instructor said you could always go into child's pose if you needed a break."

We open the door to the café next door to Satan's den. The air-conditioning hits my body like a blanket of sympathy for what I just endured.

"And be the only loser who couldn't keep up? No thank you!"

Eva sighs as we take a seat by the window. "You're too competitive."

I shrug my shoulders. "It works well in my career."

Eva laughs lightly. "I can only imagine what other lawyers must feel when they realize they are going up against you."

"They should feel shame. That means they're representing awful parents who have created an unsafe environment for their children."

I'm a family lawyer for a small firm in the city. I work tirelessly to guarantee children are taken away from abusive or neglectful parents, or a parent is given a safe space with the children, away from their abusive partner.

It's not the highest-paying avenue to take as a lawyer, but it's meaningful. I still make a decent living.

Eva leans her chin on her hand. "I don't know how you do it. Now that I'm a mother, I can't imagine seeing abusive parents for work on the daily. I'd be so jaded."

"It's not easy. There are some days the environment really sucks me into a negative thought cycle. But we aren't here to talk about my job. How's motherhood treating you? It looks good on you."

Sure, she looks tired. The bags under her eyes are a bit more pronounced. She isn't wearing any makeup, and her hair is up in a messy bun. But there's a glow to her. A sense of peace that radiates off her, like she's finally found her purpose.

"It's amazing. Exhausting. Perfect. Tiring."

"That's a whole lot of contradiction." I laugh.

"Motherhood is an entire world of contradictions."

"And Roman? Is he handling it well?"

I swear if red hearts could appear above her head at the mention of his name, there would be hundreds.

"He's the best father. It all seems so natural for him. I catch myself just staring at him and Addie all the time, wondering how I could deserve such a perfect life."

"That's bananas. You, out of anyone I know, deserve it."

I mean it too. Eva is such a kind soul. She has been my best friend since high school. We've known each other since junior high. We've been through a lot together. I love seeing her happily ever after come true. Though it does make me wonder if I'm cursed.

The dating game has not been kind to me. I always seem to attract the dicks. Men—and I'm using that word generously—who seem to have a Peter Pan complex.

"Walker is hilarious with Addie." She laughs behind her coffee cup that the waitress just filled.

My stomach clenches at the mention of her brother.

"You should see him. He holds her for a minute, then panics when she starts fidgeting."

I chuckle slightly, tired of acting indifferent about the man who ruined me. "I can see that. Walker doesn't give off *I'm a natural with baby* vibes."

"Aw, but he's sweet with her. He'll get there. He's never been around babies. I think I was the last one he was around, and he was six."

Eva doesn't know about my history with her brother. To her, it's just a friendly rivalry because we've known each other since I was twelve and he was eighteen.

"I'm so happy for you. Addie is adorable. I miss her already, but I've been so busy all week."

"You don't have to feel bad if you can't come over every week."

"I don't feel bad. I just miss her. I want to snuggle."

It's true. Addie's snuggles are amazing. I love the feeling of her warm head tucked under my chin. I swear my blood pressure instantly drops.

We eat our breakfast quickly so she can get back to Addie to nurse her.

I stroll down the streets of Manhattan as I realize I'm at an impasse in my life.

At twenty-seven, I'm too old to go out and party like I used to. It feels meaningless.

With nothing else to do this afternoon, I walk into the nearest coffee shop and buy my favorite iced coffee with caramel syrup.

I probably shouldn't be drinking all this caffeine after sweating every ounce of fluid in my body, but I need this. I need a distraction from the creeping loneliness that's been plaguing me.

Central Park is only a couple of minutes from me. In lieu of going home, I decide a walk around the park might help. Maybe it'll clear my head, give me some ideas on a good reset.

Maybe I just need a new haircut. Something crazy and daring. Not my current long blonde hair. Bangs maybe?

And just like that, I'm making an appointment on my phone as I sip on my drink. They can't get me in for three weeks, which sucks, but I guess it'll give me time to figure out what I want to do.

Bangs seem fun, but I also get annoyed if I get any hair in my face, so the idea scares me. What if they piss me off all day long?

This is what my life has come to. Obsessing over bangs as I stroll through the park by myself with no sense of direction. I need a change. I just don't know what my next move should be.

Chapter Two

Walker

"Did you hear the rumors?" Pierce asks as I make another cup of coffee in the break room.

I don't even look up, sure he's going to keep talking, like usual.

"There's a class action lawsuit underway against one of the largest pharmaceutical companies in the country."

There he goes again, though I am intrigued by this information.

"What's the number they are coming at them with?" I ask nonchalantly.

We may pretend to be indifferent, but both of us know this could be big bucks.

I grab my cup of coffee and turn around.

Pierce is smirking at me knowingly. "Five hundred million."

Fuck. Winning a case like this could set my reputation for

life. If won, the payout alone would be insane. He knows I want it. I know he wants it.

That is, if Stewart and Henry win over the client. They are the majority-owned partners of the firm. Two men in their sixties, who started this firm thirty years ago.

Pierce and I only have a small amount of equity in the company. We don't get a say in who gets assigned these cases. There are three of us that it would come down to.

Pierce, Cody, and me.

"Let's hope Stewart and Henry bring them in. It'd be a huge win for the company."

"I look forward to seeing who they see fit to take over the case," Pierce eyes me contentiously.

I clap him on the shoulder. "May the best man win."

I know he wants to shrug me off of him, but he stands tall and proud, like we're the best of buds.

It's survival of the fittest up here on the fifty-second floor of Decker and Maxfield. The polished glass walls don't just reflect city lights; they mirror every ambition, every calculated smile, every late-night strategy to climb higher. Associates hover like sharks, sensing weakness, ready to pounce on a dropped client or missed deadline.

Even partners like Pierce and me circle each other, alliances shifting with billable hours and courtroom wins. There are no friends here, only competitors in expensive suits. You either bill like a machine, bringing in million-dollar clients, or get replaced by someone who can.

In this place, loyalty is a myth, and rest is a liability.

I stroll back to my office with a spring in my step and a new objective—find Stewart and Henry to remind them who their best attorney is.

First things first. I need more information on the case that's being brought against them.

I halt at my assistant, Bradly's, desk just outside of my office.

"I need you to look into a possible class action lawsuit being filed against one of the leading pharmaceutical companies based here in the US. See if you can find out which company it is against."

Bradly nods his head. "Sure thing, Mr. Harlow. I'll let you know what I find."

Once inside of my office, I close my door and slide off my jacket. I don't have to be in court today, so it'll be a bit of a slow-paced kind of day.

I stand in front of the floor-to-ceiling window of my office, the city sprawled beneath me like the board of a game I'm determined to win. This case is my shot—the kind of high-profile litigation that could elevate me to a top-tier partner with more equity in the firm. I could be a legend in the industry.

I want it. I need it.

Though this is what I live for, I feel my body coiled too tight. What I need is a good lay. No strings, no morning-after-brunch nonsense—just sweat-slicked skin and a moan that would chase away the stress for a few hours.

I have numbers. Hell, half the women in this building would jump at the chance.

But it could be a distraction. Winning this case is what matters. It's not about the money that would come with it—I have enough money. It's about the power and prestige. This opportunity is exactly what my parents would want. A reason to brag about his son at the club.

Not sure where that came from. I haven't thought much about pleasing my parents in a while. It's been an itch of mine that I've realized is futile. Nothing impresses them or makes them proud. It's just not in their DNA.

None of that matters now. What I need to do is put my head down today and figure out who the company is. I need to find out what connection I have to them to ensure I'm the one they ask for.

* * *

It's been a day. Not only did Bradly figure out the company that is being sued, but he also got the intel that they are, in fact, speaking with us and one other firm. Stewart and Henry must be keeping this under wraps until they know for sure.

That gives me time to figure out how I'm going to convince them that I'm their guy. I've never represented a pharmaceutical company this large, but I have taken on class action lawsuits. Never on this scale before.

I walk down Park Avenue as the sun begins to set in the distance. I'm starving. I opted to skip dinner and work late, preparing for a case I'm trying to settle.

It's nothing new. Working late is part of the job. I'm not paid millions to work forty hours a week.

I pull at the tension on the back of my neck. My body has been starting to hold a lot of stress—more than usual. I just need to run on the treadmill in my gym. It'll help ease some of the muscles.

Whenever I get the time, I want to have a sauna installed in my bathroom. If I'm going to kill myself working, I might as well use some of the money to take the edge off.

I keep my head down as I walk through the lobby of my building. I hate running into some of the tenants. There are women who live in the apartments here that no doubt know I have the penthouse. They like to bat their lashes at me.

I love pussy, but not if they show signs of becoming clingy.

I ride the elevator up to the top floor and unlock my door without regarding my surroundings. Just as I'm about to close the door, I hear someone call my name.

"Walker." The soft voice comes from the hallway.

At first, I think I'm hearing things, but then there's the distinguishable sound of a baby starting to cry.

I open the door to the hall, and a woman I recall spending the night with a while back is bouncing a baby back and forth as tears run down her face.

"She just woke up," she says to me as I try to figure out why on earth she is telling me this like I'm supposed to do something about it.

Her name finally dawns on me. Amelia. A model I fooled around with for a couple of weeks. A cold chill runs the length of my body as I stare at the baby in her arms.

"Amelia," I say with a suddenly dry throat. "What is going on?"

"I can't do this anymore," she cries, barely able to speak. "I thought I was doing the right thing, keeping her, but it's just ... too much."

She takes a step toward me, but instinct has me backing away.

"Amelia, what are you saying?"

Her shoulders fall like she can't believe I'm going to make her say it. Whatever food is in my stomach from lunch begins to swirl around, threatening to come up.

"Walker ... she's yours."

I grab the doorframe as my world flips upside down with two words. *"She's yours."*

"I'm sorry. It's too much. I can't work with her. She's always crying," she rambles on while I begin to sweat even though I feel cold. "Childcare is insane, and nobody wants a baby at a modeling shoot. She's ... she's ruining my life. You have money. Family. She's better off with you."

Before I say a word, she places the baby in my arms. Instead of waiting for the elevator, she pushes the door open and takes off down the stairs.

"Everything you need is in the diaper bag." She shouts her final words at me.

"Amelia," I yell once I find the ability to speak again, but it's too late.

She's gone.

A loud shriek comes from the baby in my arms, and for the first time, I look down at my daughter. I don't know what the hell to do. Instinct takes over, and I start to bounce her up and down like I see Eva do with my niece, but it only makes her cry harder.

"Shh," I say as I look around the hallway.

There's what appears to be a stroller and the diaper bag. I grab the bag, ditching the stroller as I walk back into my place.

I place the bag on my kitchen table. With my one free hand, I look to see what's inside. Diapers, wipes, clothes, empty bottles, and a big can of something. I lift it up and read the front. Formula.

Is she hungry? How do I even feed her this stuff? I open the lid to find a bunch of powder inside. Powder. What am I supposed to do with that?

I try to read the instructions, but nothing is getting through to my brain as her screams become louder. I can't think, can't focus. Her face is now red, and her tiny hands are squeezed into fists, like she might actually punch me if I can't get my shit together and figure out what she needs.

Sweat forms above my brows as my hands begin to tremble. Okay, I can do this.

I take a deep breath and read the can. Two ounces of formula per four ounces of water. What the hell is even an ounce?

I stare at her, then at the can, then at her. She's in complete hysterics now, like she knows she was left with the most incompetent person on the planet.

"I'm sorry," I whisper to her desperately. "I don't know how to be your father."

My heart thunders in my chest. My throat tightens, making it hard to breathe.

I need to call someone. I can't do this alone right now. My parents would freak out if I told them about this. Just another thing to ruin their image.

Eva. My baby sister. She would know what to do. She has one of these of her own. Shit. I can't put this on her. Roman told me she was struggling with adjusting to the lack of sleep, not getting nearly as much as she needs.

This is the last thing I want to put on her.

I open my phone and scroll through my Contacts, all while the screams hit levels I didn't know were possible.

But all I see are clients. Business associates. Friends. Hookups. None of these people will do.

Then I come across *her* number. I only have it because she's my sister's best friend and we connected while Eva was in the emergency room a while back.

But she does know babies—I assume. She must at least know more than I do.

Does she hate me?

Yes.

Does she have reason to?

Yes.

Do I have any other option at this point?

No.

I click on her name, Jessie Turner, and place the phone to my ear. I try to bounce the baby up and down as I walk around the room.

She answers on the third ring. "Walker?"

"Jessie ..." I breathe a sigh of relief. "Thank God you answered."

"What's going on? What's that noise in the background? Is that a baby?"

"Yes. I need your help."

"Is that Addie? Are you at Eva's? Oh my God. Is everything okay? They wouldn't let you babysit, would they?"

I take serious offense to that. Why wouldn't my sister trust me to babysit my niece? Then I look down at my own daughter, wailing in my arms.

"No, Jessie. I'm not watching Addie. I just ..." I struggle to get the words out. "Can you come over?"

There's a moment of silence. I look down at my phone to see if I lost the call.

"Jessie?" I ask desperately.

"I'm here. Sorry. I'm, um ... you want me to come over?"

"I promise I'll explain when you get here. I really need someone. Please. I'm begging you."

"Uh, yeah. Sure."

Instantly, there's a sliver of relief that forms in the pit of my stomach. Though the screaming baby prevents any type of real relief.

"Oh, thank you. Thank you!"

"Sure. Uh, where do you live?"

I don't know why that makes me stop in my tracks. "You don't know where I live?"

She sighs audibly. "No, Walker. Not every woman in the city is obsessed with you. Some of us couldn't care less about things like where you rest your head at night."

"Hilarious. I live on Park Avenue—432. Penthouse on the ninety-first floor. Please," I beg as the baby continues to wail.

I am starting to wonder if something happens to a baby if they cry too long. What if I hurt her?

"Hurry," I add.

"I'm coming, Walker."

The phone goes dead. I throw it on the couch and look down at my daughter. I'm the worst father in history. Not even five minutes with her, and she's hated every second of it. I don't blame her. I wouldn't want to be around me either.

Ten minutes later—the longest ten minutes of my life—a knock at my door has me nearly tripping over my own feet to get to it. I open the door, breathing heavily. Jessie stands in front of me in jean shorts and a yellow tank top.

Even with a screaming baby in my arm, I notice how good she looks. She always does.

"Thank God you're here." I open the door all the way.

She follows me into my place as I lead her to the kitchen where every bottle and its pieces are scattered all over the counter.

"How do you feed a baby formula?" I ask as I grab a handful of items and let them fall back down. "What is all of this stuff?"

"Walker ..." Jessie ignores my question and stares at me like I've lost my damn mind. She would, too, if she were in my position. "Why do you have a baby in your arms?"

"She's ... my daughter." The words feel strange to say out loud.

Her eyes bug out of her head. "You have a *daughter*?" She starts to stutter over her words. "H-h-h-how? When?"

I'm in no mood for these kinds of questions. Now is not the time.

I look down at the baby. "Jessie, can we talk about that later? Why won't she stop crying?"

She rolls her eyes—rolls her damn eyes at me like I'm the problem. "Give her to me."

I obey and hand her over. She places her against her chest and tucks the baby's head under her chin, where I was holding her like a football. She doesn't exactly stop crying, but it's definitely not at the decibel it was when she was in my arms.

I feel irritated by that.

"Okay," Jessie says calmly. "Read the back of the can. How many scoops to ounces?"

What the hell? How does she already know about that shit? She must have babysat a lot. This is not common knowledge.

"Two scoops to four ounces. How much is four ounces?"

"It's on the bottle. We just need to fill the water up to the four-ounce line, then put in two scoops."

Of course it's on the bottle. If I'd had a moment of silence, I would have been able to figure that out.

"Now what?" I ask once I'm done.

"You need to put that bottle nipple into the disc and insert that blue tube under the disc. Close it up. Shake. We can see if she's okay with colder water. If not, we need to heat it up."

Just as I'm done shaking it, she tries to hand the baby to me.

I back away. "What are you doing?"

"I'm giving you your daughter back."

I shake my head back and forth like a toddler throwing a tantrum. "She doesn't like me."

I think I detect a brief moment of sympathy from Jessie before annoyance takes over. "Come here. Let's go sit on the couch."

I follow behind her, not sure how I'm going to get through the evening. What if she leaves me? I'll die. She can't leave me.

Chapter Three

Jessie

I feel like I'm dreaming. This doesn't feel like reality. A reality where Walker is a father and he's asking *me* for help. I don't even know how to digest any of this. But that's for another time. This poor baby in my arms needs to be soothed.

I sit down on his couch. He stands in front of me, holding the bottle.

I look down at the spot next to me, then back up at him. "Sit down, Walker."

The fear in his eyes is potent. I can feel it in my bones. He has no idea what to do. And he thinks she doesn't like him. I don't like this guy, but I know he needs me to be kind at the moment.

"Walker, it'll be okay."

With that, he takes a deep breath and takes a seat next to me. Even in this situation, his nearness puts my skin on high alert. I despise that my body still reacts this way to him.

I shift myself so I'm facing him. "Put your arms out. I'm going to help you through this."

He obeys, and I place his daughter in the crook of his arm. She starts to cry harder, and he sits up like he's about to freak out.

"Stop!" I say sternly. "We just need to put the bottle nipple in her mouth."

I place my hand on his then help him lower the bottle to her lips. I move the nipple over her lips so she can taste the food in between her screaming.

Her eyes open immediately, and she begins sucking. I don't let go of his hand yet, not until I am confident that she is taking the bottle and not going to spit it out. When I'm sure she won't refuse the bottle, I take my hand off him and lean back in my seat.

He still looks tense, afraid to move a muscle, as he holds the bottle to her mouth. Not gonna lie; my blood pressure was through the roof with the crying. I understand why it's so stressful. My body finally starts to settle.

"There you go," I say as she continues to suck down her milk. "She was just hungry."

"Is she gonna cry again after this?" he asks, terror written all over his face.

"Eventually, she is. She's a baby. That's how she tells you she needs or wants something."

He doesn't like that answer. But I'm not going to lie to him. I watch him watch her, and the questions begin to come flooding back to me.

I have to ask, "Walker, did you know about her?"

His eyes meet mine. "Of course not. Do I look like someone who wasn't caught off guard with a baby? I had no idea."

I glance around at his penthouse. That's true. Not a trace of evidence that shows he is prepared to take care of a baby.

"Where is her mother?"

"Gone," he says distractedly, staring down at his daughter with a sense of curiosity.

"Gone? Where did she go?" I ask quickly.

She'd better come back soon. Walker doesn't know what the hell he is doing. That much is clear.

"Gone, Jessie. She dropped her off an hour ago and told me she couldn't do this anymore."

"Are you serious? She just ... left her daughter with you? For, like ... good?"

His shoulders tense. "Yes. She left her with me, Jessie."

"What kind of person does that? Where did you meet her?"

He looks at me with contempt. "A bar. She's a model."

I roll my eyes so heavily that it gives me a slight headache. But it's just so typical of him. He's such a man-whore.

"Go ahead. Spit it out," he growls at me.

"What?" I question.

"Tell me I had it coming. That it was only a matter of time that my man-whore ways caught up with me."

I'm slightly taken aback by how well he sniffed me out. Am I that transparent?

It's his turn to roll his eyes—at me. The nerve. "You call me a man-whore literally every time you see me."

"Yeah, well, maybe if you didn't have a different girl on your arm every time I see you, I wouldn't have to."

"You don't have to call me anything. It's called being a polite person."

"Oh, please. You are anything but polite to me."

"That's because you're a raging bitch to me."

I gasp. "How dare you call me a bitch, you egotistical asshole!"

Before he can respond, he abruptly looks down at the baby, who is now finished with the bottle. "Oh my God. Is she gonna cry? What do I do now?"

Seriously, I've never seen anyone more incompetent with a baby.

"You need to burp her."

He tries to hand her off to me again. "You do it."

"Given the fact that it looks like your daughter is here to stay, I'd say you need to learn these things. Just put her over your shoulder and pat her back until she burps."

But the moron literally puts her hips on his shoulder.

I grab the baby and scoot her down his chest until her head rests near his shoulder. "Like this. Now pat her back."

"I'm gonna wind up hurting her, aren't I? You can already tell how screwed I am. And what about my job? I can't take care of a baby and be a partner at my firm. I have the potential to score one of the biggest cases of my life. I should be working right now."

There he is. The corporate attorney who only cares about money and prestige. Not the guy I remember growing up with. The one who would tell me all about law school, talking about how he was going to change the world while I hung on every word. Use his powers for good. Fight for the ones who couldn't fight for themselves.

I don't know when it all changed.

"There are more important things than money and cases. Like your innocent daughter lying in your arms right now. Why don't you think about something other than yourself for a second?" I snap.

He continues to pat her back, then she lets out a loud, wet burp. Before I see the evidence, I can tell she spit up by the horrified look on his face.

I can't help it. It makes me smile. I like seeing him suffer.

He tries to look over his shoulder. "What the hell is that? Why am I wet?"

I let out a laugh. "She spit up on you. Serves you right for being a dick."

"Jessie, this is my career. I was just given a newborn baby on a Thursday night with no information or plan set in motion. Have a little sympathy."

I snort. "You're barking up the wrong tree if you're looking for sympathy. Why did you even call me in the first place?"

His eyes, which normally hold so much confidence, meet mine with sheer desperation. "I can't bother Roman and Eva right now. You know if I told Eva, she would drop everything. But she has her own one of these at home that's causing her to lose sleep."

"True. I'd prefer you didn't put this on her right now. But what about any of your other friends?"

"They're probably just as clueless as me."

"You guys are all a bunch of duds."

He looks less than amused.

I smile. "Sorry."

She's been quiet for a couple of minutes in his arms. He seems to notice the same thing, with a slightly different reaction.

"She isn't crying. Why isn't she moving? Is she dead?" He sits up straight, panic flooding his body again.

I lean back to see that her eyes are closed and she's breathing softly. "Oh my gosh. You need to chill. She's sleeping."

He really doesn't know a damn thing about babies. I don't know what the hell he is going to do, but I think my job here is done.

"Well"—I clap my hands and stand—"I guess we're done here. Good luck with that, Walker. I wish you the best."

"You're leaving?" He stands quickly. "You can't leave. I need you."

"What exactly do you want me to do? You now know how to feed and burp her."

He moves in front of me so I can't take another step. "What about everything else? If you leave, I'll have to call Eva. I don't want to, but I can't do this alone."

Of course I don't want him bothering Eva, but I'm not sure what he's asking of me.

"What about your parents?" I ask, wondering now why they weren't his first phone call.

"I can't." His words come out on a choke of emotion. "They would lose their minds and tell me to do something crazy, like drop her off at the fire station. A doorstep baby isn't good for our family image."

Shit, he's right. His parents aren't exactly the warm and fuzzy type. And there's an odd part of me that's proud of him for stepping up and trying to figure this out. I just can't believe I'm the only one he feels he can rely on.

But I watch him, standing in front of me, begging me for help, his daughter cuddled underneath his chin, and I know I'm going to say yes. I've always been powerless to my pull to him, no matter how much I hate it—and him.

"Fine." I sag my shoulders in defeat. "What is it you need?"

He swallows hard. "Stay the night. Please. Help me get set up with some kind of ... I don't know ... routine."

"So, you're keeping her?" I question.

"I mean ... what else am I supposed to do? She's my *daughter*. Her mother just *abandoned* her. I don't see any other choice."

His dark blue eyes have always been like ocean waves that could take me down with just one look.

I've managed to keep my distance from him for years. Spending the night in his place, with his daughter, feels dangerous. I shouldn't do it.

But I've never done what I should do where Walker is concerned.

Chapter Four

Walker

I know it's not the smartest thing to do, asking Jessie to stay with me. There are many reasons why I've kept my distance from her over the years. But I'm desperate. I need her help. And I trust her.

She stands in front of me, arms wrapped loosely across her torso, biting the inside of her cheek as she considers what I'm asking. All I can do is stand and wait, hoping she agrees. Because if she doesn't, I don't know what I'll do.

"I'm not promising more than tonight." She points her finger at me, but all I feel is relief.

At least I know I can make it through the night. Tomorrow is an entirely new beast.

"Thank you, Jessie," I sigh.

She looks around my place. "So, what is it that you have?"

I point to the diaper bag. "That's all—what is in there. Oh, and a stroller in the hallway."

Her eyebrows rise. "That's it? You can't even make it through the night with that. We need to go to the store. Now."

"Now? She just fell asleep. Where do I even put her to go shopping? Can I just carry her into the car? Is that safe?"

"Shit. No. She needs a car seat. Okay." She takes a deep breath in and then lets it out. "I'm going to run to the store."

She grabs her purse off of my counter.

"Ugh, you're gonna just leave her here with me ... alone?"

If looks could kill, I'd be dead.

"Seriously, Walker? You want my help? I'm helping. Yes, I'm going to leave you alone with your daughter for, like ... an hour."

I gulp down the mountain of anxiety that creeps in at the thought of being alone with her for an entire hour. "Okay. I'll just ... hold her like this, I guess."

She rolls her eyes. "Do what you gotta do."

She holds out her hand, as if I'm supposed to give her something. I raise my eyebrows in question.

"Credit card, dummy. I'm not paying for this shit."

"Oh, right." I turn around and stick out my butt. "Wallets in my pocket."

She reaches in, and—I'm not gonna lie—the warmth of her hand on my ass is nice. Even in a moment of panic, my body reacts to her touch. It just proves that this is a stupid idea, being this close to her for an extended period of time.

"Which one?" she asks as she opens the wallet, apparently completely unaffected by touching me ... there.

"Um ... the black one right there."

Another eye roll from her. "Of course you have a black Amex."

What a surprise. A snarky, judgmental comment from the world's most annoying woman. If she wasn't saving my life right now, I'd have something to say back.

Instead, I watch her walk out of the door. I look around the silent penthouse, decorated with high-end furniture in every corner. It's not a kid-friendly space. She sighs and wiggles in my arms, and I instantly freeze.

Please, don't wake up. Please, don't wake up.

Then she lets out a slow sigh and softens back in my arms.

Thank God.

I look around the room for somewhere to put her down to sleep. The only place that looks semi-comfortable is the couch, but I don't think that's a good idea.

I'll just sit back down on the couch like we were before. Maybe if I keep her in my arms like this, she won't wake up.

An hour later, my front door opens. I shoot off of the couch because, instantly, the noise startles the baby, and she starts wailing in my arms.

Jessie strolls in with a luggage cart from downstairs that's filled to the top with boxes and bags.

"What the hell, Jessie? You woke her up by barging in like an animal."

"Babies cry, Walker. Get used to it. It's gonna happen ... a lot."

She struggles to get the cart over the wedge of my doorframe. No matter how hard she pulls, her effort is futile.

"Ugh, here, take her. I'll get it."

I hand her my baby, hoping she can figure out why she's crying. While I pull the cart inside and start to unload all of the items into the family room, Jessie goes to the diaper bag and gets out a fresh diaper and wipes.

"Okay, Einstein. Come here." She motions for me to follow her to the kitchen table.

She places some kind of mat down, then puts the baby on top.

"What?" I ask.

"You need to change her." She points.

I know she's not going to let me get away with not doing this. I might as well suck it up and get it over with. A terrible odor hits my nostrils.

"Eww, Jessie. I think you need stronger deodorant. You stink."

She giggles next to me with delight. "I think that's coming from her."

My eyes bug open. "Did she ..."

I can't even say the words.

"Pretty sure she did. You did just feed her an hour ago."

I look down at the baby, who seems a bit happier, placed on her back, but is still whining lightly.

"What's her name?" Jessie asks.

"I haven't a clue," I state as I reach down to look at whatever contraption she's in. "How do you get this thing off?"

Jessie walks me through the process as she rummages through the diaper bag. "She must've left something for you. I can't believe you don't even know her name. That's messed up, Walker."

I cringe at the stuff inside her diaper, breathing through my mouth the entire time. "What's messed up is that a little thing like this can produce such a pile of grossness."

"Aha!" she cheers. "Bingo."

I toss the dirty diaper aside and place the fresh one underneath her, like Jessie told me to. Seriously, this is disgusting.

"What are you yapping about over there? I'm trying to focus."

"Birth certificate. Social Security card, pediatrician information. It looks like her name is ... Elise. Aww, that's cute. Eli." She bends down and kisses the baby's nose. "You look like an Eli."

Once she's done and changed, I pick her up, and she starts to fuss and cry again.

"Now what?" I ask.

"Oh, I bought some pacifiers. Let's see if that works."

Jessie runs over to open a package and cleans the thing off in my sink. Meanwhile, I look down at her birth certificate.

Elise Harlow.

Amelia gave her my last name. Was she ever planning on keeping her?

"Here," Jessie sings as she approaches.

She places it in Eli's mouth, but she doesn't seem to have any interest. Only Jessie doesn't give up. She tries again, and it breaks through Eli's screaming enough to get her to suck on it.

Miraculously, she starts viciously chomping on the pacifier.

"Also, I ordered dinner. I haven't eaten yet, and if that continues ... I'm going to get angrier and angrier," she admits. "I got you something, just in case."

"Thanks. I haven't eaten yet, but I don't have much of an appetite at the moment. I'm feeling kind of sick to my stomach, to be honest."

She grabs a big box off of the cart and begins to open it. "Well, you should eat something. You're gonna need your energy tonight."

"What are you opening?"

"It's a pack and play. It's somewhere for her to sleep. It has a little bassinet on top and a changing station right next to it."

What I think is going to take hours, instructions, tools, and a lot of fighting between the two of us takes Jessie minutes to put together.

"What in the world just happened? How did you get it together so quickly?"

"I know, right? I'm impressed with myself. Clearly, parents aren't messing around with how easily they need this shit to come together."

There are two little contraptions on top of the crib. I don't understand what each one is for.

"What am I looking at here?" I ask as I stand over it.

"This one is where she sleeps, and this one"—she points to the one with a plastic bottom—"is where you change her."

I lean down slowly and place her in the bassinet like she's a bomb that could go off at the slightest movement. By some miracle, she doesn't wake up. It's probably all the crying she's done. I'd be exhausted too.

As I stand next to Jessie, we both peer down at my daughter as she sleeps snuggly in her new bassinet.

I turn around and glance into a bag from the store. "So, what exactly did you buy? It looks like the entire store."

"It's not like you can't afford it." She joins me, hands on her hips.

I ignore the dig. "What do we need to get through the night?" I ask.

She goes straight for a box and opens it quietly. "First things first. This sound machine. It'll drown out any noise that might startle her awake."

I freeze in place. I don't want that.

"Open it now," I whisper, refusing to move until she puts in the batteries and dangles it off of the pack and play.

"Okay, I say, let's get the changing station ready. Diapers, wipes, clean clothes. Then we can set up a bottle station for the middle-of-the-night feedings."

My heart sinks. "Feedings? More than once? How often do babies eat?"

"A lot. And they poop a lot," she says with a wink.

"You don't have to enjoy my misery so much." I push her arm as I open up the diaper box as quietly as possible.

She pushes me back—harder. "It's much deserved, assface."

"Why didn't I just call Eva? She'd be a whole lot nicer to me."

"Because you apparently have a heart, though it might be the size of a pea. She's tired. I just talked to her this morning. Addie had them up most of the night."

After we set up everything she thinks we'll need for the night, the dinner she ordered arrives. We sit on opposite ends of the couch, eating quietly as we watch Eli sleep.

I can't believe I'm already shortening her name, but I did like the sound of it when Jessie said it.

I'm lost in thought through most of dinner, trying to force down the contents of the food, though my body still feels like it's stuck in fight-or-flight mode.

Like she knew I just finished dinner, Eli begins to cry. I throw my plate in the sink and make another bottle—instructed by Jessie, of course.

When I walk back into the room, Jessie has her changed into a small floral sleeper-looking thing. It's cute with its footies. She has Eli cradled under her chin and is slowly bouncing her around the room.

My heart beats erratically in my chest at the sight of the woman I swore I could never have, soothing a baby I never knew existed until tonight.

She must sense my presence even though I haven't made a noise, but she looks up and locks eyes with me. We don't say anything, and I don't move. I swallow down the feelings I've kept secret for years.

"I can take her," I say through the thickness in my throat.

"No, I'll feed her. Why don't you move this pack and play in your bedroom while I do? She'll need to sleep in the same room as you."

I nod my head and do as I was told. I didn't realize she needed to be in my room. I'm never gonna get any sleep tonight.

I walk back into the family room, where Jessie is now sitting on the couch, feeding Eli.

"You should get ready for bed now while she's content," she says to me without even looking up.

I roll my head around my shoulders, hoping that'll relieve some of the mounting tension. I don't even know how to process all of this. I went from spending the day with the possibility of scoring a case that would make me the most-sought-after corporate attorney in the city if I won to changing diapers and making bottles for a baby I hadn't known about. All with a woman who hates me—and who, I'm pretty sure, thinks I hate her.

Nicole Baker

If she only knew ...

Chapter Five

Jessie

Eli is precious. She sucks ravenously on her bottle nipple, taking down her formula like a champ. She has one tiny little hand wrapped around my thumb while her eyes remain on me.

As soon as she's done, I pull the bottle from her and rest her on my shoulder to burp. I forgot to grab one of the many burp cloths I purchased, but that's okay. A little spit-up never hurt anyone. Though Walker's reaction to it would have made you think so.

He's been a total spaz since I got here. I like to give him a hard time, but I don't think anyone would be calm in a situation like this.

As Eli lets out a loud burp, then snuggles into the crook of my neck, I wonder how in the world her mother could have given her up.

Just goes to show Walker's type. He's never known how to pick a good one. I've seen the women he's had on his arm. Tall, leggy, blonde. Makeup so thick that you wonder what their face looks like when it's off. Definitely after his money and power. His looks don't hurt.

He walks back into the room, wearing gray sweatpants and a tight black shirt, and my entire body is engulfed in flames. The shirt does nothing to hide his biceps or the sheer size of his chest. Eighteen-year-old me is freaking out right now. Luckily, twenty-seven-year-old me is here to put a stop to it.

He stands in front of me, running a hand through his tousled hair. Shit, where did twenty-seven-year-old me go? She's nowhere to be found right now. I could really use her ability to cut through this fog of attraction with her snarky comments.

Instead, I stare up at him like a damn fool. This is why I shouldn't be alone with him. I haven't lost control of keeping my hatred in the forefront of my mind for years.

"Your turn," he says, breaking me from the voodoo spell he had on me.

"For what?"

"Getting ready for bed. I can take her."

He stretches his arms out. I stand up, and we awkwardly try to maneuver around one another to exchange Eli. He has a woodsy, spicy scent that's distracting. I've always been a sucker for the scent of a man.

He places her in the same upright position she seems to enjoy, and I stand in front of him awkwardly as I realize I don't have anything to sleep in.

"Um, I didn't expect to be spending the night," I admit, feeling suddenly shy, which isn't my personality.

Walker is the only one who brings this side out in me.

I hate feeling this vulnerable.

"Oh, right," he says as he bounces her slightly and pats her back. He already seems slightly more comfortable with holding her than when I first got here. "Follow me. You can borrow something."

That's a bad idea. Wearing his clothes is what girlfriends do. But I'm not trying to sleep in his air-conditioned penthouse in my shorts and tank top. It's cold in here. And I like to be comfy in the middle of the night.

Walking into his bedroom feels strange. He opens a drawer and pulls out black sweatpants, handing them to me.

"They're big, but there's a drawstring so you can tighten them around your waist." Then he opens another drawer, this time pulling out a gray Columbia shirt.

"I get your ratty old college shirt?" I say to lighten the mood.

"Yes, I've gone down on plenty of girls in that thing. I thought you'd like it."

I toss the shirt at him, and he laughs as he hands it back to me.

"I'm just kidding."

"Are you though?" I ask, feeling like it's more probable that he did.

He sighs as he pats Eli's back some more. "Just go change. You can use my bathroom right behind you."

I change as quickly as I can, not wanting to let myself think about the fact that it's his clothing that's draped around my body. I walk back out into his bedroom to find him pulling the covers on his bed down with Eli asleep in his arms.

The sound machine has been moved to his bedroom as well as everything he needs to change her in the middle of the night.

The swaddle that I purchased is draped over the pack and play.

"You should swaddle her and get some sleep now while you can," I whisper. "Where am I sleeping tonight?"

He looks at his bed and back at me like the answer is obvious. "Right here."

I lean forward, hands on my hips—an attempt to convey the utter disbelief that I'm feeling. "Umm, I'm not sleeping in your bed with you."

You would think I just told him his puppy died with the look he's giving me.

"What? But I need you. How will I know whether to feed her or change her or what she needs in the middle of the night?"

"I'll sleep on the couch, you big baby. Come get me if you need me."

I go to turn around, and he's in front of me before I can even make it out of the room.

"Please, Jessie. I *can't* do this alone tonight. I know we have a history. I know it's ... complicated."

I huff at his word choice. That doesn't begin to describe it.

"But I'm begging you ... please help me get through this. I'll put pillows in between us. I just ... I can't do this alone tonight. I need you."

Beat me over the head. What a guilt trip. Watching the man I've secretly longed for saying this to me while snuggling his baby girl on his chest? It's really not fair.

"Ugh, fine. Just for tonight." I point a finger at him, hoping to drive home how serious I am.

I can't do this longer than one night. I may hate the guy, but he's still stupidly attractive. Lines can get blurred pretty damn fast.

I walk him through how to swaddle Eli. She is totally conked out, not budging at all throughout the process. I hope this is a good sign for how long of a stretch she'll sleep tonight.

Walker placed the pack and play right next to his side of the bed. He climbs in next to her. I walk over to the other side, my heart feeling like it's going to beat out of my chest.

I crawl under the covers, lying on my back, mirroring Walker's position next to me. We both lie in silence.

I wonder what he's thinking about. Is the idea of sleeping next to me even something that gives him pause?

Who am I kidding? He made his feelings clear that night. This isn't affecting him in the slightest. That's why I have to guard my heart.

I may be willing to give him my time, but I'll never give him the chance to hurt me. Not like last time.

Chapter Six

Walker

I feel like I got punched in the face. What the hell happened last night? Eli woke up, like, seven times. Each time—whether it was changing her, feeding her, trying to soothe her—it took forever to get her back to sleep.

I doubt I got more than three hours of sleep.

This is the second cup of coffee I've pounded in the last hour, and it's still not even six. I need another spot to put her in the morning. I've been holding her on the couch for an hour, terrified to wake her up.

Jessie is still sleeping in my bed. She punched me in the arm around four when I begged her to help again. I'm just so much calmer when she's with me, even if she's not doing anything. But I want her to get some sleep, so I'm not gonna wake her.

I tossed and turned for a while last night. Between having my daughter to my left and Jessie on my right, my brain was full of distractions.

You would think the punches and curse words she shells out to me, and me alone, would make me sour toward her. But, damn, they make my dick hard. What I would give to punish her for all the times she's come at me. A delicious punishment that would end with my cum all over her body.

Fuck. I need to stop it. This is why it took me so long to fall asleep.

Now that I managed to make it through my first night, I have another dilemma to tackle today. Who is going to watch Eli during my court appearance this morning?

My eyes immediately look at the door to my bedroom. Jessie is my only hope. If not, I have to ask Eva. I don't want to put two babies on her plate. But I can't miss it. It's the initial conference for my breach of contract suit. The judge will set timelines for everyone, and this judge doesn't take kindly to not respecting his time.

Getting on his bad side this early could be devastating.

I place the empty cup of coffee down on the coffee table and scoot back on the couch. I could probably have a dozen coffees and still feel tired. Eli snuggles closer to me, and my heart skips a beat. It felt like an intentional move to get closer to me. My daughter—taking comfort in me.

This is the first time I've had a moment to myself with her, without crying or panic at the forefront of my brain. It's an overwhelming feeling.

Am I going to be a good dad? Am I going to do this ... for real? Try to be a single dad?

It seems impossible. Not with my career.

But I do have a lot of money. I just need to find a good nanny. I could make it work.

I *should* make it work. She already had a mother give up on her.

I take a deep, shaky breath as I realize I've just made my decision. I'm going to keep her. I'm going to raise her.

I'm not ready to tell anyone yet. I feel like I need to get a routine together before I start to answer everyone's intrusive questions. I first need to feel confident in my ability to actually do this before I tell others.

Jessie startles me when I see her standing in the doorframe of my bedroom. She looks gorgeous with no makeup and crazy hair on the top of her head. Wearing my clothes.

Bitterness fills my veins because I can never have her, not without telling her, and I can't do that. But I can't be with someone holding such a big lie between us. It would eat away at me. I've accepted the fate of my life. Life is a bitch. It kicks you in the ass any chance it gets. It's better this way. Living in my misery is easier than hoping.

"Morning," she croaks in a scratchy voice.

"Morning. There's a pot of coffee made."

"Thank God." She walks past me and pours herself a cup before joining me on the couch.

"You look tired," she says as she looks me up and down from across the couch.

"What the hell happened last night? That can't be normal."

She smiles behind her coffee cup. "I'm pretty sure it is. Especially at her age." A weird look crosses her face. "How old is she exactly?"

I shrug my shoulders. "I don't know."

She stands up and comes back with a paper in her hand. "She was born on June 26. So, she's a month old. Yeah, I'm pretty sure four-week-olds can be up a lot at night. Talk to Eva. She'll tell you all about it. Awww." She freaks out, holding a hand to her heart.

I look at her a little crazy, wondering what could make her this excited.

"Walker, Addie was born June 23. They're cousins, born three days apart. How cute."

I never thought about that. My sister and I have babies the same age. Cousins.

"Eva is gonna freak out." She smiles widely.

"Yeah. I'm, uh, I don't want to tell her yet."

Her face falls. "Why not?"

I sigh, annoyed that I have to explain this already. "Because ... I want to have the ground underneath my feet before I field a million questions about how I'm going to manage this new ... life."

She bites her lip as she seems to ponder my words, then looks at me skeptically. "Does this mean ... you're taking care of Eli?"

Fear settles in the pit of my stomach. This isn't how I saw

my life going. I wish I'd never met Amelia. "I have to. I'm her father."

The shock written all over Jessie's face annoys the fuck out of me.

"Wow. I'm kind of stunned."

I roll my eyes. "Shocker. Jessie didn't think I was capable of taking care of my child on my own."

"Hey." Her eyebrows turn down at me. "That's not fair. It's just ... you live a certain way. You've never really seemed like the kind of guy who could live life worrying about someone else."

Of course that's what she thinks of me. For being such a perceptive person, she sure has missed a lot about why I am the way I am. If only she knew. But that's wishful thinking because I'm taking my secret to the grave.

"Gee, tell me how you really feel about me."

She shakes her head in irritation. "Never mind that. We're getting off topic. You can't keep this from Eva for long. *I* can't keep this from her for long."

"I just need to figure something out. Like ... a nanny. Where do I even get a nanny?"

"This is New York City. There are agencies with a slew of nannies everywhere."

"Really?" I ask. "That's great!"

She chuckles. "Yeah, great."

I scratch the back of my head nervously, knowing I need to

convince her to help me until I find one. "About that. Um ... until I find a nanny, I ..."

Her head tilts to the side, and then it dawns on her. "No, I've given you more of my time than your dumbass deserved."

"Please!" I beg, rubbing a hand over Eli's back, hoping she stays calm enough for me to have this conversation. "I'm begging. Begging! I can't do this alone. I have a court date today." Before she can go off, I continue, "It's just an initial conference. It'll take an hour. Are you in court today?"

When she doesn't answer immediately, I know the answer.

"If you watch her this morning and afternoon, I'll come home right after court and start looking for a nanny."

"What's in it for me?" she asks, seemingly calm for what I'm asking of her.

Her question throws me off-kilter. "Huh?"

She leans forward. "What's. In. It. For. Me?" she says slower, like I'm a moron.

"I don't know ... the knowledge that you helped out a desperate man in need?"

She shakes her head. "Nope, not good enough. You're not a man. You're a man child."

Fucking hell. She is such a stubborn woman.

"Fine. Shopping spree on me this weekend."

She pouts her lips. "Hmm. Interesting. What's the spending limit?"

"I don't care. Spend all of my money."

"Wow. You are desperate." She sits up and puts her coffee cup down. "Okay. Deal. I'll help you until you get a nanny if you take me shopping this weekend."

Relief washes over me like a tide—but just as quickly, it ebbs away, leaving uncertainty in its wake. Just because I've decided to take care of Eli on my own doesn't mean I think I'm capable of it. Doubt floods my mind, making it hard for me to think about what my next step is.

"Deal. And just so we're clear, we aren't telling Eva yet."

"If she comes right out and asks me, I'm not going to lie."

I groan at how frustrating she is. "Fine. If Eva point-blank asks you if you are helping me take care of my secret child that I just found out about, you can tell her."

Proving how crazy this woman is, she nods her head in agreement, satisfied with my response.

I look down at Eli, sleeping soundly on my chest, then up at Jessie.

"Just put her down in her bassinet. I'll go get her if she cries while you're getting ready."

Damn, she knows me too well.

By the time I'm ready, I have to check my watch while walking back into the living room to see how long I took. Because, based on what I see you'd think I was gone for hours.

There's a swing already set up in the corner, and Eli is

currently lying down on some blanket thing that has toys dangling over her head.

She's kicking and waving her arms while making sounds.

Jessie is lying on the ground next to her with a smile on her face. "I know, Eli. Mr. Cat sure is funny, isn't he?"

"What is that thing?" I ask as I tie my tie, now standing over both of them.

Jessie looks up at me, but instead of answering, her throat bobs as her eyes look at me from head to toe. My jaw clenches because I know exactly what that look means, and I need her to stop giving it to me. Not unless she wants me to drag her into my room and fuck it off her pretty little face.

I've only got so much self-control. If she is going to openly ogle me, we're going to have issues.

"It's a mat," she finally responds, shaking off the moment.

"I didn't know she could make any other sounds besides crying," I admit as she continues to babble on the mat. I look down at my watch, knowing I've got to get out of here to get shit done before court. "I gotta go. I'll be back around one."

I glance down at the mat and Eli. "Don't, like … step on her or anything while she's down there."

Jessie gives me the death stare. "Get out of here before I step on your face."

I chuckle at her cruelty. There's my girl.

Bradly stands tall just as I'm walking into my office, following me in quickly.

"Sorry I'm a little late. Last night was ... hectic," I say vaguely.

He glances out the window to see if anyone is coming, then turns back to me. "Word is, the pharmaceutical company, Solentra Biotech, has officially hired us."

Heat surges through my veins like fire. My fists clench on instinct as I bite down hard. This is not what I wanted to hear first thing this morning.

"Thanks for letting me know," I answer.

I fall down into my chair as he backs out of my office awkwardly. Normally, I would be thrilled to hear this news and have him sitting down with me to construct a game plan immediately.

But I need time to process this news. I still need to reach out to an agency this morning to hire a nanny and prep for my court appearance. Then I'm supposed to be done for the day to relieve Jessie.

How am I supposed to find time to plan and execute a strategy to convince Stewart and Henry that I'm their guy? Am I their guy? This is a big case. It will require a ton of hours.

I massage my temples as I try to fight off the headache that's appeared as well as the foggy brain from lack of sleep.

I just need to get face time with one of them this morning. That will have to be enough until I can gather myself and figure out next steps.

I walk to the other side of the floor, where their offices are located. As luck would have it, they are talking by Stewart's door, just outside of his office.

I grab an empty file from the top of a filing cabinet, trying to look like I have a purpose for my venture. "Stewart, Henry ... nice to see you this morning."

"Walker, we were just talking about you," Stewart admits.

"All good things, I hope," I reply as I pat him on the back.

"Always." He chuckles. "I'm sure you've heard the news. I know there've been rumblings around the city about it. There's no keeping it a secret."

I smile, shrugging my shoulders. "I guess congratulations are in order. That's a big case for this firm."

Henry nods his head. He's the more serious one of the two. "It is. It's going to take some time to figure out how to staff such an important case for the firm."

Here's my in. "I know this case is going to be brutal—layers of science, red tape, and media heat. But I thrive in messy. Give me the lead, and I'll not only win it; I'll turn it into a showcase for what this firm does best."

Stewart's eyes light up while Henry's face doesn't change a bit. At least I know I got one of them feasting off of my words.

"I knew you were a spitball," Stewart replies. "Didn't I tell ya, Henry?"

Henry looks between the two of us. "We have a lot of talent in the office and a big decision ahead of us."

I don't want to push him too hard and scare him off. I need to get out now while Stewart is still on my side. "I'm sure whatever you decide will be the right move. I'll catch you guys later."

I walk back to my office with a sinking feeling in the pit of my stomach. What if they do choose me? I'm going to need a live-in nanny at this point to raise my daughter for me. This case would take up every waking hour of mine for months.

Unfortunately, I have too much on my plate today to agonize over what-ifs. First thing is finding a nanny.

Chapter Seven

Jessie

Eli has been a gem all morning. She took a long nap in her bassinet after her bottle, which gave me time to take a shower and change back into yesterday's clothes, minus the dirty panties, which I stuffed into my purse.

There are few times in my life when I lose control of myself and agree to things that I shouldn't, but this morning was one of them.

Agreeing to help Walker until he finds a nanny isn't just a minor inconvenience; it's a catastrophe waiting to happen. I can already sense the old feelings that I've shoved deep down inside of me making their way back up.

Seeing him doing something so mundane as tying a tie this morning should not have rendered me momentarily speechless. It was as if he were moving in slow motion and the world around us ceased to exist.

Not. Good.

But that's the Walker effect. He's always had this magnetic energy around him that my mind and body seem to be in tuned with in a way I've yet to experience with someone else.

Too bad that kind of chemistry is wasted on a man who sorely disappoints me every chance he gets.

The front door opens, and Walker comes rushing in like he's jacked up on cocaine. He marches toward me as Eli rests on my chest while I try to get a burp out of her.

"Uh, is everything all right?" I ask as he paces back and forth.

"It's fine. Everything's fine," he spits out quickly. "Why do you ask?"

His jacket and tie are gone, sleeves rolled up, and the top three buttons of his shirt are undone. His hair is disheveled.

"Um, you have a strange amount of energy."

He doesn't stop moving the entire time. It's unnerving to watch.

He motions at me with his hand like I'm crazy. "It's no biggie. The first five cups of coffee this morning did nothing to curb how tired I was, so I drank four energy drinks."

My eyes probably look like a cartoon character who was just run over. "Walker!" I whisper-shout so I don't scare Eli. "That's insane! You're gonna have a heart attack."

"It's fine, Jessie. I talked to my senior partners this morning, got in good face time with them for an upcoming case that I want assigned to me, I prepped and got ready for court, AND," he says loudly after a pause to breathe, "I got on the phone with the top nanny agency in the city. Had to pull some strings, talk up the big names that I know, but she's sending over a nanny for me to interview tonight."

I've never seen him like this. He is normally so cool and collected, like nothing can penetrate his icy exterior. I'm not sure I feel comfortable even leaving him like this while I go home. But I need to go home. I need clothes. I have to get some work done. I need space to get back to the Jessie who doesn't give a fuck about the asshole in front of me. Right now, she's fading away, and I don't like it. It's disconcerting.

"Are you going to be okay if I leave?"

He stops for a beat. "You're coming back though, right? Remember the shopping."

A laugh bubbles out of me. "Yes, I remember the shopping. I'll be back after dinner for bedtime."

"But I need you here to help interview the nanny. I don't know what questions to ask."

"You're a corporate lawyer at one of the most prestigious firms in the city. You can't come up with some questions to ask a nanny?"

His face falls. "No. Like, what if I forget to ask something important? Something that could mean life or death for Eli?!"

The mere idea has him pacing around the room again like the Hulk, ready to transform. I can't watch him like this; it's painful.

"Fine. What time is the interview?"

"Six," he replies quickly.

"I'll be here. Just calm yourself down before I hand over Eli. You're too worked up."

He stops and breathes in, counting to himself, then exhales, all while keeping his hands on his belly.

"What the hell are you doing?"

"I don't know. Some belly-breathing thing that we did in yoga. Eva made me go one time. Told me it would help with my stress at work."

"Ugh, yoga."

He opens his eyes and looks at me curiously. "Don't like yoga?"

"I like yoga just fine. Hot yoga, which Eva dragged me to the other day? That's another story. I hate hot yoga more than I hate you."

"Wow." He chuckles to himself. "That's a pretty high standard it had to beat. I feel honored to have fallen from number one on your list. Thank you, hot yoga."

I try not to smile, but I know the smirk is written all over my face. He smiles back at me, and there's a pause as we seem to lose ourselves in a moment where all walls have been dropped.

Then Eli fusses in my arms. It breaks the spell and reminds me how easy it can be to forget why I don't like him.

I stand from the couch now that he is a bit calmer, then hand him Eli. "Here you go. I'll be back before six."

I don't wait for a reply. Instead, I grab my purse and march out the door, desperate for fresh air. The moment I hit the streets, I feel like I can breathe again.

This is dangerous. I shouldn't be doing this. It's already messing with my head. I should text him now and tell him the deal's off. I don't need that shopping spree, though I would love to spend his money. Being a family lawyer who does a lot of pro bono work doesn't pay very well.

But I'm comfortable. I can afford a decent place in the city and live a modest life while helping those who don't have the money to help themselves. It works for me. But it doesn't leave room for an amazing wardrobe.

I want to back out ... and yet I know I won't. I'm weak. I have a soft spot for him. I care too much about him to leave him high and dry. That's the unfortunate reality of the predicament I find myself in.

* * *

Luckily, I have an amazing boss. Lorain was very understanding when I told her I had some personal matters to attend to this week. I told her I would do as much work as I could from home—that being Walker's home.

I know I can't tell Eva the news, but I need somebody to talk to. The only other person I can think of is my dad. He's always the sound of reason in my life. Someone who can smooth out the rough edges that shape me.

As I pack a suitcase to have at Walker's I pick up my phone and dial his number.

He answers on the first ring, like usual.

"Hey, Jessie girl. I've been thinking about you," he says cheerfully.

I chuckle. "You always say that when I call."

"What can I say? I think of you often."

His response warms my heart. "Aw, I don't believe you, but I appreciate it nonetheless."

He laughs. "How've you been? I've been wondering when my favorite daughter was gonna come home to visit next."

"I know; I know. I'll definitely be home for the holidays, Dad."

"It'd be nice to see you before then."

I sigh. I know I need to go home more often, if only to see him. Whenever I think about going home though, I hear my mother's incessant judgments about how I choose to live my life.

"I'll try," I reply to soothe him for the time being. "But I actually was calling because I need to vent."

His tone shifts to one of concern. "Something wrong, sweetie?"

"I'm fine. It's just ... I'm helping a friend out with something. It's big ... and I promised to keep it from Eva until he was ready. But it's a lot."

"What could you possibly need to keep from Eva? Who's asking you to do this?"

"Walker," I bite out with frustration.

I dive into a long-winded explanation of how we got to where we are today, which is me currently throwing clothes into a suitcase aggressively.

When I'm done talking, I stand, hand on my hip, in front of my bed, waiting for his reaction.

"Wow," he replies neutrally. "That's ... not what I expected."

"I know. It's absolutely crazy. And he is acting like a baby himself, not able to figure out how to make a bottle or change a diaper. Now, he claims he doesn't know how to interview a nanny and needs my help."

Dad catches me off guard by chuckling on the other end of the line. "That's not that crazy."

"What do you mean? Of course it is," I demand.

"Men don't have that natural instinct when it comes to babies. If he hasn't been around a baby before, I can see why he would feel helpless. I certainly would."

"Get out of here. You're a great dad. A natural."

"I appreciate that, but I can assure you when your brother was born ... I was terrified. I didn't know a thing about what to do with a baby. I was afraid I would hurt him somehow."

I roll my eyes. I wanted my dad to make me feel better. This isn't what I had in mind.

"I'm just saying," he continues, "go easy on the guy. He has a lot on his plate at the moment and could use a break. I think it's great that you're helping him. He's a good kid. I've always liked him."

It may come off as completely immature, but I'm not thrilled about the fact that my own father likes the one man who doesn't deserve his approval. If only he knew the way Walker has treated me. How he uses women and tosses them out like they mean nothing to him.

Since I can't exactly share our whole sordid history, I decide getting off the phone is my best bet. I'm in no mood for a Walker praise fest.

"That's great. Hey, Dad. I'm sorry, but I have to run."

"All right, Jessie. I miss you."

"Miss you too. I'll talk to you soon."

I hang up the phone and hang my head in defeat. Am I the only one who's seen the dark side of Walker? It's like everybody around me thinks he's this stand-up guy. It's frustrating, being his sister's best friend. I wish I could just hate the guy and never see his face again.

But even I know those words aren't exactly true. There's a deep, sick part of me that is glad I still have a reason to keep him in my life. What kind of twisted torture is that? I think I might need to see a therapist about this. It can't be healthy.

I get to Walker's place fifteen minutes later, knocking on his door with a big suitcase and tote bag. He opens the door, and my body instantly forgets how to breathe.

He is standing in front of me in low-hanging black athletic shorts. That's it! Nothing else! Lines and lines of tanned muscle everywhere. Ridges on his stomach, on his arms, his chest.

When I finally have my wits about me, I realize he looks pissed. I should be the one who's furious. He has no right, parading that kind of body in front of me.

"Jessie"—his deep voice pulls me from my thoughts—"don't look at me like that."

It's like a slap in the face. It feels like I'm eighteen all over again. The pain is sharp and piercing. "Fuck you, Walker."

I walk in past him and try my hardest not to cry right here in front of him. I don't understand why the idea of me and him together is so repulsive to him.

A flashback from nine years ago hits me like a sudden force to the chest.

I'm so happy my parents agreed to a joint graduation party with Eva. Having it at her parents' house means that I get to see Walker. He's staying for the weekend, then going back to the city, where he is currently in law school.

I love picking his brain when he comes home. I've known him since I was twelve. Back then, I was a scrawny kid who idolized boy bands and didn't know the first thing about law.

But after taking a class sophomore year as an elective, I became enamored. I still remember the case that broke me and solidified in my mind that this was what I wanted to do for a living.

One night, when Walker was visiting home from undergrad, I talked to him about it after Eva fell asleep. We talked until four in the morning. I told him about how the case kept me awake at night, wondering how our legal system could have failed someone so drastically.

It was about a girl whose mother had passed years prior and she was left with a drunk, abusive father. Even though her aunt petitioned for custody and there was plenty of evidence of abuse and neglect, the court favored the father with money and power.

I saw so much of myself in the girl. Not in the family living situation, but when they described her as a person. My entire world is filled with people with too much money and power. What if I needed the law to save me? Not from my dad—he would never do anything to hurt me. But what if something happened to him and I was left with my mom? She could marry someone who hurt me. Who would help me then?

Walker confided in me that night. We talked about his reasons for wanting to be a lawyer. He, too, has parents who are mixed up in money and power. He's seen the unjust world where the rich bought their way through business deals and illegal activity.

He wanted to become a force of good.

And throughout all of it, I couldn't stop staring at his lips. The way his muscles flexed when he talked so animatedly.

It was the first crush I had that made me realize the effect a guy could have on my body. And I've been in love with him ever since.

We talk all the time now when he visits. He's become a friend. I love the way his face lights up when I walk in the room. It makes my heart race and my chest feel like there's a brick on top of it.

I spot Eva across the lawn, standing underneath the tent that her parents had set up for the party. It's being catered by the number one–rated company in the city. Only the best for their daughter. I'm just happy to be along for the ride. My dad does well, but not as well as her father.

She's arguing with her mom about something—I can tell. The way she waves her arms around so dramatically. She doesn't talk to her mom like that unless she's upset.

The entire night, my eyes are peeled, looking out for Walker. I've been such a mess that I've barely spoken to any of our friends, just walked circles, like a vulture waiting for its prey.

I feel his presence before I see him. Every nerve in my body feels like it's on fire. I turn around and spot him talking to his dad and mine. They are all laughing about something. I find my legs moving before I can stop them. I should play it cool—not seem so desperate, but I'm powerless to these feelings that he ignites in me.

Before I get there, his tall, leggy ex-girlfriend, Natalie, pops up on his right. She makes a big show of kissing Mr. Harlow on the cheek and wrapping an arm around Walker's, linking them together.

Ugh, I hate her.

She was around a lot when I was younger. They dated on and off in college, both attending Columbia. She's home now, likely desperately looking for a man with money to marry. Little does she know, Walker isn't like the rest of the men in this town. He isn't after money and power.

I can't watch her worm her way back into his life. I shift my weight to my heel and peek to the right, where I spot some high-school friends. I don't even want to talk to them right now, but it's better than my heart shattering piece by piece as I lose the man I've dreamed of to someone older and prettier.

I finally decide to get another Shirley Temple at the bar, tempted to beg them to put a shot in it, when all the hairs on my arms begin to stand.

"Congratulations." His warm breath tickles my ear.

I momentarily close my eyes, unable to comprehend how something like that makes me feel more than any of my high-school boyfriends were able to invoke.

I turn around and smile up at Walker, no doubt with adoration in my eyes. "Hey, you." I reach up on my tippy-toes and give him a hug. "Thank you."

"I can't believe you two are going to college in different states," he says as he sticks his hands in his pockets. "How are you going to survive without each other?"

I tuck a piece of hair nervously behind my ear. "Well, I'll have one of the Harlow siblings in the same city as me."

He chuckles. "That's true. NYU—that's a huge accomplishment, Jessie. I'm so proud of you."

I begin to fidget with the gold necklace that hangs between my breasts. His eyes immediately fall down to my hand, then home in on my chest. I specifically wore this dress because my boobs look awesome in it.

This is the first time I think I've ever caught him ogling me. I want to do a celebratory dance but need to be cool.

Instead, I run my fingers up the inside of his forearm and

take a step closer. "Are you going to make sure nothing happens to me in the city this year? It's a scary place."

His throat bobs as his eyes move to my lips, where I bite down on my bottom lip.

Before he can respond, Natalie appears like a ninja in the night. "I lost you for a second," she says to Walker.

He doesn't take his eyes off me. "Yeah, looks like it."

She looks me up and down with disdain. I know that look from a girl when I get it. She's threatened. By me. I feel like a million bucks.

"Congratulations, Jessie. Aww, you are so cute. Going off to college. Still so young though." She pulls on Walker's arm. "Hey, let's go say hi to my parents. You haven't seen them in ages."

He doesn't look like he wants to go, but Natalie has him falling backward away from me without his response.

The rest of the night plays out completely different than I expected. Natalie won't leave his side.

I give up on my dreams of tonight being the night for something to happen around midnight.

Instead of going home, Eva begs me to spend the night. "Please." She clasps her hands together in front of me. "I leave for Chicago in seven weeks. Our sleepover nights are limited."

Even the thought makes my insides tense. "You're right. I don't want to think about that right now. Let's have a slumber party like we used to. We can round up a big tray of leftover desserts and put on Dirty Dancing."

We race to her bedroom with a big tray of desserts that are impossible for just the two of us to consume. She changes into her pajamas, and I rip off my dress and steal a tank top from her, leaving me in just my black panties and her white top.

About halfway through the movie, I look over to find Eva snoring with a piece of cheesecake hanging out of the side of her mouth.

My first thought is, This is why she is my best friend.

My second is, I wonder what Walker is doing. He's probably asleep.

I can't help but replay our conversation tonight over and over in my head. From the way his eyes roamed my body to the feel of his skin on my fingertips.

I wanted tonight to be something special.

It dawns on me that this will probably be the last time I sleep at their house with Walker here.

He's already one year from getting his law degree. And who knows where the wind will blow for me and Eva in our next chapter? This is it.

If I want to take a chance on what I feel for him, tonight is the night. I want to show him that I'm not innocent or just his younger sister's best friend. I'm going off to college now. We'll both be attending school in the same city. We can make it work.

With a renewed sense of confidence, I tiptoe out of Eva's room and down the hallway, until I'm standing outside of Walker's room. I press my ear to the door. I don't hear anything. I take one last deep breath and slowly turn the knob to the right, then push it open.

It's dark. I can barely make out his form lying in the bed as the moon casts a subtle light on him. I walk to the edge of his bed. His covers are at his waist. He isn't wearing a shirt. My body instantly reacts to the smooth edges of his muscles.

My instincts take over from here. I'm not even thinking. Just doing what I want. What my body wants. I sit down on the bed and let my fingers glide over the soft ridges of his abs. They flex under my touch.

I push the covers down, revealing a pair of tight black boxers. The outline of his dick is huge. I'm no virgin by any means, but I wouldn't call myself experienced. I still feel slightly intimidated at the sight of a man's dick.

Not now.

I am practically salivating over the idea of touching him, of being the one to bring him to the height of pleasure.

My fingers move back to his abs before running lower to the waistband of his boxers, brushing back and forth. He groans and lifts an arm above his head, but doesn't wake. His dick is harder now, growing by the second.

I should wake him first, but I'm too transfixed. I wrap my fingers around him and stroke it over the material. He's thick. My fingers don't fit all the way around him.

I feel his hand on my shoulder.

"Fuck, that feels good," he groans.

That's all the motivation I need. I push his boxers down, revealing the most perfect dick I know I'll ever see. There's a bead of pre-cum, and I immediately need to know what he tastes like. I lick around his tip until I get all of it on my tongue. His moan tells me he likes it.

I've only given a handful of blow jobs before. All I know is what I've looked up on the internet.

I decide to just go all out, see what he likes. I wrap my lips around him and glide them down as far as they can go until he touches the back of my throat, making me gag.

"Goddamn," he exhales. "You can take so much of me."

His words spur me on. I suck up and down vigorously, letting him gag me each time. His hands fist into my hair as he makes almost-painful, choked sounds.

"Yeah, just like that. Take it deeper," he demands in a deep, groggy voice. "Choke on it like a good girl."

I've never been talked to like this. My panties instantly become wet as a moan escapes my throat. I wrap my hand around the base of his dick, where my mouth doesn't reach, then move it up and down in time with my mouth.

My tongue slides around his dick, trying to hit every spot for a taste.

"Fuck, I'm gonna come so fucking hard. Where did you learn to do this?" he growls.

I feel a pulsing sensation in his dick before his cum shoots out in warm, rhythmic jets.

I take all of it down, loving every single drop. We're both breathing heavily when I pop off of him and crawl upward until we're face-to-face.

His hands find my cheeks, and his lips crash against mine. It's ... everything. My heart soars into my throat, joy and disbelief tangling in my chest.

His mouth moves over mine like a man who knows what he wants and takes it. It's like I've never truly been kissed until now. He grazes my cheek, then trails down my neck, breath hot against my skin.

"Where did you learn how to do that, Natalie?"

My body locks. Every nerve inside me snaps taut.

What did he just say?

My stomach plunges as the name echoes inside my head.

"Natalie?" *I whisper.*

He jerks back like I burned him, nearly falling off the edge of the bed. He's panting, wide-eyed. His hands hover near his mouth, like he's trying to erase what just happened.

There's a beat of silence. Then it drops.

"Jessie?" *he growls—different now. Hard. Sharp.* "What the fuck are you doing?"

I blink. My lips still tingling from his kiss.

He is out of bed and pulling his boxers back up in the matter of seconds. His hands tangle in his hair as he rocks back and forth, like he's trying to wake from a nightmare.

Humiliation floods me. My face burns. My heart—God, my heart—shatters.

He jumps off the bed and begins pacing across the room, dragging both hands through his hair.

"You're my sister's best friend," he spits. *"You ... you just graduated high school, Jessie. Jesus."*

"I—" My voice is small, shaky. *"I thought—"*

"You thought what? *That this was okay? That there was something here?" He laughs bitterly, but there's no humor in it. Only rage. Only guilt.*

I can't speak. I can't even look at him.

"I should've never—" He bites the inside of his cheek, then turns away from me. "This was a mistake. All of it."

Tears sting my eyes, but I refuse to let them fall. He won't even look at me now. Because to him, I'm a child. A mistake.

And I don't understand why the rejection feels laced with something deeper, like he's breaking apart from the inside.

But I know he won't tell me.

He just shakes his head as I walk toward his door. "We can't, Jessie. Ever."

I don't ask why.

Because I already feel like I'm not enough. And I don't think I can survive hearing the truth if it's worse than that.

The memory always hits like a sucker punch, no matter how many years pass. I've replayed that night more times than I care to admit—searching for something I missed, some hidden clue in his expression, in his voice.

But the only thing I've ever found is silence.

He never gave me a real explanation. Never let me in. After that, he just stopped talking to me altogether. Despite my best attempts at moving past it.

And maybe that's what hurts the most. Not that he rejected me, not even that he mistook me for someone else.

But that he ruined a friendship over it. He never apologized for the outburst or how it'd made me feel.

I hate how he looked at me like I was a mistake he couldn't afford to face.

I was eighteen. He was twenty-four. I get it; the timing was awful.

But I'm twenty-seven now. And he's still acting like my existence is a problem he can't solve.

It's not about the age gap anymore.

So, what the hell is it?

Chapter Eight

Walker

I can't do this right now. I have a million things on my mind. I'm about to interview a nanny. A complete stranger I'm supposed to trust to take care of my daughter. I know my words came out harsh and strong.

But I'm hanging on by a thread, trying to keep my feelings for Jessie buried down deep, where they belong. I can't have her looking at me like that.

I close the door behind me and find her standing by the window in my family room, head down. She isn't moving, like she's caught in thought. Then I see a tear slip down her cheek, and I don't think I've hated myself more than I do in this moment.

Eli seems happy enough, so I put her down in the swing and fasten her in. I walk to where Jessie is and stand right behind her. I'm close. Too close. But I'm not worried about anything but her.

"Jessie," I whisper.

She straightens her back and wipes at her cheek.

"I'm sorry."

She spins around, peering up at me. I see the cracks in the tough facade she has built over the years. She wasn't always like this with me. Once upon a time, I was on the receiving end of her smiles and affection. It was always the highlight of my day.

Now, I'm the reason for her tears. Though I decided long ago we could never be together, it still kills me to know I've caused her pain.

"I'm fine," she replies bitterly.

I sigh heavily, wishing I could reach out and touch her. Offer some kind of comfort. But I know if I do that, I'll want more. And I know she isn't fine. I know her.

"I didn't mean to come off so ... rude," I admit, though I know I'm not saying the right things.

Nothing but the truth is going to ease her pain, and I can't tell her the truth.

A harsh laugh escapes her. "I get it now. Just the idea of us makes you sick. Message received."

I tilt my head as I look at her quizzically. She thinks I'm pushing her away because I'm not attracted to her. I slam my hands against the window above her head. Fuck, I hate that I'm in this position.

"Let me make one thing clear," I growl, our lips a breath away from each other. "If I could have you, I wouldn't hesitate for a second. You're not just the sexiest woman I've ever seen; you're the kind of woman who ruins every other woman for me."

I hear her sharp intake of breath.

"Why can't you have me?" she asks softly.

My forehead falls to hers, and I shake it back and forth. "I can't go there. It's not my place to tell. Just know … I've thought about what it would be like to finally be able to claim you as mine. And I'll think about it until the day I die."

Eli begins to cry, giving me the much-needed excuse to pull away from her before I do something I regret. I stop the swing and unbuckle her. She begins to soothe herself a little as soon as I pick her up.

I wonder if that possibly means she trusts me a bit. Maybe she finds comfort in me. Is that all it takes to gain the trust of a baby—twenty-four hours?

I feel Jessie's eyes on me. I'm afraid to meet her stare, but I gaze her way despite my uncertainty. Her arms are crossed as she leans against the window, watching me bounce Eli. She doesn't say anything. I don't say anything.

It feels like she's making a decision in her mind right now. I shouldn't have admitted that to her. It just makes things more complicated. But I couldn't let her think I wasn't interested. Fuck, I am so far beyond interested. I'm desperate.

Suddenly, a knock on the door brings me back to what my priority at the moment needs to be.

Jessie's eyes open wide. "Is that the nanny?" she asks.

I cough to clear my throat. "Yes."

"Here." She rushes over to me. "Give me Eli. I'll get her settled so you can start."

A fifty-year-old woman is waiting at the door for me. She's divorced, and her kids are grown up and out of the house. The interview goes by quickly, Jessie helping me with the questions.

When she leaves, I order us dinner, and we talk about what we thought as we eat. Eli is asleep in her swing.

"What did you think?" I ask as I swirl pasta on my fork.

She shrugs her shoulders. "I actually really liked her. She was nice and seemed like a very trustworthy person."

I nod my head. "The vetting process at the agency is extremely thorough. Her background is clean. What do you think about her nannying style?"

"She doesn't believe in letting the baby cry or self-soothe. I like that. I think she'll tend to Eli's needs well."

"I do too." I pause. "Do you think it's bad that I want to hire the first nanny I interview? Should I do more interviews?"

"I don't think you need to interview for the sake of interviewing. If it's a top-tier nanny agency, I think you're just looking for an agreement on how to nurture the baby. If you think you've found that, why not hire her?"

"That's true. I do like her. I felt comfortable around her. But I'll sleep on it."

I'm relieved that she isn't acting different toward me after what I confessed to her earlier. Maybe we can just let it go and pretend I never said anything. If she knows how I feel, how much I want her, things could get complicated.

Next thing I know, Eli wakes from her swing with a roaring scream. I jump off the couch and swoop her up. After I warm a bottle, which she refuses, I try to give her a pacifier.

"Maybe change her," Jessie offers from the couch.

I'm sweating at this point as panic takes up residence inside of me. I want to scream at Jessie, but I decide to bring Eli into my bedroom and change her. She wails even harder during the process and is no closer to being happier by the end. I pick her up and bring her back into the family room.

"Great advice, Einstein," I bark at her. "Now she's more upset."

Was that harsh? Yes. Is it hard to say the right thing when there's a screaming baby in your ear? Absolutely.

I try to bounce her up and down, but nothing works. I thought I'd started to figure it out. Either feed her, change her, or get her to sleep with a pacifier. This isn't part of the rotation. I feel out of control and completely useless.

Jessie stands up and extends her arms. "Here. Let me try."

I offer Eli to her, disappointed that I wasn't able to calm her down. I thought I might be capable of doing this single-dad thing on my own. Now, I'm not so sure.

Jessie makes her rounds, trying the same things that I did, but to no avail. She glances at her watch.

"You've got somewhere to be?" I quip, the crying beginning to get to me.

"I think this is the witching hour. Eva was telling me about it at breakfast the other day."

Now she's just talking crazy. Has the crying already made her go mad?

I extend my arms. "I think I should take Eli back. I don't know what you're talking about, but I don't want any voodoo magic around my child."

She stops bouncing Eli up and down. She stares at me in disbelief for a fraction of a second. Then her head falls back as she laughs boisterously. I cross my arms across my chest, not amused at all. I don't see how what I said was in any way humorous. Not to mention that my baby is still inconsolable, and neither of us can figure out what's wrong.

"Walker," she says in between her fits of laughter, "*witching hour* is a phrase they use to describe a specific time period where a baby cries and is difficult to console."

I feel heat spread across my face, realizing my assumption might have been a little extreme. She continues to laugh at my expense, and the sheer volume of it distracts Eli enough to calm her down.

She realizes it at the same time, looking down at my daughter with affection. "Is that what calms you down? Me laughing at your silly daddy?"

"Maybe it was your obnoxious laugh that scared her silent," I quip, not liking her and my daughter teaming up against me.

Jessie seems amused. "Why don't you go hide your candles? You wouldn't want me having access to those. I might break out in a ritual."

"Joke's on you. I don't own candles," I reply, then take Eli out of her arms. "Finish your dinner."

She shrugs her shoulders and falls down to the couch and grabs her plate.

An hour later, Eli is bathed, changed, fed, and in her bassinet in my bedroom. I walk out of my bedroom and literally fall face down on the couch as I let out a loud groan.

Jessie is sitting at the edge of the large sectional, her legs resting on the coffee table.

"How am I even functioning?" I sigh into the couch cushion.

She pats my head like I'm a damn child. "You'll get used to it. According to Eva, your body gets used to lack of sleep eventually. I would recommend not downing coffee and energy drinks."

I lift my head. Her bare legs are inches from me, tanned and toned. She must have changed into pajamas while I was getting Eli down. I shake my head and slam it back down on the cushion.

"Fuck my life," I growl to myself.

On top of being sleep-deprived, I've got Jessie's legs taunting me in my own home—reminding me what I want, but can't have.

"Oh, get over it, you big baby. Everyone goes through this with newborns."

I growl and roll over to my side. "Want to watch a movie or something?"

"Sure. FYI … I'm sleeping on the couch this time. You made it through last night. You can figure it out tonight."

I don't fight her on that. It's definitely for the best. I don't need any more temptation. She hasn't brought up what I said earlier, making me wonder if what I was admitting even sank in.

Chapter Nine

Jessie

I look over at him snoring on the couch, his broad chest rising and falling rhythmically. His words have been running on replay in my mind for hours. Eli's scream fest was the only time I was able to get it out of my head.

Now I lie next to him, our heads only a foot apart.

The way he looked tortured as he kept his hands off me, I felt the struggle inside of him; it was transparent.

And how he described it ...

He would die, wishing he could claim me as his.

My pussy clenches when I recall it.

He was so ... direct. Just like the night I'd tasted him. The words he spoke were so dirty, so honest. It'd made my insides melt from the scorching inferno it generated.

To this day, no man has ever spoken to me like that during sex. Walker is not only brave enough to match my fire but daring enough to burn even hotter.

His Redemption

But why can't he have me? What is holding him back? What can't he tell me?

Back then, I had just turned eighteen. I could possibly see why he would hesitate, though he didn't have to be such a dick about it. I was young and sensitive.

It can't be my age.

Ugh, I'm so frustrated. I've spent so many years hating him, thinking he was the spawn of Satan, for treating me so poorly. For pretending like I never existed after that night. I told myself time and time again that he just wasn't attracted to me, no matter how much that hurt. No matter how many times I swore I caught his eyes drinking me in with appreciation.

It's what drove my hatred all these years, fueling it for the next time I saw him—the anger from knowing that my body reacted to him so viscerally while he was indifferent to me.

But that's all gone, taken away from me in an instant. Vanished in a painstakingly sexy moment, where he had me pinned up against the window like he was seconds away from throwing caution to the wind and owning my body.

Somewhere in the middle of the night, I'm startled awake by Eli's wailing. I look over at Walker, who shed his clothes sometime in the night, all the way down to his black boxer briefs. His beauty fuels my anger.

I reach over and punch him in the stomach.

"Ughhhhh," he grunts in agony.

Honestly, I didn't punch him that hard. It's an overreaction.

He looks around like he doesn't know where he is. Once it dawns on him what's going on, he sits up.

"You could have just nudged me awake," he bites out as he stomps away in a daze.

I nod off back to sleep until Walker's presence wakes me again. He is pacing around the room, right in front of the coffee table, with Eli over his shoulder as he pats her back.

I take this time to watch him in the soft city glow coming from the window, casting him and Eli in a blanket of light. The way he sways back and forth with her chubby little fist caught under her chin. My heart cracks open even more, leaving crevices for him to sneak back in. I know this isn't good. I just need to get through a couple more nights. I'm sure by then he will tell Eva, and everything will be okay.

I'll be back at home and far away from him. I'm sure everything will go back to normal.

***

The glow of the laptop at night is starting to strain my eyes. I reach into my bag and grab my blue light glasses.

Today was crazy. I spent the morning with Eli while Walker went to work, and then we switched.

We are now sitting on his couch, working, while Eli sleeps in the other room. The monitor is sitting between us, the white noise machine sounding through the device.

I reach for the glass of wine and take a sip as I look up at the episode of *The Office* playing in the background.

Walker has on his glasses and is scowling down at his laptop like it just insulted his mother. I find it amusing to watch. He begins typing aggressively, each finger pushing harder than the last, until I'm afraid the keys are about to start flying across the room.

"Is everything all right over there, buddy?" I ask curiously, my smirk hiding behind my glass of wine.

"Everything's fine," he bites out as he continues to abuse his keyboard.

"Doesn't seem like it," I press, wondering what the hell has him so worked up.

He stops typing and looks over at me. "What makes you say that?"

"I don't know. Maybe the fact that if your keyboard could speak, it would be begging for mercy."

His jaw moves from one side to the other as he seems to work out what he wants to say, and then he takes a long, defeated breath.

"It's this damn case that our firm just landed. It's a once-in-a-lifetime kind of case, one that could make me the most-sought-after attorney in the city if I won."

"And you want it assigned to you?" I assume, realizing where this is going.

"I'm the best one for the job. I can do this. I can win this case. I just don't know if my hours this week are going to cost me the opportunity."

This week? If this case is as big as he is claiming it is, he would be working hours not suitable for a single father. Eli needs him. She can't have a mother who abandoned her and a father who is gone most of the time.

"If you did get awarded the case, you wouldn't be able to work your usual late hours. Not with Eli."

He runs his hand through his hair, then bangs it down on the couch, startling me. "Fuck. I can't let this opportunity go by."

I study the hard lines on his forehead as his anger emanates throughout the room. "Once upon a time, it was your dream to be a lawyer who helped the underdog. Not for the money. Not for the fame. But to help those that couldn't help themselves."

He slams his laptop shut and tosses it to the side. "Yeah, well, dreams are not always meant to come true."

His eyes look up and down my body in a way that makes me think he might be talking about more than just his work. It sends shivers up my spine.

Then his eyes dart down to the baby monitor. He picks it up and holds it to his ear, like he might have missed a noise. He's done that about thirty times since we sat down. It makes me smile.

"What are you smiling about?" he asks.

I shrug. "I'm silently judging your paranoia. Don't mind me."

He crosses his arms across his chest in defense. A giggle bubbles up before I can stop it. His forehead creases as his eyebrows rise.

"I'm not being paranoid."

I lean back into the couch, watching him sneak yet another glance at the baby monitor glowing on the couch between us. He wasn't even subtle about it—like if he stared hard enough, he could will the little green bars to stay steady forever.

A smile tugs at my mouth. "Yes, you are. If you're going to stare at that thing like it's a bomb about to go off, I should just confiscate it."

Before he can react, I snatch the monitor and lean away, holding it out of his reach.

He lunges forward instantly. "Hey, give it back."

I shake my head, laughing, leaning away from him as he reaches for it. "Nope. Consider this an intervention."

The couch cushion dips as he lunges, and I let out a squeal, twisting out of reach. He grabs for it, but I extend my arm farther behind me, arching out of his way. His hand closes around my wrist instead, warm and unyielding.

The laughter catches in my throat. Suddenly, he is braced over me, his weight close enough to press me into the cushions. My chest rises and falls against his, the monitor forgotten between us, my pulse loud in my ears.

His gaze meets mine, and for a second, it isn't teasing; it's dark, steady, too intense.

"You think this is funny?" he asks, voice rougher than it should be.

My mouth goes dry. My free hand flattens against his chest. Heat bleeds through his shirt, through my palm.

I swallow. "Maybe," I say, trying to sound breezy, even though my pulse is racing.

His grip loosens, but doesn't release. His thumb brushes lightly over my wrist. The shift in his touch sends a shiver down my spine. He is so close that I can see the faint stubble along his jaw, can feel the heat of his breath against my cheek.

It isn't about the monitor anymore. It's about this—him over me, the way the air appears to thicken, the awareness crackling like static between us.

The baby sighs faintly through the monitor speaker, and the soft sound startles me back into reality. My head snaps toward the device still clutched in my hand, and his gaze follows.

For a heartbeat, neither of us moves. Then he eases back just enough to give me space, though his eyes stay on me, like he hasn't quite decided to let go.

And, God help me, I'm not sure I want him to.

Chapter Ten

Walker

The sexual tension between us just continues to grow with every breath we take in the same room. If Eli hadn't interrupted the other night, I'm sure I would have kissed her. It's all I've been able to think about.

My body is in a constant state of arousal when she is around. I don't know what's happening to me. It's like no matter what she is doing, it turns me on. Even watching her wash bottles was giving me a boner.

I feel like we've gone back in time to when we were younger and I didn't have control of my own horniness. Forget being productive at work. My current clients are lucky their cases are slam dunks for me because I don't think my brain could focus long enough to read through hours of evidence and case law.

Which presents a pretty big problem, considering I'm gunning for the largest case of my career.

Yesterday, while Jessie watched Eli in the morning, I got

some more face time with Stewart and Henry. They asked where I'd been this week.

It's been four days, and they've already noticed that I'm not clocking twelve-to-fourteen-hour days, like I usually do.

I lied and told them my mom was sick. It's a shit excuse, and I know I'm going to hell for it, but I panicked. What I should have done was tell them the truth. I should tell them about Eli. I know it's the right thing to do. It also would effectively take my name out of the running for this pharmaceutical case.

Tonight is my final night with Jessie here. Tomorrow is Friday, and there's no reason for her to spend the night on the weekend. I know if I get her to myself for too long, I'm going to do something I'll regret.

That's why I've made a reservation for us to go out to dinner with Eli. Though at this point, I wonder if being in public could stop me from finally taking her in my arms and kissing those delectable lips.

Just as I'm pulling my shirt that's covered in Eli's spit-up over my head, my front door opens. It's weird, knowing Jessie has a key to my place and just walks in whenever she wants. I like it—and that's a fucking problem.

"Walker," she calls from the other room.

Eli is out there in her swing. She probably won't last long. I just gave her a bottle, but she seemed squirmy, like she wanted to move around. I just needed to come in here and change real fast.

"I'm in here," I shout as I toss my shirt into the hamper and open my drawer.

"I was thinking that maybe"—her voice sounds like it's getting closer—"Eli should ..." She's now standing in front of me.

It's the same damn look she gave me the other day when I opened the door without a shirt on. It's dangerous because it tells me just how affected she is by me, even when she pretends to hate me.

"Eli should?" I say to try and keep the conversation moving.

Maybe if we both pretend we don't want to fuck each other's brains out, the energy between us will settle.

She squeezes her eyes shut for a moment. I try not to smile, thinking if only she knew what I would do to corrupt her if I had the chance. If seeing me without a shirt on creates such a reaction, I can't imagine what would happen if I got a chance to lick her sweet little cunt.

Fuck, now I'm hard.

"Dinner!" I nearly shout, startling her and making her jump back in surprise.

"What?" she asks hesitantly.

I cough and nervously clear my throat as I try to save face. She's the only person who can garner such intense emotions from me. I'm not used to feeling like this.

"Dinner. Um, I made reservations for us to go out to dinner," I reply, trying to maintain a sense of indifference. "I thought getting out of the apartment would be good for Eli."

"Oh, um, yeah. That sounds great. Dinner." She shifts uncomfortably on her feet. "I'll just go, uh ... get changed first if that's okay."

"Yeah, totally. Get changed. I'll be out there in a minute."

She nods her head, then backs away slowly, like she has whiplash and is still trying to figure out what just happened.

I realize I'm going on the closest thing that might ever come to a date with Jessie. For some odd reason, my stomach twists at the thought.

I close my T-shirt drawer and walk into my closet. After taking too many minutes to decide, I land on a plain black button-down with jeans. Nice but can pass as casual with little effort.

I race into my bathroom to put on extra deodorant, run some more paste through my hair, and squirt on some cologne.

When I walk back out to the family room, Eli is starting to grunt and groan in the swing. I take her out and scan the room as panic sets in.

What the hell do I bring out to a restaurant?

Shit. This was a bad idea. What if she's hungry? Or needs a diaper change? Or poops up the back of her pajamas like she did yesterday? Where will she sleep if she gets tired?

"Okay, I'm ready," Jessie calls from behind me as she exits my guest bathroom. "What's wrong?" she asks immediately.

"What do you mean?"

"You look like you saw a ghost."

I look around the room, not sure how to respond. "I don't know what to pack. How do people bring babies to restaurants? I might need all of this stuff." I gesture around the room, slightly dramatic.

She brings her hand up to stifle her laughter. "You just pack a diaper bag."

"With all of it?" I ask.

She grabs a bag and throws a few different onesies in it, diapers, and wipes. Then she measures two bottles with the formula and packs a bottle of water. I just stand and watch, thinking she is the only one I would have wanted to experience this past week with.

It's been a roller-coaster ride of emotions, but having Jessie around makes everything better.

"Where will she sleep?" I follow up with when she stands in front of me with the diaper bag.

"The stroller. They allow those in restaurants, you know."

I nod my head. "Okay, that will work. Maybe we can walk her there in the stroller and get her asleep."

"Now you're thinking like a dad." She smiles.

We buckle Eli into the car seat that slides into the stroller, then ride the elevator down to the street. Luckily, I actually thought about the logistics of how hard it would be to travel far with Eli, so the restaurant I booked is only a couple of blocks away.

It only takes us five minutes to get there. Eli fell asleep almost instantly. Jessie said noise and movement knock most babies out. I guess that's what makes bedtime such a horrible time with babies. Quiet and still.

I'm surprised how easily we get settled at our table with Eli's stroller parked right next to us. The moment I sit down and realize it, I take a deep breath.

Jessie opens her menu and peeks over at the sound of my sigh. "I think I can actually feel the relief in that sigh."

I chuckle to myself as I grab the menu in front of me. "I might have been internally panicking the entire way here, wondering about everything that could go wrong."

"Let's get you a drink. You need it."

"You're not wrong about that," I reply. "But I think we both need it. How about we share a bottle of wine?"

She raises an eyebrow. "You trying to get me drunk?"

I smirk. "It's not like it's hard. You're such a lightweight."

Her mouth falls open. "Rude."

I shrug. "You're not denying it."

Just then, the waitress—a tall brunette—approaches. She smiles down at the stroller. "She's precious. Congratulations."

I look over at Jessie, realizing she thinks Eli's ours. Together. Jessie's throat bobs as her eyes catch mine. She doesn't know what to say.

"Thank you," I reply.

It's not worth correcting her. Plus, a part of me wants it to be true. I might never have Jessie, but maybe tonight, I can pretend it's real.

"I think we are going to share a bottle of the 2010 Chianti," I tell the waitress.

We decide to place our orders quickly as well, just in case we're on borrowed time with Eli.

After the wine is poured and we wait for our food, I can't stop looking across the table at Jessie. I know this is supposed to be a night where I keep her at arm's length, but the idea of treating this like a real date is too tempting.

"Tell me something," I ask her as I lean back in my seat.

Her forehead scrunches, like it always does when she's confused. "What do you mean?"

"I mean ... tell me something about yourself that I've missed over the years. You know, with all this hate between us ... I know there's tons of stuff in your life I've missed."

I can see she is skeptical of why I'm asking. I don't blame her. For years, I've kept my distance, treating her like the plague in order to protect her. Now, I'm too close—and I want more.

"You've missed a lot in the last nine years, Walker."

"Nothing like the present to change that," I challenge as I take a sip of wine. "I'll go first if you'd like."

Her lips purse with interest as she leans her elbows on the table. "Fine. I'll go if you go."

I match her posture, our faces now only a foot apart. The urge to reach across the table and tuck a piece of hair behind her ear is strong, but I resist.

I scrub my chin as I think of something that she doesn't know about me that might give her a glimpse into a part of me not everybody knows. "Hmm, I forgot my birthday three years in a row. I never realized it until I got home and saw a message from Eva, wishing me a happy birthday."

Her eyes bug open as her hand lightly hits the table. "Walker, that's awful. What about your parents?"

I cock a brow at her. "Come on, Jessie. You know my parents. They're too busy to remember something like their kids' birthdays."

"What about the guys?" she asks.

I shrug. "They're busy too."

"Well, that's just sad. That's no way to live your life. That's not a flex, Walker."

"I never said it was. It was just the first thing that came to mind."

I wonder why it's what came to mind. Is it that, underneath everything, it bothers me that I never remembered my own birthday or had anyone in my day-to-day life who did?

I don't hold it against the guys. We don't remember shit like that. Even if we did, we aren't the type to call the other up to tell each other it's our birthday.

But I remember Jessie and Eva always made such a big deal out of one another's birthdays. It made me smile to see how easily they showed affection toward each other.

Her head shakes back and forth, like she is still in disbelief at my confession.

"Your turn," I tell her.

She places her wineglass on the table and sits up straighter. "My turn. Okay, let me think."

She mimics my gesture earlier and scratches her chin. I can't help but laugh at her performance, leaning forward curiously as I wait.

"Okay. I've got one. I have an Excel spreadsheet, ranking each dessert I try in the city."

"Every single dessert?" I ask to clarify.

She giggles and nods. "Every. Single. Dessert."

"You're kidding?"

"Nope. Not kidding at all. It's long. Extensive. I give them star rankings from one to five and explain my reasoning."

I find that incredibly endearing and very like Jessie. She's always loved her sweets. "I think that means we need to get a dessert tonight. I'll help you rank it."

"You mean, you don't think that's the most pathetic thing you've ever heard?" She snorts before she takes a sip of wine.

"It's a cute kind of pathetic," I tease.

She tosses her napkin at me, and my head falls back with laughter. The waitress interrupts with our dinner, which is exactly when Eli decides to grace us with her presence. I scoot the stroller closer to me to pick her up and instantly notice the foul smell coming from her.

"I think I need to change her," I tell Jessie. "Where's the restroom so I can change her diaper?" I ask the waitress.

She looks at me awkwardly. "Oh, there's only a changing table in the women's restroom. Maybe your wife can change her?"

I nearly fall out of my seat. "There's no changing table in the men's room?"

"Uh, no, sir. I'm sorry."

How in the hell am I supposed to change my daughter's diaper? Is this some kind of rule everywhere? What about a single dad like myself? Am I not allowed to take my baby out?

I start to panic as I realize the world might not be set up for the convenience of my and Eli's situation. This was a mistake. I shouldn't have been so bold, thinking I could handle going out after only one week with a baby.

"I'll take her, honey." Jessie smiles knowingly at me. "You do so much already."

She stands up and takes Eli from my arms, then grabs the diaper bag. My knee bounces up and down nervously as I watch her disappear with my baby that I apparently can't take care of in public.

By the time they're back, Eli is happy as a clam. I take her from Jessie and prop her up on my lap.

"You eat," I tell her. "I don't want your food to get cold."

I grab a slice of pizza and take a bite, the taste not even registering in my brain.

"Hey," Jessie calls from across the table, pulling me from my thoughts. "It'll get easier. Not every restaurant will be like this. This one is apparently stuck in the dark ages."

"So, when I go out to dinner, it'll be a toss-up on whether or not I can take care of my baby?" I reply with a bitter taste in my mouth.

The sympathetic look on her face tells me everything I need to know.

The rest of the evening sinks under a heavy weight. What I thought I needed—a distraction, a way to smother the fire of my longing—turns out to be something else entirely. I'm forced to see the truth—I have a hard road ahead of me as Eli and I try to carve out our place in a world that was never built with us in mind.

Chapter Eleven

Jessie

I've been in a weird mood all day. It started as soon as Walker came home from work at lunchtime. I knew it was the end of my time with him and Eli.

The moment I handed her back to him, I grabbed my bags and rushed out before he could see the tears pricking my eyes. I felt like a fool. I had spent one week with them. There was no reason for me to feel so emotional about it.

The entire walk to work, I cursed myself for letting my heart get mixed up in Walker again. I'd thought I buried my feelings deep enough that they'd never resurface.

And yet spending the week with him—watching him become a father—it was impossible not to crack in half as he took on the role with no questions asked.

I glance down at my watch. It's after seven, and I know I need to go home. Just thinking about going back to my place depresses me.

I need to shake this.

With Eva at home with the baby, I know I have to find another alternative.

I reach for my phone and send out a text to my friend Melissa. We went to undergrad and law school together. We go way back, having known each other since we were eighteen. She's a lawyer at a large firm here in the city.

Me: Tell me you're out right now. I need a drink.

As I pack my things into my brown leather bag, I feel the fear pressing against my chest. It took me years to stop thinking about Walker every night before I went to sleep. I can't let this happen again.

My phone beeps. I nearly knock it off my desk as I fumble to open it.

Melissa: You're in luck. Just got done having a drink with our new clients. They're the worst humans on this planet. Come join me. I need another drink to recoup from the last hour of my life.

I text her back as I walk out the door.

Me: Tell me where. I'll be there soon.

On the way to the restaurant, I decide to call my dad, and just like always, he picks up on the first ring. He always drops everything he's doing to take my calls. I've told him time and time again that he doesn't need to do that.

"Hi, Jessie girl."

I smile at the familiar greeting. "Hi, Dad."

"How's it going? Have you had a good week?"

"Oh, you know, it's been ... different. I've spent every night at Walker's, trying to help him out. Tonight is my first night back to my normal routine."

"Ah, poor guy. Are you sure he's gonna be okay tonight?"

"I'm sure he's fine, Dad. He caught on pretty quick. I'd thought he was a lost cause, but he's really stepped up."

"I'm not surprised. Good kid, that one. He's going to be a terrific father."

"Yeah, he might not know it yet, but I think so too. Anyway, how are you doing? Any plans for the weekend?"

He sighs. "Oh, your mother has our calendar filled with social events. I tell ya, she has more energy now than when I met her."

Typical. Social status is very important to my mother. She has always put it at the top of her list of priorities—frequently over her responsibility as a parent.

"Why don't you just tell her you don't want to go? It's your life too."

He chuckles. "Because I love her and want to make her happy. Plus, it's easier to go with the flow. Oh, she's right here. You want to say hi?"

Before I can respond, insisting I have to go, he hands her the phone.

"Hello? Jessie?"

"Hi, Mom. How are you?" I ask, bracing for the answer.

She goes into a five-minute tangent about what Barbara down the street said about their friend Nancy. By the time she's done, I'm standing outside of the restaurant, desperately trying to figure out how to get off the phone.

"Oh dear, look at the time. We have to be at the Walshes' house in thirty minutes. I'm so sorry, but your father and I must go. Talk to you soon. Love you."

Instead of dwelling on how little I have in common with my mother, I walk through the doors to the restaurant to find Melissa waiting at a high-top table just to the left of me. She waves and smiles enthusiastically as soon as she spots me, then holds up a glass of white wine as I approach.

"I ordered your favorite," she tells me as I sit.

My shoulders sag with relief. "You're the best. Thank you." The first sip goes down easily, the stress of the day slowly melting away.

"Rough day at work?" she asks.

"I wish," I reply as I take another sip.

What I wouldn't give to be dealing with work-related stress at the moment. There's always a solution or an end to it eventually. There are distractions after work, like friends or my favorite TV shows to offer comfort.

But I know what it's like to cry myself to sleep over Walker. There's nothing that makes it better.

Her tone turns more serious. "Is everything all right?"

She knows about Walker. I told her all about it my freshman year of college, when I was consumed with my feelings of regret and embarrassment.

"It's ... Walker."

Her eyes widen with disbelief. "Walker? Like *Walker*, Walker? The same Walker who broke your heart and made you feel small and insignificant?"

I lean my elbow on top of the table and let my forehead fall to my hand. "Ugh, yes. That one."

"What the hell did he do now? I thought you hardly saw him despite Eva living here now."

"I didn't. Not until he called me, panicking, last week."

"He called you? The nerve of the asshole. What did he want?"

"It's the craziest story, Melissa. You're never going to believe it."

"Try me," she replies, crossing her arms across her chest.

I run through the entire week of events. Every. Single. Detail. Even him pressing me up against the wall, nearly kissing me, and telling me how badly he wanted me, but couldn't have me.

Her hand is resting on her chest, as if the story physically struck her. Her other hand is stuck in motion halfway to her mouth. "You're kidding me. Jessie! Holy shit!"

I raise my glass, then take a sip. "Yep! Hence my desperate need for a drink."

"And so ... like ... now what? How are you feeling about all of it?"

I glance away, the pain rising to my chest. I try to blink away the tears that hit my eyes.

Her hand rests on my arm. "I'm sorry, Jessie. I know how hard it was for you to get over him the first time."

I meet her eyes. "I don't think I ever really got over it. I just buried my feelings."

She nods in understanding. "I don't get it. What does he mean, he can't have you?"

A bitter laugh escapes. "Who knows? He won't talk about it. I thought it might have been how young I was at the time, but that doesn't make sense. That wouldn't be an issue now. But he's still acting like there's something holding him back." I shake my head. "It was easier to hate him when I thought he just didn't want me. Now ... when he acts like it's torture to stay away ... I feel ... shit ... angry again, I guess. But in a different way."

"That makes total sense. Of course you're angry. It's not fair for him to be so vague with you. And to call you, of all people, to drop everything and help? Ugh, asshole."

I should jump on the bandwagon and vent my frustrations. Calling him an asshole worked a decade ago, but I don't feel that way anymore. Deep down, I'm glad he called me. I loved every second of my time with him and Eli.

I drag a hand through my hair, frustrated with the whirlwind inside of me. It would be easier if I could just shut it all off, pretend that none of it mattered to me. But the truth is, he's tangled into everything. Every quiet moment when I let myself imagine what could be. And no matter how hard I try, I can't untangle myself from him.

"But he's not an asshole. It was easy for me to tell myself that all these years. It kept the anger at bay so I could make it through another day without him. But now ..." I say as I wipe away a tear. "Now, it's like that dam is broken. I got a glimpse back into his soul, and I can no longer pretend."

"So, what are you going to do?"

I sigh as I face my new reality. "Nothing. There's nothing to do. I just have to ... feel my feelings."

The waitress walks by us, and Melissa stops her. "Hi. Can we get two more glasses of wine, please?" She turns back to me. "In that case, we need more alcohol."

A quiet laugh tumbles from my lips. "I'm sorry. I didn't mean to make this night so depressing."

She turns her head to the side as her gentle eyes hold mine. "That's what friends are for. We sit through the depressing times, even if there's no solution, and help ease the pain."

Melissa does her best to distract me for the next couple of hours. We laugh and reminisce about old times as we get tipsy off our three glasses of wine.

The laughter fades the moment I hug her goodbye and walk home to my apartment. The silence in my bedroom presses in, too heavy, too sharp. The memories, the questions, the ache in my heart—it all comes rushing back to me as I lie in bed. I sink further into my pillow, wondering if tomorrow will feel any different ... or if the morning light will only make the weight of it all harder to bear.

Chapter Twelve

Walker

"All right, Eli," I say as we ride up the elevator together, her lying in her stroller, "this is going to be a new adventure for us. I don't know how long we will be out, but it's really important. I need you to be a good girl so we can spoil Jessie. She saved our butts this week and deserves it. Can you do that for her?"

She smiles up at her kitty hanging from her car seat.

"I'm going to take that as a yes," I reply as the elevator comes to a stop and the doors open.

We just had our first morning alone together without Jessie's help. She started bawling her eyes out during my shower. I had to run out wet and naked to soothe her in her bassinet, shampoo in my hair and dripping down my body.

It was ... quite the experience.

I had a minor panic attack, where I thought there was no way in hell I'd be able to live my life again until Eli was in kindergarten. There was a good hour of catastrophic thinking that led to difficult breathing before I splashed cold water on my face and snapped out of it.

I am now fully showered, suds and all washed out of my hair. Both Eli and I are fed and just went to the bathroom—hers was in her diaper, but I'll still call it a win. Maybe one less poop explosion to clean out in public.

I've never been to Jessie's apartment before, but I've had her address for years. I've known her address in the city. I might have had to keep my distance, but I've always been close enough to know she's safe. I never liked her living by herself in this city.

But I gave up the right to have a say-so in the matter.

I raise my hand and knock it against her door. After about a minute, I glance down at my watch. It's eight thirty in the morning. Could she be out somewhere already?

I knock again and wait. The door swings open, and I'm met with a pair of tired green eyes looking back at me. She's in nothing but a T-shirt that's hiked up way too high, giving me a glimpse of her silky thighs.

I stand there, in awe of just how damn beautiful she is, hating my dumb luck that the only woman in the world I would die to have happens to be the one whose world I could crumble in less than a minute.

"What are you doing here?" she grumbles groggily.

My eyes drag up and down her body. "What are you doing, answering your door, dressed in next to nothing?"

She rubs one of her eyes as she yawns. "I didn't really think about it. I'm tired."

I push through the door and close it behind me, Eli still cooing up at her cat.

"That's your excuse? You're tired? What if I was a delivery guy? I could've taken one look at you and forced my way into your apartment."

She smiles softly. "You did do that."

"That's my point, Jessie. It's not safe. Don't ever do that again."

"Good morning to you too," she says with her all-too-familiar attitude, then bends down and smiles at Eli. "And good morning to you, sweetie pie."

"Dammit, Jessie," I growl because her ass cheeks are hanging out. I close my eyes and hang my head back. "Please go put some clothes on."

"How about you tell me why you're here first?" she replies defiantly.

I open my eyes, hoping she's standing straight up again—and thankfully, she is. "We're going shopping. Remember? It was part of the deal."

"Walker, you don't have to do that. I'm not going to make you spend your money on me."

I place my hands on her shoulders and turn her around. "Get your butt in your room and get changed. We are going shopping. I will not take no for an answer."

I push her into her room.

She turns around, scoffing at me. "You're so bossy."

My brows furrow. "Don't make me show you what bossy looks like."

I turn around before I fuck her against the wall and give her bossy.

I scan her apartment, noticing just how cramped it is. The kitchen barely fits two people, no table in sight. She probably eats standing at the counter or perched on that small sofa in the living room.

But this is the life she's chosen—simplicity over ambition, passion over paychecks. And damn if I don't respect her for it. I've been clawing my way toward power for years, chasing my father's approval like it was the only prize worth winning. The cruel truth? No matter what I accomplish, it's never enough for him. Maybe it never will be.

Jessie walks out, dressed casually in light jeans that are ripped at the knees, white sneakers, and a white T-shirt with gold jewelry.

"Okay, I'm ready. Where are we going?"

"I figured we'd start off on Fifth Avenue, then maybe make our way over to SoHo," I tell her as I push the stroller to the front door.

When we get into the elevator, I watch her as she shifts her weight from one side to the other nervously.

"Are you nervous?" I ask curiously.

She looks up at me with big doe eyes. "This feels weird. I don't want to take your money. And ... I don't shop at these places. I've never had the money."

I reach for her hand and give it a squeeze, finding it impossible to let go. Without thinking, I thread my fingers through hers. The simple connection feels more natural than breathing.

"I want to spoil you today. And I'll make sure everybody treats you like the most important person in the room."

The air in the elevator turns thick as I rub circles on her hand with my thumb. She doesn't answer. Her eyes hold mine, and she stares at me like she's trying to figure me out. I'm sure none of this makes sense to her.

Then the doors open, and the moment is broken. She pulls her hand away and adjusts her shirt.

We hit up a café first to grab a coffee and pastry for breakfast. Eli fell asleep on the stroller ride there and has been knocked out ever since. We drink our coffee as we walk to Fifth Avenue.

I have a couple of appointments set up with the stores on Fifth to get us started. I want someone to be available to Jessie's beck and call. She can try to deny it all she wants today, but I know she really wants to take me up on this. The size of her apartment just shows how little her company is paying her. She deserves this shopping spree.

She deserves *everything*.

She might not know it, but I follow her career. I know just how many families she's helped or children she's saved from an abusive or neglectful parent. She really is living out her dream that she's had since high school.

We step into a cathedral of fashion, two soaring floors,

draped in endless rows of clothing that seem to stretch on forever. A woman in a blue pantsuit meets us at the door.

"Hello." She smiles with her red lips. "Welcome. How may I assist you?"

I can feel the nerves radiating off Jessie, so I wrap an arm around her waist and pull her against my side. "Hi. My name is Walker Harlow. I have an appointment."

Jessie cranes her neck, then looks at me with confusion written all over her face. I wink at her, which just seems to fluster her more. A deep chuckle escapes from my throat. I like disarming her usual tough facade. This is the Jessie I remember. I've missed her. We used to have so much fun together.

"Oh, hello, Mr. Harlow. We have you all set up in our private changing room. My name is Roxanne. I'll be working with you today."

I nod at her. "This is Jessie. You have my permission to spoil her rotten. No limit today."

Her subtle excitement doesn't slip past me. I know they work on commission.

"Of course. We will make sure she is well taken care of. Please, follow me."

We are escorted into a private area in the back of the first floor with a long cream couch, a floor-length mirror framed in gold, and a black curtain off to the corner.

The coffee table in front of me has a bottle of chilled champagne and a charcuterie board. I roll the stroller in front of the couch off to the corner to keep it out of the way, then take a seat.

"You just sit and relax. Jessie and I are going to go have some fun." Roxanne smiles brightly, then grabs Jessie's hand.

Jessie looks at me like a deer in headlights. I pull out my phone and begin to sort through work emails. This is not like most Saturdays. I usually get in a solid eight-hour workday. Sunday is much of the same—maybe a five-hour day if I'm feeling run-down.

An email sent early this morning catches my eye. It's from Stewart, one of our majority-owned partners. He's requesting a meeting with me on Monday morning.

I know it's about the high-profile case. He doesn't do one-on-one meetings unless he's discussing major business. We have nothing else on our docket worthy of a meeting with him.

I'd usually go into the meeting with confidence, knowing I was the best choice and showing it with how I carried myself. I'm not so sure now. I wonder how much they noticed of my absence this week. Hopefully not the full extent that I was actually gone. I could've been in court, and they don't generally micromanage, but it's still leaving me feeling rattled.

I wanted to get more face time in with Stewart and Henry. Who knows what Pierce has accomplished with my time away? Probably shit-talking me left and right.

I toss my phone to the side in frustration. Last week, I was at the height of my career with nothing but possibilities.

Today, I'm grappling with the weight of choices I never saw coming, wondering if I've already lost everything I've worked for.

The bottle of champagne rests on the blistering cold ice. I scoot to the edge of the couch and grab it out of the bucket, then pop it open. The pop of the cork is sharp, but not sharp enough to silence the reminder that my life is slipping out of my hands.

Just as I'm pouring the second flute for Jessie, she walks back into the room with Roxanne following behind her, rolling a rack filled with clothes.

My eyebrows rise as I take in all of the items. "Wow. You gathered all of that quickly."

Roxanne smiles enthusiastically. "It's my job. Plus, this one has a figure to die for. I may have gotten carried away with my excitement to dress her."

Jessie's shoulders are no longer at her ears. She seems to have relaxed back to her normal posture. "Roxanne is amazing. She's my new favorite person."

Eli cries in the stroller. I stand up and wheel her closer to me, then pull her out. "I think she's offended that *she's* not your new favorite person."

Jessie's lips turn down. "Eli girl, you're my most favorite. I'm so sorry."

She takes her from my arms and gives her chubby cheek a big kiss. My heart flips over in my chest. It stirs something deep within me, equal parts warmth and ache. She fits so easily into this moment, into our lives, that it's almost too easy to imagine a future that isn't mine to hope for.

"She's precious," Roxanne gushes as she grabs Eli's little hand and rubs her skin. "You two made one beautiful baby girl."

It's like pouring salt in the wound. I grab my champagne glass and take a large sip while Jessie smiles as she holds Eli in her arms.

"Oh, I'm not her mother. Walker and I are just ... friends."

"Really?" Roxanne asks, not even trying to hide her surprise. "Well, you could've fooled me." She grabs two large handfuls of clothes. "Anyway, I'm going to hang these in your room behind this curtain. While you try some of these on, I'll go find some more options."

With Roxanne gone, Eli starts to wiggle and whine in Jessie's arms.

I reach into the diaper bag and pull out a bottle. "Here. I'll take her. She needs to eat. You go ahead and begin the fashion show."

She hands her back to me. "Fashion show? You don't seriously think I'm modeling this stuff for you?"

"Of course I do. I'm here to help you. Don't you want my opinion?"

"Your opinion or your smart-ass remarks?" She crosses her arms across her chest.

I place the bottle in Eli's mouth and lean back against the couch. "Can't it be both?"

She rolls her eyes. "Ugh, you are so annoying."

"I think you love it." I smile confidently up at her.

She tries not to smile, but I see the hint of one tugging at the corner of her mouth.

"Get your cute butt in there and try some clothes on."

Instead of fighting me on it, she actually spins around and walks into the changing room. The curtain closes, and I focus back on Eli, who is sucking down her bottle.

When she comes back out, she's wearing a white sheath dress with a mandarin collar with a matching belt at the waist with a gold buckle. She looks like a high-powered attorney, ready for a day in court.

"Classy," I tell her as she walks in front of the mirror.

"It's nice. I'd be terrified to eat anything in it, but I do really like it."

She cranes her neck as she continues to look at herself from different angles. Her curves are pure perfection. The mound of her ass is accentuated flawlessly in the dress.

"Looks like it's going in the yes pile."

"Maybe. I don't want to go crazy here, Walker. Maybe a dress or two."

I laugh loudly at the absurdity. "Babe, we aren't leaving here until we have enough to fill your closet. Next one. Time is ticking."

The next ten items are amazing. I say yes to all of them, but she's a bit more critical, saying her hips look too wide in one. She actually says she feels fat in another. It takes everything in me not to lose my shit on her for ever uttering such words. I love her curves, but I'm trying to be respectful and not force her to like something she just isn't feeling.

Roxanne continues to bring in stacks of clothes. I'm on my second glass of champagne and finding that I'm actually having a good time. Who knew shopping could be fun?

Though it might not be the shopping I like as much as watching Jessie show off her killer body to me over and over. And there's nothing better than watching her smile and laugh, enjoying my company as well.

Eli hung out for the first hour but is now conked out again in the stroller.

"This is a nice pantsuit, right?" she asks, once again in front of the mirror. "Would you be intimidated if I walked into the courtroom, wearing this?"

My eyes roam the length of her body in the fitted gray pantsuit. "Intimidated? Babe, the jury wouldn't stand a chance with you in that suit—hell, I wouldn't either."

"Okay, I guess this can go in the maybe pile."

Oh, and after all this time, she is still hanging on to this maybe pile, like she might win this battle of monitoring how much we spend. It's sweet that she thinks I wouldn't spend my entire life savings to make her happy.

"Okay, I thought we could switch to some evening wear." Roxanne marches in animatedly. "Time to sex you up for a night out on the town."

Fuck. Roxanne hangs her new choices in the changing room, then runs out to start picking shoes. Hopefully nothing too sexy. I don't need to be sporting a hard-on in the store.

"Thank you." Jessie smiles. "I don't know when I'll need sexy clothes, but I'll give them a try."

Roxanne walks away, leaving us alone again. Eli is still sleeping soundly in the corner.

"Here we go. Another round. Are you bored out of your mind yet?" she says as she reaches for the curtain.

"Miserable," I joke, too afraid to tell her it's the best Saturday I've ever had in my life.

She pulls the curtain closed. It takes a minute for me to notice, but she didn't close it all the way. There's about six inches of open space at the end. With her back to me, she unbuttons her jacket and discards it on the bench in front of her. Her black lace bra holds up her breasts, revealing her creamy skin.

I should look away—I know I should. But instead, I watch. The gap in the curtain gives me just enough of her, and when her eyes find mine in the mirror, the air shifts. Surprise flashes across her face, yet she doesn't turn or pull the curtain closed. She simply holds my gaze, her expression softening into something else—a quiet curiosity that roots me to the spot.

Her hands work the button at the top of her pants, and then she slowly drags them down her legs inch by inch, her eyes not leaving mind for a second. I break the contact. She's wearing a thong, and each creamy cheek is now showcased in front of me like a forbidden temptation—one I have no business staring at. Heat coils low in my stomach, my pulse pounding in my ears as I fight every instinct screaming at me to close the distance between us.

My dick strains in my pants. I adjust myself to make room for my growing erection. Her eyes watch me as she steps out of her pants on the floor. Standing now in nothing but her panties and bra.

Her hand reaches behind her back, working to unclasp her bra. I can't breathe as I watch. Waiting like I might combust if she doesn't let it drop. Her breath hitches as her bra slips away, but she doesn't move to cover herself. Instead, she holds my gaze in the mirror, daring me to keep looking.

The sight of her soft curves and flushed skin, those hard peaks drawing me in—it's enough to undo me. She's flawless. I swallow down the desperation I feel to suck her nipple into my mouth and coax it with my tongue.

Roxanne breaks the spell I'm under when she comes rushing in with a high-pitched voice. "Okay, I'm back with some amazing shoes." She places stacks of boxes outside of the curtain. "If you need to see some of those dresses in heels, I have a selection for you right out here."

Jessie is fumbling around in the dressing room, reaching for a dress frantically. "Thanks, Roxanne," she replies with a bit of guilt in her voice.

I shift around uncomfortably as I take a few subtle deep breaths, trying to gather myself.

Roxanne stands anxiously on the other side of the curtain. "Let's see what you've got. I can't wait to see you in these dresses."

Jessie pulls back the curtain. She looks breathtaking in a shimmery gold dress that molds to her body, pushing her breasts up to peek over the top in a tantalizing way. It's short, cutting off only a couple of inches below her bottom. Her silky white thighs are on display again.

Jessie stands in front of the mirror.

Roxanne clasps her hands together. "You look ... stunning," she gushes. "I knew this dress would be perfect. Your body was made for this dress."

She's got that right.

"What do you think?" Jessie eyes me in the mirror.

I clear my throat. "Trouble. That's what I think."

"It's a keeper. We must put it in the yes pile. Let me see if I can find some jewelry that goes well with it."

"Oh, no. I don't need—"

"Perfect, Roxanne. We definitely need jewelry," I cut in.

Roxanne walks out, winking at me as if she's onto me. Jessie has already gone back into the dressing room. Just before I can take a seat, the curtain opens.

"Umm, I can't seem to unzip the dress."

"I think I can manage that," I say coolly, though nothing inside of me feels that way.

I follow her back into the dressing room, not sure what makes me close the curtain behind me. She faces the mirror with a nervous energy radiating off of her.

"I don't know how I managed to zip it up in the first place." Her voice cracks.

"I don't mind helping." The mood has shifted, like we are

right back to where we were five minutes ago, when she was undressing for me.

My dick hardens instantly. My fingers barely touch her skin when her body visibly shivers. If the faintest of touches gets a reaction, I can't imagine how she would react to my tongue against her clit or my cock buried in her pussy.

The thoughts take me away to a place where I think maybe one touch is okay. We both clearly want it.

I drag the zipper down all the way to the bottom, where the top of her thong is exposed. That's it. My job here is done. But instead of moving, we connect in the mirror again. Her chest is rising and falling rapidly.

She drags the straps off of her shoulders, but the dress doesn't go anywhere, still molded to her. I grab the straps myself and pull them down, waiting for her to tell me to stop. When she doesn't, I continue to move them down, and the top of the dress begins to descend around her breasts.

I watch in the mirror as her breasts pour out of her dress. I work it all the way down to her hips, just past her thighs, letting it fall to the ground.

The tension in the room could drown us both, heavy and undeniable. My hand rests on her stomach just above her belly button. I pull her back against my body so she can feel what she's doing to me.

Her jaw falls open as my dick rests in between her ass cheeks. I growl with anger and resentment. I should be able to touch her. She was meant to be touched by me.

My hand slowly edges up her stomach until my fingers

caress the bottom of her left breast. Before I can move any further, Roxanne's voice echoes outside the curtain.

"Jessie, you just have to try this dress on."

My hand freezes, then drops. Jessie steps forward and covers her chest, suddenly self-conscious about being naked in front of me. Roxanne reaches into the room and holds the dress out.

"Thanks, Roxanne. I'll give it a try," Jessie mumbles frantically.

I wait until it sounds like Roxanne is out of the room, then peek out to confirm she is gone. Before I take a seat, I check on Eli, who is still sound asleep. I have the traveling sound machine playing on top of the stroller, which must be drowning out our voices enough for her to sleep.

Jessie comes out in another tight dress that leaves little to the imagination. This one is a floor-length red, but the slit cuts all the way up to her hip. Her long, toned legs are on display every time she takes another step toward the mirror.

"Wow," I breathe out.

"You like it?" she asks.

Roxanne walks in, ruining the moment again. I'm beginning to think she's doing this on purpose. "Jessie ... that dress."

"I know." Jessie smiles. "I've never owned something like this. It would be perfect for a fancy dinner. I just need to get myself a date."

"I'm sure you'll have no problem with that."

They continue talking and laughing, but I can't hear the words. The pulse of my anger is ringing in my ears. How did I not think about this? She's going to wear the clothes that I pay for to go on a date ... with another man.

I can't shake my anger for the rest of the day. We spend another hour looking at shoes and jewelry, but my mind is elsewhere.

By the time we get to the counter, Eli is awake, and Jessie is holding her to keep her happy. As instructed, Roxanne has rung up everything in the maybe pile and more.

"This is too much, Walker. I don't need all of this. You absolutely cannot buy it all."

"Good thing it's not about what you need," I mutter, handing the associate my black card. My tone is sharper than I intended, but I don't take it back.

She frowns, stepping closer, lowering her voice. "I mean it. The dresses, shoes, work clothes ... it's too expensive."

"Then consider it my problem, not yours."

Her lips part like she wants to argue, but the words die under the weight of my glare. She sighs and shakes her head, defeated while the associate bags everything up.

The anger still simmers in my chest, but beneath it all, there's something else that I can't shake—the gut-wrenching fear that she'll walk out of here, wearing everything I bought ... only to belong to someone else for the night.

Chapter Thirteen

Jessie

Nothing about today has gone how I planned it. I didn't really believe that we were going to go shopping. Sure, in the moment, I was all for taking his money. But as the days passed, I knew I wasn't actually going to take him up on the offer.

Little did I know, he was going to show up at my apartment with Eli in tow, ready to spend the day watching me try on clothes. I was confident that as soon as we started, he would regret his decision. But, no, he had to be all supportive and fun. It seemed like he was actually enjoying himself.

And now—fuck, now—my entire world has been flipped on its axis after what happened in the dressing room. Those moments were hotter than all of my sexual experiences combined.

The way he looked at me like I was the only thing in the world left me breathless. The energy between us was so overwhelming that it felt like the ground shifted beneath my feet.

It just proved what I'd thought since I was eighteen—us together would be explosive. I'd felt it in my bones back then, and today only made me sure of it. But I can't let it happen again. Not if he's still saying that we can't be together.

Just as we step outside onto the sidewalk, his phone rings. He pulls it out of his pocket and groans.

"Who is it?" I ask.

"My sister."

He goes to put the phone back in his pocket, but I stop him.

"What are you doing? Why don't you answer?"

"Because she already texted me last night. She wants me to stop over. And I can't do that until I tell her about Eli."

For all the things this man makes me feel, he still manages to annoy the crap out of me. Eva is the most supportive person in this world. I don't understand how he can be so afraid to tell her. His parents? Now, they're a different story.

"You pick up that phone right now and tell her we're on our way."

His eyes open wide. "Excuse me? What makes you think I'm ready to tell—"

"If you don't tell her, then I'll march my ass over there right now and tell her."

His jaw drops. "You wouldn't dare."

I see him scan the bags that are taking over both of our arms, deciding whether or not to throw the fact that he just spent the equivalent to my entire year's salary on me.

I raise my eyebrows at him, daring him to go there when he all but forced me to do this today despite my protesting. His shoulders sink as he presses a button on his phone and brings it to his ear.

"Hey, sis," he says with a hint of displeasure in his voice.

I can't hear what she's saying on the other line, but when he hangs up a minute later, he shoves his phone back into his pocket.

"There. You happy? Looks like I'm heading over there now."

I smile triumphantly. "Perfect. And don't think I'm missing this. I want to be there to make sure you don't chicken out. Plus, I need me some baby Addie time. Oh my gosh!" I jump up and down as we walk in the direction of their penthouse. "Addie and Eli get to meet. They're going to be the best of friends. Aww, this is so exciting!"

He pushes the stroller and sighs, but I see the corner of his mouth tip up. "I'm glad one of us is excited."

Since we don't have a car seat base, we are forced to walk fifteen blocks with the stroller while carrying ten large shopping bags stuffed to the top. My arms are killing me.

"My arms are gonna fall off. I can feel them going numb," I cry as we reach the halfway point.

He looks me up and down, then rolls his eyes. We both seem to know how to get on each other's nerves.

"Here," he says as he stops. "Give me your bags. Just push the stroller."

"What? You're not going to carry all of these," I argue.

"Dammit, Jessie. Do you want me to help or not? You can't complain about carrying them *and* not carrying them."

"Fine." I extend my arms and let him start to peel them off of me, exposing the red marks underneath each handle. "Be my guest."

Once he has all of them covering his arms, I grab the stroller and begin to push. Eli is still awake as her eyes look all around her, probably trying to figure out the noises of the city.

"Hi, baby girl." I smile down at her. "Are you excited to meet your cousin?" Despite knowing she has no idea what I'm talking about, I continue to talk to her. "You're going to love her. I bet you two become the best of friends. Just like me and your auntie."

We finally get to their building and take the elevator up to the top floor. Walker seems slightly agitated as he pounds on the door. The door swings open seconds later.

Eva is holding Addie, who is snuggled up into her mama's neck. Her smile fades as she looks between me and Walker, then down at the stroller.

"Ummm, hi," she stutters as her eyes continue to bounce between us and Eli. "Come in."

The second she closes the door behind us, Walker drops the bags to the ground and rubs his arms, which are no doubt hurting.

Roman walks into the foyer and gives Walker a hug. "Hey, man. Thanks for coming." He glances at me, doing a double take. "Oh, hey, Jessie. I didn't realize Eva had called you too."

I bite my bottom lip, suddenly feeling extremely awkward. Why isn't Walker saying anything?

Roman's head crooks to the left. "Are you babysitting?" he asks casually as he notices the stroller.

I look over at Walker, who is standing frozen, like a statue. "Umm, kind of. I have babysat this little one before."

Roman seems completely unfazed. He clearly has no idea what's going on. Eva, however, knows there's something up.

"What's going on? What are you and Jessie doing together, and since when do you babysit? And what in the world are all these bags for?"

Walker pulls at his neck. "Uh, I think we should maybe sit down. I have a lot to explain."

"Did I miss something?" Roman asks.

I try not to smile as Eva huffs and rolls her eyes at him.

"Wouldn't be the first time. Come on in."

She turns around and walks into the family room with Addie still asleep on her chest. She takes a seat and absent-mindedly rubs soothing circles on Addie's back. Walker takes Eli's car seat out of the stroller, and I follow him slowly into the family room.

Silence falls upon the room as we all sit on different ends of the sectional sofa. I peer into the car seat and notice that Eli is starting to make weird faces and scrunch her body. She's about to lose it. Walker had better spill it before Eli freaks out.

"So"—Roman claps his hands together—"is this where you tell us that you two have finally pulled your heads out of your asses and gotten together?"

"Roman!" Eva scolds. "I can't believe you said that. And be serious. They hate each other. Jessie literally can barely be in the same room as him."

Roman laughs loudly while Eva looks over at us.

"Right?"

I look at Walker, who is staring at the carpet. I swear I have no idea how this man is a successful corporate attorney.

I can feel my face redden at the question. "Walker ..." I bite through clenched teeth.

He takes a deep breath, then meets Eva's eyes. "Jessie and I are just friends."

Yikes. Him starting with that feels like someone rubbing salt in the wound. I know it's true, but after what happened earlier, it's still hard to hear, especially from his lips.

"And the baby's name is Eli." He pauses. "She's my daughter."

For a beat, no one breathes. The words hang in the air, heavy and impossible to ignore. Eva's mouth falls open, her eyes darting between Walker and me, like she's waiting for one of us to laugh and say it's a joke. Roman leans back on the sofa and crosses his arms like he's deciding whether or not he believes it.

Eva finally finds her voice. "Your daughter?" she repeats.

"Yes, my daughter."

"H-h-h-how?" she follows up.

Walker chuckles lightly. "I think you know the answer to that. I only found out about her last weekend. A girl I'd hooked up with a couple of times dropped her off at my door. Told me she couldn't do it anymore."

"Fuck," Roman exhales as he realizes Walker isn't joking.

"Yeah." Walker nods his head. "That was pretty much my reaction."

"She just ... dropped her off and took off?" Eva asks. "I thought that stuff only happened in the movies."

"Apparently not," he responds.

Eva turns her attention to me. "And how do you factor into this?"

"Umm, he called me, freaking out. He needed help."

Eva's face falls. "You called Jessie for help, not me?"

I see the look of betrayal in her eyes. Eva and Walker are siblings, but they are also close. They have always been there for one another. She's hurt that he didn't call her first.

Walker looks crushed, knowing he hurt her. "I'm sorry, Eva. I didn't want to stress you out. You have enough going on. The last thing you needed was to worry about helping me figure my own mess out."

"I could have helped you," she replies softly. "And how was Jessie your second option? No offense, babe. I love ya. But I figured Walker would know better than to ask you to help since you'd rather make his life harder than easier."

Walker and I both look at each other and smile.

"He's not so bad," I reply, then look at her. "Plus, I told him not to bother you. He needed help. Like, a lot of help. I spent the entire week at his place."

"You did? Seriously?"

"It was only because I was afraid for the safety of this little one if I left him alone with her."

Roman chuckles. "Yeah, I can see that."

"And you didn't call any of your friends or Mom and Dad?"

"Mom and Dad? Really?" Walker questions. "I needed help. Not a lecture."

She bites her bottom lip and smiles. "Okay. Fair point."

"And don't get me started on my friends. I couldn't take Roman away from you, and the rest of the guys are as clueless as me."

Eli decides she has had enough and lets out a loud, shrieking scream. Walker moves to grab her, but I swat his hands away.

"It's fine. I'll feed her. You guys talk."

I reach for the diaper bag that he brought over and pull out a bottle.

"Do you need to use our bottle warmer?" Eva asks. It's sitting on the counter by the sink.

"Yeah, that'd be great. I'll be right back."

By the time I'm back, Eli is sucking down her bottle in my arms. I take a seat and tune back into the conversation.

"June 26. Are you serious?" Eva squeals. "Our babies are three days apart?"

Tears are now streaming down her cheeks. I knew she was going to be over the moon after the shock wore off.

"I can't believe it," Roman adds. "How are you handling everything? What's the plan with work, going forward?"

"Well, I've already hired a nanny. She starts Monday. Honestly, I still have no idea how I'm going to manage all of this. My work isn't conducive to being a father, let alone a single father."

"We're here to help," Eva says with her hand over her heart. "I'd love to help watch Eli. She's my niece. I want to be there for both of you."

I can see the emotion rise up in Walker, who is currently trying to hold it back. "Thanks. That means a lot."

Once everything settles down and both babies are awake, they wind up putting them next to each other on the carpet. Eva is obsessively taking pictures and talking to both girls about all the fun they are going to have.

But my mind keeps slipping back to the dressing room. To the feel of his hand on me, burning my skin as he inched closer and closer to my breast. My skin breaks out into goose bumps as I envision the way he looked at me and the feel of his hard length pressing against my back.

I force myself to smile, to pretend everything is normal. But the second his eyes hit me from across the room, I know ... nothing about us will ever be the same again.

Chapter Fourteen

Walker

It's bright and early on Monday morning, and I'm waiting for Stewart and Henry to show up in the conference room for our meeting. I'm not sure what exactly is in store for me, but my legs are bouncing up and down with restless energy.

I just handed Eli over to a complete stranger, and now I'm expected to be able to focus on work like nothing happened. Marietta Monticelli—Mrs. M for short—seems like a great nanny, but that doesn't change the fact that I don't know anything about her.

It's amazing how quickly you can become protective and attached to a child. I already know I'd do anything for Eli.

That scares the hell out of me.

Henry and Stewart walk into the room, closing the door behind them. I wait in silence as they both take a seat across from me.

Henry nods at me first. "Walker. Thank you for meeting with us."

"No problem," I reply, keeping it short.

"Well, we're not going to beat around the bush here," Stewart says casually, as if having these conversations is nothing to him. "We are struggling to find the right guy to give our Solentra Biotech case to. It's no surprise there. You and Pierce are top-notch lawyers who do a lot for this firm. It doesn't make our decision easy. So ..." He looks over at Henry.

"So"—Henry picks up where he left off—"we want to hear each of you out. Tell us why you would be the best guy for this case."

My throat tightens as I picture Eli's soft, chunky fingers wrapped around mine this morning when I fed her a bottle. Affection pulls at my chest.

"Uh ..." My voice cracks. I clear my throat. "This case ..." I try to gather my thoughts as they look at me with blank faces. "This case will not be won easily. No pharmaceutical case is. It takes courage and stamina, and most importantly, it takes someone who can anticipate the opposition's next move. I've proven those skills time and time again. If you pick me, I'll give everything to this case, to the company."

Lies. It all feels like bald-faced lies. Because as I think about all the hours it would take, I picture missing Eli's firsts along with it.

I can't keep selling lies. The words dry up, and all I can do is sink back in my chair, the weight of my silence heavier than any argument I could've made. Their eyes flick to each other, and in that instant, I know—I've already said enough and far too little, all at once.

I don't miss the look Stewart gives Henry before he meets my eyes. "I see. Short and sweet. I think I can respect that. Thank you for your time, Walker. We'll be in touch."

I should tell them about Eli. It's the right thing to do, but instead, I watch them stand from their chairs and leave the room. My hands drag through my hair as I realize I just lost this case. There's no way they'll hire me after that lackluster argument.

I'm sure Pierce will talk their ear off about all of his accomplishments. They will be begging him to shut up by the end of it. He will show his passion and drive.

But I have passion and drive. I can win this case. It's just ... bad timing. And yet I know cases like this one are unicorns. I may never get an opportunity like this again in my career, and I just panicked and ruined it all in the span of five minutes.

I slam my hand down on the table, then push the chair out and storm through the hallway.

"In my office ... now," I growl to Bradly as I walk past him.

He follows me in immediately and closes the door behind him. The realization of what I just did begins to settle in, and my anger continues to build.

"Fuck," I swear as I rip off my tie.

"Did they give the case to Pierce?" he asks as he remains by the door.

"No, but after that meeting, they sure as hell will be giving it to him."

He looks at me like he doesn't recognize me. Like I'm not the same boss he had just a week ago. Truth is, I'm not. I've never felt so lost and suffocated before. Life has always been laid out for me. The next turn carved out ahead of time. I'm not sure how to handle this, not knowing what tomorrow will bring.

"What happened?"

I sigh and let myself collapse down onto the couch in the corner of my office. "I've got a daughter, Bradly."

He shifts uncomfortably. "I'm sorry I didn't know that. Is everything all right with your daughter?"

A bitter laugh escapes me. "It's okay. I didn't know I had her until about a week ago. She's just over a month old. Her mom dropped her off at my door and took off."

There's no hiding the shock; it's written all over his face. "And that's why you were out so much last week."

"Right." It feels good to finally tell somebody at work. "Do you think anybody noticed?"

He shakes his head. "Not at all. You are out all the time between court and meeting with clients. If they noticed you weren't in the office as much, they probably think it's for work."

"I froze in the meeting. They wanted me to tell them why I was the best one to take the case. All I could think about was my daughter. I have no idea how I would manage both, to be honest."

"Maybe it's for the best. There will be other cases."

My eyes catch on the Empire State Building, standing tall and proud in the center of the city. Once, it was the tallest, the crown of the skyline. Now, it's just another giant, overshadowed by something newer. The thought stings. Maybe we're not meant to hold the top spot forever. Maybe it's not about being the best forever but knowing when it's time to let go.

A dark cloud falls over me. "Yeah, I'm sure there will be," I reply as I continue to gaze out. "I trust this secret will remain between us."

"Of course, Mr. Harlow."

I turn my head toward him. "Thank you, Bradly. Let's get back to work. We've still got clients to take care of."

He nods his head in agreement and leaves me alone to sulk. The once-competitive light that shone within me, driving me to be the best, feels dulled. I can't shake it the rest of the day.

* * *

On Wednesday morning, it was announced in a company-wide email that Pierce would be handling the Solentra Biotech case. I had known it was coming, but the news still carved a deep wound inside of me.

Facing him in the break room when I went for another cup of coffee was torture. His smug smile. Shaking his hand and congratulating him were physically painful.

Three days into this working-single-father gig, and I know there's no way in hell I would have been able to take that case.

Mrs. M has been great. She texts me pictures and updates while I'm away, and I've found that they're the only thing getting me to the end of the day.

I've made sure to be home by five thirty each day to be back for Eli.

I pour myself a glass of wine and pull out my laptop to get back to work. I had to work until one in the morning last night to manage my workload, but I've survived so far.

Eva is going to take Eli this weekend so I can do whatever I can to get ahead of my work. She's already talking about going shopping with them and buying them matching outfits.

Shopping. The word brings me back to last weekend with Jessie. Not only was it the most fun I'd had in a long time, but that moment in the dressing room was the hottest I'd ever experienced—and I'd experienced a lot.

She was so bold as she willingly undressed in front of me, daring me to do something about it. And, fuck, I almost did. If we hadn't been interrupted, I would have taken her right there in front of the mirror.

My dick twitches in my pants at the memory. I've stroked myself to that memory four times already, and it hasn't even been a week since it happened.

But it's also her presence that I've found myself longing for all week. Having her here last night would have soothed the ache after finding out Pierce got the case.

It's made me consider if my secret is worth spending a lifetime apart from her.

I look down at my takeout, not much of an appetite anymore. I just got home from work not long ago, and Eli is hanging out on her mat on the floor. She starts smiling up at the talking elephant I added to the top of it. My heart swells in my chest. She's never smiled like that before—so intentionally.

I grab my phone off the coffee table and snap a picture of it. I should send it to Jessie. She would love it.

No, I can't. I need to draw the line in the sand. Opening up the gate for us to start texting each other could only lead to more blurred lines. The fact that I'm even considering exposing my secret is proof enough that I'm getting too close.

Only hours later, after Eli is asleep in my room and I'm lying on the couch after working, I start to think maybe it wouldn't be so bad if I texted her. It's just a text. She would want to see the picture. I should be proud of my daughter, not afraid to brag about how cute she is.

That solidifies it. I open up our recent text strand and attach the picture, then send it to her.

She answers immediately.

Jessie:Ohhh my gosh!!! Look at that smile!!! She's the cutest!!!

I smile at my screen.

Me:I do think I made a pretty adorable baby.

Jessie:Ugh, of course you make this about you.

I chuckle to myself. Typical Jessie response—though I guess I deserved it.

Me:Would you expect anything less?

Jessie:Not at all. You are so predictable.

Something about her calling me predictable doesn't sit well with me. I'm predictable when it comes to her because I need to keep my distance. I can't fly by the seat of my pants and do what my instincts are when I'm around her.

I'm tired of it. Just once, I want to take her by surprise. To show her I'm the guy she used to know before everything changed.

Me:Oh, yeah? Predictable? Is that what you thought when I was touching you while you stood, naked and begging for me, in the dressing room?

My heart rate accelerates as a thrill runs through me. No more beating around the bush. We're not going to let that moment pass by without acknowledging it.

But a reply doesn't come through right away. After several minutes, I begin to panic, wondering if I pushed it too far, when my phone lights back up.

Jessie:Please, I wasn't begging.

Jessie:You were the one who couldn't keep your hands off me.

Jessie:And I'm on my knees when I beg.

Fuuuck. Picturing her on her knees in front of me has my cock pushing through my sweatpants right now. I can't help it. I reach down inside of them and pump my fist up and down over my straining dick.

Me:Don't think I don't remember what that mouth of yours feels like, wrapped around my dick. Pure heaven.

I continue to stroke my cock as I bring myself back to that night. She was so greedy as she sucked on me like I was a damn Popsicle melting in the sun.

Jessie:Funny how you cling to that night. Too bad you'll never get my mouth again—you wouldn't survive it twice.

I come on my stomach as I read the text. Anger and relief mix together to cloud my thoughts. I can't help but laugh. Leave it to Jessie to bring me to the edge like that, just to shove it in my face.

Chapter Fifteen

Jessie

Eva opens the door, wearing a yellow sundress, her hair down in loose waves. I'm not sure I got the memo that we were supposed to look cute. I'm wearing jean shorts and a black tank top. At least my hair is down, and I have on some makeup.

I extend my arm and hand her the bottle of wine. "I'm underdressed. Is this some fancy dinner party?"

She smiles brightly and grabs the wine as I walk into their penthouse. "Addie slept through the night last night. I finally had enough energy to shower and do my hair. I had to jump on the opportunity. Plus, she's six weeks now, and the doctor gave us the green light to have sex again. Roman is ready to pounce on me."

My head jerks back. "Uh, are you sure you want me here?"

She chuckles and links her arm with mine. "Please, he needs to work for it. If he's good tonight, I'll reward him."

We walk into their kitchen, where Roman and Walker are each holding a baby. I nearly trip over myself. Every time I see him, I forget how beautiful he is.

My heart beats against my chest like it's trying to make an escape.

"Oh, hi. I didn't realize you would be here," I say as we join them around the island.

His eyes appear to glow with delight, like he can sense my nerves and enjoys seeing me squirm.

His lips turn up. "You got a problem with that? Do I make you uncomfortable?"

I scoff. "No. I was just saying I didn't realize you'd be here. No need to be a dick about it."

He cocks his head to the side, studying me. I'm not sure why I'm being so defensive. I'm reverting back to my old behavior, where being mean to him feels like the safest way to deal with the tsunami of emotions I'm experiencing.

"And they're back." Roman chuckles to himself.

I look at him with what I hope is a murderous stare that conveys how much I will hurt him. He doesn't seem fazed. He just winks at me.

Eva laughs. "All right, calm down, everybody. Let's have a nice evening together. It's my first adult night since I had Addie."

Roman walks over to the oven and peeks inside. "Lasagna is almost done. Should be another fifteen minutes, and then we'll let it sit for another fifteen to cool down. Let's have a drink out on the terrace while we wait."

I follow them outside onto the terrace that has a breathtaking view of the city. The sun is beginning to set over the Hudson, which gives me chills to see. I don't spend much time in penthouses, so these views don't come along very often.

The terrace has several sofas and chairs with big black cushions on top. I settle onto a chair that's diagonal to a long couch, where Eva and Roman just sat down. Walker takes the chair next to mine.

I can smell his cologne from here. A distractingly woodsy scent that always makes my body break out in a shiver.

It's hard to even look at him so I look past him toward Eva, who is now holding Addie while Roman pours each of us a glass of wine.

It was just the other night that he told me my mouth was like heaven. I wanted to be angry, but all it did was turn me into a quivering ball of desire. For years, I had wondered if he could tell I was inexperienced. Maybe if I had done a better job, he wouldn't have pushed me away.

To know the truth about him enjoying it, for him to describe it like that, it just made me want to do it again. I've learned a lot over the years. I want to show him what I can do. I want to drive him wild.

I want him to look me in the eyes this time and know it's my mouth wrapped around his thick cock.

Roman pulls me from my thoughts and hands me my glass of wine.

"Thank you." I smile as I take it from him.

The first sip goes down so smoothly. I forgot I'm at a billionaire's penthouse, so I'm probably drinking a bottle that cost more than my electric bill.

Addie and Eli instantly decide to make their presence known as they both begin to wail.

"She's probably hungry," Walker announces casually. "I'm going to go in and feed her."

Roman stands and takes Addie from Eva. "I'll give her one of the bottles you pumped in the fridge. You enjoy yourself out here. We'll call you in when dinner is ready."

Eva hands over Addie, then turns to me and winks. As soon as Roman is out of earshot, she whispers, "Odds are in his favor so far. I think he might be getting lucky tonight."

I chuckle, then reach for my glass on the coffee table. "Cheers. To at least one of us getting lucky tonight."

She laughs. "You don't have anybody you're ... interested in?"

The way she says it, it's like she knows something that I don't. She looks over her shoulder at the guys, then back at me.

"Umm," I drawl, not sure how to answer. I can't tell her I've been pining for her brother since I was a teenager. "Not really. Same old boring dating life."

"Hmm," she hums, "that's too bad."

I get the feeling that she's trying to push me to talk. She can't possibly know that there's something simmering between Walker and me. I haven't told her anything. Walker definitely wouldn't say anything.

Thankfully, she lets the subject go, and we start jabbering about celebrity gossip—a favorite pastime of ours.

Roman eventually calls us in for dinner. We walk into a perfectly set dinner table. I take a seat at the round table.

"Where are the girls?" Eva asks.

The guys point toward the family room, where one is on a mat and the other is in a swing, both seeming perfectly content for the moment.

"It's a ticking time bomb over there. I don't know how long we have before one of them loses it," Roman says.

I'm impressed. The guys have everything under control.

We all plate our food quickly, knowing we don't have much time. About halfway through the meal, things take a turn.

"Jessie"—Roman looks at Eva and winks—"how do you feel about blind dates?"

Walker coughs, choking a bit on his wine before recovering. I'm thrown off by his question. It feels completely out of left field.

"Uh, I don't know. I've never really thought about it. Why?"

He lifts a shoulder nonchalantly. "I've got a friend I think you'd hit it off with."

"Oh, interesting. Um ..." I stall as I try to find the right words.

No, I'm not interested. Not when the only man I've ever burned for is sitting to my left, occupying every space in my mind.

"Oh, Drew is very attractive. You definitely should meet him," Eva interjects enthusiastically.

Roman side-eyes her. "Easy there. Don't go drooling over my friend."

Eva rolls her eyes. "Chill yourself. I only have eyes for you. I'm just telling my friend here that she should consider it."

Walker drops his fork on the plate, and a loud clatter echoes around us. He seems visibly agitated. I peek over at him, then back at Roman.

Walker sighs but doesn't say anything. He has some nerve, getting upset over me being set up. He doesn't get to push me away and tell me he can't be with me, then get angry at the idea of me being with someone else.

"You know what? I'd *love* to," I reply confidently. "You can give him my number."

I look over at Walker, who is now staring daggers at Roman. Roman smiles triumphantly back at him while I try to figure out if there's some kind of game being played here that I'm not aware of.

"Yeah, I'm sure Drew would just love dealing with your smart mouth," Walker mutters under his breath.

"Excuse me?" I shift forward in my seat, stunned that he just said those words out loud.

Before he can answer, one of the babies begins to cry. Not long after that, the other follows suit. Addie and Eli seem to be battling it out for who can scream the loudest.

While Roman tries to soothe her, Addie takes the opportunity to spit up all over him.

"Shoot. I'll go get a burp cloth," Eva tells him before running over to the corner of the room.

While she begins to wipe up Roman's shirt, Walker places a pacifier in Eli's mouth and tries to soothe her. She seems reluctant to take it, whining every few seconds.

I suddenly don't feel like I can finish my food, my appetite stolen with the bitter taste in my mouth. I push out my chair.

"Um, I think I'm going to take off. You guys have your hands full. Thank you so much for dinner, Roman. It was delicious."

Eva gives me an apologetic smile. "I'm sorry. We'll get better at this hosting-with-a-baby thing eventually."

I wave my hand at her. "Oh, stop it. Next time, I'll provide the food so you two can have a break. I'd say my place, but it isn't big enough to host."

"Take care, Jessie. I'll be in touch about Drew," Roman adds as Eva continues to wipe up the spit-up all over him.

"Bye, Walker," I say through clenched teeth. "Have a lovely evening."

His piercing stare sends goose bumps up my spine. "I'll make sure you get home safe."

I start to head toward the door, not understanding why he even cares. "I'm fine, Walker."

"I said"—he raises his voice as he places Eli in the stroller, then grabs his diaper bag and slings it over his shoulder—"I'll make sure you get home safe." He waves over his shoulder. "Thanks for dinner."

The room feels too small, too hot. I let out a breath, trying to push away the storm brewing inside. Instead of fighting him, I hold open the door so he can push the stroller out.

We wait in silence for the elevator, the air between us thick with unspoken words. When the doors slide open, the quiet follows us inside, pressing closer than the steel walls ever could.

The space feels charged, the silence crackling like static before a lightning strike. I keep my eyes fixed on the glowing elevator numbers, refusing to look at him, though his presence presses against me with a force that steals my breath.

If this is how he is going to be, I would rather he not walk me home. I've been living alone in this city for years; I know how to take care of myself.

"I'm fine getting home on my own," I say lightly.

He lets out a grunt. "No."

I'm fed up with his attitude. I don't deserve this kind of treatment when he's the one putting us through this. "Let me be clearer. I don't want you to walk me home."

He shifts his body until he is towering over me. I crane my neck to meet his piqued eyes. For a beat, he just looks me up and down, as if he's sizing me up. I swallow back my fear of trying to face off with him when I'm so consumed by the fire his presence engulfs my body in.

"Let. Me. Be. Clear. I am walking you home whether you like it or not."

My jaw falls slack. I'm shocked at the nerve of this man. I

point my finger directly into his chest as hard as I can. "*You don't get to tell me what to do.*"

He stumbles backward but catches himself, though he doesn't seem pleased. I begin to pull my hand back, but he grabs my wrist and pushes me up against the wall of the elevator.

His lips are a breath away from mine. My anger mixes with lust. It's a push-and-pull that is making my panties uncomfortably wet.

"Don't push me right now, Jessie. I'm not in the mood. Let me get you home safe, and then you can go on your little date with Roman's friend."

I knew he was pissed about that. I try to shove him out of the way, but he gets back in my space.

"Don't you dare act like you get a say-so in who I date. You made it pretty clear where we stand, so you don't get to have an opinion on the matter."

"You don't know what you're talking about," he says, which sounds like a warning. "Nothing is clear about where we stand."

"Oh, I disagree. You're the one who has this big bad secret that he uses as an excuse because he's too chickenshit to be a man and take what he claims he—"

Before I can finish, his mouth crashes down on mine, swallowing the rest of my words. The force of his kiss steals the air from my lungs, but it's the hunger behind it that sets me ablaze. His hands grip my cheeks as his lips devour mine.

I fist his shirt and yank him closer, slamming his chest against mine. His teeth catch my bottom lip, a sharp sting that makes me gasp before he soothes it with his tongue, sliding deep and tangling with mine. Heat surges through me, and a helpless moan tears free, betraying just how badly I want him.

We are both ravenous as our lips continue to devour each other. He abruptly stops the kiss, then leans his forehead against mine, our breaths mixing together in the space between us.

"Come home with me," he demands as his hands move down my arms until they find mine.

My brain is still reeling from our kiss, making it hard for me to think or formulate any kind of coherent thoughts.

"Please," he continues. "I don't want to think about it. I don't want to talk about it. I just want to fucking worship your body tonight. To make you mine."

I should say no. I should tell him to fuck off and stop messing with my head. There are plenty of things that I should be saying at this moment.

Instead, I find my lips moving before I can stop them. "Okay," I whisper just as the elevator doors open wide.

Chapter Sixteen

Walker

I'm like a man on a mission on the way to my place. I only live two blocks away, so it only takes a couple of minutes, but my strides are long, making it hard for her to keep up with me.

I extend my hand behind me, and she willingly takes it. Something in me has officially snapped. I can no longer think of a single reason good enough to stop me from claiming her tonight.

I know it's stupid. I know nothing has changed. I'm not sure what tomorrow holds, but I might lose my mind if I don't get my hands on her body.

We ride the elevator up as Eli lies happily in her stroller with her pacifier. As soon as we walk into the apartment, I nearly sprint to the kitchen to make Eli's bottle. My body is crackling with pent-up sexual energy, lips still burning from our kiss.

In record time, I have Eli changed and the bottle warmed.

I turn to Jessie. "I'm going to give her this bottle. Hopefully, she'll fall asleep while taking it. Please," I beg, "don't leave."

She smiles softly. "I'll just put on a show while I wait."

I walk into my bedroom and put the sound machine on and turn it up to the second-highest level, hoping it will drown out any noise we make in the other room.

I sit on the chair I ordered the other day and get comfortable as I feed Eli her bottle. By some miracle, she downs her bottle and falls into a milk coma instantly. I've noticed when she hits this level, she's out like a light—at least for a couple of hours.

Being as gentle as possible, I stand up and softly place Eli down into her bassinet. She doesn't budge or wiggle, which is a good sign. I tiptoe out of the bedroom, closing the door behind me, then reach for the monitor receiver and turn it on.

Jessie isn't on the couch, and I begin to panic as I scan the room.

Did she leave?

Then I catch her walking my way from the kitchen with a glass of wine in her hand and a smirk on her face.

"I hope it's okay." She holds up her glass. "I could use a glass of wine."

I nod my head as I watch her hips sway as she takes her steps. My fists clench with a desperation I've never felt before. It feels like the last decade of holding back has finally hit a brick wall. All my feelings are about to come bursting out of me with reckless abandon.

She takes a sip of her wine, and I watch her throat bob as it goes down. My mouth is suddenly dry, starved for another taste of her lips.

The right thing to do would be to let her sit down and enjoy her wine first. But I've waited far too long. I close the distance between us. She watches carefully with each step that I take. When I finally reach her, I grab the glass and put it down on the end table sitting on the side of the couch.

Then I wrap an arm around her waist and slam her body against mine. She releases a quick breath as our lips are now centimeters apart.

"I'm trying to control myself here, Jessie," I admit as my other hand runs up along her arm until it rests on her cheek, my thumb rubbing along her jawline. "I don't know how to tame these feelings raging inside of me. If I kiss you, I won't be able to stop. If you don't want this, you need to tell me now."

She closes her eyes and shakes her head, then opens them back up. "I should tell you to stop."

My heart nearly crumbles into a pile of pieces. I've already lost my chance with her. It's too late. She knows I'm not worth the risk.

"But," she adds, which slowly puts some of the pieces back together, "I don't want to. Don't tame anything inside of you, Walker. Give all of it to me. I want all of it."

Her words do me in. All the resolve inside of me is gone, replaced with pure desire. I slam my lips on hers in a searing kiss that instantly sends a chill up my spine.

I don't take my time starting with a soft, slow kiss. This is primal. It's almost ten years of pent-up desire crashing through me in a single kiss, fierce and unrelenting, as if I could devour every second we've ever lost.

Our tongues mix together, hers matching mine with just as much power and force. I grip her head tightly and move it to the side so I can deepen our kiss, then walk her backward until her legs hit the couch. She falls backward, and I tumble down with her, both of us refusing to break our contact.

She gasps against my mouth, and I pull back just enough to look into her eyes.

"You feel that, Jessie?" My voice is rough, dangerous. "That's me barely holding back. You push me one more inch, and I won't stop. You'll be mine—every part of you. Do you understand me?"

She trembles, but her lips part in a soft moan. "Walker..."

"Say it." I press my growing cock down onto her pelvis to show her just what she does to me. "Tell me you want me to take control. Tell me you want me to ruin every thought of any other man touching you."

Her nails dig into my shoulders, her eyes wide and pleading. "You've already ruined me."

"That's it," I growl, dragging my mouth along her jaw and to her ear. "You belong to me, Jessie. Only me. And I'm done pretending I can hold back."

I move my tongue down her neck. She whimpers, and my dick strains. My hand moves up her stomach and massages her breast through her shirt. She thrusts her hips up and grinds herself against me.

I growl against her soft skin as I move slowly down her body with my lips until I reach her chest. I look up at her, and the burning flames of her desire are evident in her eyes.

"Baby, I might just come in my pants the second I get a taste of your pussy. I've dreamed of licking your cunt far too many times."

She bites her lip as she lets my words wash over her. I grab the bottom of her shirt and lift it up and over her head, then unsnap her bra and rip it off her, tossing it across the room.

"Fuck yes," I say to myself as I finally get a close-up view of her perfect tits.

Instead of instantly feasting on them, like our kiss, I massage one as I gently bring my tongue to her left nipple and circle it around the entire perimeter. She gasps as soon as my wet tongue touches her there.

I flick her nipple and press my teeth down and bite it just enough to cause a twinge of pain before I soothe it with my tongue. Her body is already trembling below mine—so responsive to me. I continue to play with her nipple, eventually moving over to the other one to give it the same treatment.

By the time I'm done, she is a complete mess as she pants with every single tug and swirl. I slowly glide down her stomach, dragging kisses down her side, and then I bite down on one of her hips. Everything about her is sexy.

Every single inch is worthy of my complete praise and

attention. I could spend hours savoring all of her, but right now, there's one area I need to get my mouth on.

I place one last kiss below her belly button, then unbuckle her shorts and drag down the zipper. As I pull them down, taking her panties along with them, she shimmies her hips to help me get them off.

I grab her right thigh from under her leg and lift it up and over the couch so it's hanging off the edge and gives me the most perfect view of her glistening pussy.

I feel nearly paralyzed with complete and utter infatuation. There's no way this is really happening. After so many years of depriving myself of having her, being here in this moment, it feels like a dream.

My eyes meet hers, and I see such trust in them. She is bare to me and in a compromising position, but I see her desire burning through.

"Jessie," I mutter as I swallow down the emotion building inside of me. "You're fucking perfect. I can't believe I finally get to taste your sweet pussy."

I look down at her, and this time, I see her leaking as her arousal drips to her ass. Fuck, she's feeling aroused, just at me seeing her like this. My dick pulses in my jeans, begging to come out and play, but I ignore it.

This is all about her.

My index finger finds the wetness as it drips onto her back hole, and then I swirl it around the opening, teasing the idea. Her eyes open wide, and I smile.

I sure as hell want to, but right now, I need to make her come. Instead, I drag my finger back up and let it glide through her folds until it reaches her clit. Then I begin to move it back and forth against her swollen bud.

I dip it down an inch, back to her lips, and slide two fingers inside. She's tight. Her walls push against my fingers. I move them up and down, hitting the spot I know will drive her wild.

I watch her face contort and change as my fingers take her to another level. She moans and closes her eyes. I take this opportunity to surprise her, leaning down and wrapping my lips around her clit and sucking it.

A groan breaks free from the back of my throat the moment I get a taste of her. She tastes better than I could have ever imagined. She gasps and pushes her hips up, shoving her pussy further into my face.

I fucking bury my face as deep as I can into her, moaning like a damn fool, but completely unable to control it. Her legs begin to tremble as I feel her walls clamp up.

The moment I go back to sucking her clit, she goes off. Gripping my hair and holding me in place as she whispers unintelligibly. Each wave of her release is a gift that I cherish as I softly lick and move my fingers until her hips hit the couch and her body goes limp.

I pull away, the evidence of her release all over my lips and chin. I want her to taste herself on me. Proof of what we just did together.

I crawl up her body and crash my lips down onto hers, moving them slowly this time as I let her taste the evidence of her arousal. Our tongues meet again. Her hands move slowly under my shirt and up to my chest. Her fingers mix with my hair, and then she moves her thumbs against my nipples.

It makes my entire body break out into goose bumps.

Her hands trail down and begin to unbutton and unzip my pants. Before I know what's happening, she pushes my chest, breaking our kiss, pinning my back against the couch. I right myself so I'm sitting up. She slides down to the floor, kneeling in front of me.

"What are you doing?" I ask through choppy breaths.

She pulls down my pants and boxers, my cock springing free, and slides them all the way down to the floor.

"I want a redo of our first night together," she says. "This time, don't push me away."

Her words strip away every defense I've built, leaving nothing but the man who's always belonged to her.

"I tried once, and it damn near destroyed me. Never again."

With that, she wraps her fingers around the base of my cock and gives it a long, hard tug. She pushes my dick back and rubs my balls with her other hand as she continues to stroke me.

I bite the inside of my cheek in a desperate attempt to act like I'm not already coming undone by a couple of strokes of her hand.

"At night," she whispers as she works both of her hands, "I sometimes touch myself to the memory of your thick cock in my mouth."

My jaw falls slack. Not only is the image hot as fuck, but her talking so dirty to me while touching me is making my dick strain with desire.

"You were my first. I'd never done that before," she admits, then raises herself higher on her knees and begins to move her mouth to my tip.

I fist my hair, then rub my eyes with my temples. "Fuck," I growl. "I was your first cock baby?"

She stops with her mouth near my tip, nods, then wraps her lips around me and swirls her tongue. My head falls back against the cushion as I release my breath on a groan. Shit. Knowing it's her mouth on me makes it feel ten times better than anything I've ever felt.

For several minutes, she just plays with my tip, sucking on it, licking it, running her soft lips over it. I've never seen someone fucking make out with the tip of my dick, but it'll be burned in my brain forever.

She looks like she is exactly where she wants to be—my dick in her mouth. I love that.

Then she flattens her tongue against me and slides her mouth until I hit the back of her throat. She lets out a moan, and I nearly burst my load inside of her.

I run my fingers through her hair as I watch her glide back up my shaft, then move back down. Her lips are tight, and her tongue moves around me with each pass.

"Baby, I'm fucking close already," I admit, feeling slightly embarrassed. "You're just too good at this."

She smiles with a mouthful of my cock, then takes it up a notch. She moves quickly up and down as she takes as much of my cock that will fit and pumps the rest of my dick with her hand. She slurps, sucks, and moans while tears fill her eyes with each gag.

Then it happens. I feel the first release of cum that hits her throat, followed by several other thick bursts—filling her mouth full of my release. She watches me the entire time, taking all of it without batting an eye, then slides off and swallows slowly as she wipes the side of her mouth.

I don't miss a beat. I lean forward and slam my lips down on hers—this time, it's me tasting myself on her. I pull her up, so she straddles me, then focus on slow, deliberate kisses as my hands fists themselves into her hair.

I'm not sure how long we make out. Long enough that when she pulls away from me, my lips feel slightly bruised. I hold on to her for dear life, trying like hell to make sure this memory will forever replace the old one.

Her forehead falls to mine, and she moves her legs so she can sink further down onto me. Her bare pussy now rubbing against my dick, which immediately becomes hard. He knows he's right there and can sink into heaven with one little push.

But before we can even think about that, Eli's soft cries ring through the receiver. She's only fussing at this point, but I know I will need to go in there and get her back to sleep. Jessie's eyes hold mine for a moment. I can tell she's about to leave, and I can't bear the thought, not after what we just did. I need to be close to her.

"Spend the night with me," I beg as I run my hands up and down her arms.

She worries her lip as I watch her contemplate what she should do. I know there are more questions than answers about us at this point. I understand her trepidation. But that doesn't mean I can help the fact that I have lost all ability to fight my feelings anymore.

"Please. I don't want to be apart from you after all of this. I just want to hold you," I admit.

Her chest rises and falls with a long, deep breath. "Okay," she whispers.

I lean forward and kiss her forehead. "Good. I'm going to go see if I can rock her back to sleep. Why don't you come with me so you can grab something from my dresser to sleep in?"

She follows me into my bedroom, pulling something from my dresser and disappearing. After a couple minutes she comes in wearing a T-shirt of mine that goes down to the top of her knees.

Emotion catches in my throat.

She reaches for Eli, who is still fussing in my arms. "I'll take her. You get in bed and rest. You've gotta be exhausted."

"You don't have to. That's not why I'm asking you to stay."

She smiles. "I know that. I want to. I miss her."

I stand up and hand Eli over to Jessie, who looks down at my daughter like she already loves her. I rub my chest as it begins to feel tight, like it's breaking in two.

The moment I lie down in bed, despite Eli still making little whimpers, my body reminds me just how tired I am. I try to fight sleep until Jessie comes to bed, but I lose the battle within minutes.

Chapter Seventeen

Jessie

The smell of coffee and something amazing wakes me from my sleep. I roll over onto my back and stretch my arms over my head. I open my eyes, and for a second, I forget where I am. Then I look around and see the bassinet in the corner and yesterday comes crashing back to me.

A smile takes over my face. Last night was incredible. We didn't even have sex, but it was the best orgasm of my life. He was so attentive to me, listening to my body and what it liked. I felt him adjust if I moaned or gasped.

The way he looked at me, like I was a piece of treasure.

But even as the memory warms me, a knot twists in my chest. He's made it clear that he can't be with me. There have been no promises. There is no future. Just stolen hours that are starting to leave me aching for what I know he'll never allow himself to give.

I should walk away. Protect myself before the inevitable happens. Before he shuts down and pushes me out of his life for good. But I can't. Not when he touches me like I'm the only thing that matters. Not when he looks at me as if I'm his salvation, even while swearing he can't be mine.

So, I let myself sink in the memory, even knowing it's dangerous. Even knowing my heart is already halfway broken just by loving him this much.

I throw the covers off me, shocked that I slept so well last night.

After I got Eli back to sleep and crawled into bed, Walker was out. I knew he must've been exhausted. This has been a lot for him, but the way he has taken on the role as her father has been amazing to watch. It's hard not to fall for the guy when you see him with Eli.

She only got up one more time in the middle of the night. As Walker was feeding her a bottle, I heard him calmly whispering to her as I went in and out of sleep. I'm hoping that means he got some decent sleep too.

A glance at the clock tells me it's already nine in the morning. Shit. He's probably been up for hours.

I open the door and walk to the kitchen, where he is standing in front of the stove in nothing but his low-slung sweatpants. Why the heck is that so sexy? I press my thighs together as I watch his back muscles strain with each move he makes.

As I walk further in his direction, he cranes his neck and glances over his shoulder.

A smile takes over his face. Swoon. I'm toast.

"Morning, beautiful. Are you hungry?" he asks, then turns around.

Eli is slung to his chest in some kind of tan material that I missed when I was too busy checking him out. It's not at all what I would have expected to see after spending the night with Walker for the first time.

Well, the first time after we fooled around.

I cover my mouth as a laugh breaks free. Then I meet him in the kitchen, where I see Eli is looking around wide-eyed, like this angle is something she has never seen before.

I bite my lip to keep from laughing more, but Walker's grin is so damn smug that it sets me off. He catches me, shaking his head like I'm trouble, and I swear the air between us crackles all over again.

He leans close, voice low and teasing. "Careful, Jessie. You keep looking at me like that, and I'll forget breakfast exists and take you into my room to give you a proper punishment."

My laugh tumbles out again before I can stop it, warm and reckless, because, God, it feels too good to be wanted like this by him. He raises his eyebrows with a warning that he might just be serious.

Is it wrong that I want him to punish me? I've never been punished before. Would he ... hurt me?

Moisture pools in my underwear. I close my eyes to try and get rid of the images dancing around in my head.

He shakes his head and turns around, mumbling to himself

about not having enough willpower. Then he pours me a cup of coffee and hands it to me.

"I assume you still take it black," he says as he extends his arm.

I take the cup from him cautiously, wondering how he knows a detail like that. I don't get the words out before he answers it for me.

"I know everything about you, Jessie. All these years you think I've been indifferent, I've been memorizing you in silence."

He can't say things like that. It's too confusing. I don't know how to separate my feelings when he's confessing such intimate details of his own.

"Thank you," I reply, voice cracking.

"I've got pancakes, eggs, toast, fruit, and bacon." He nods over his shoulder.

"That's all?" I ask sarcastically.

He tucks my hair behind my ear. "I wanted to make sure I fed you properly. Plus, I've got a ton of energy. This little one slept great. That's the most sleep I've had since she came around."

"What can I help with?" I ask as I take a sip of coffee.

I normally like to sit and enjoy a cup while doing nothing to give my brain time to wake up, but I suppose that goes out the window with a baby.

"Nothing. Take a seat at the island. Food will be done in a minute."

He goes back to cooking, and I prop myself up on a barstool and enjoy my view of his back again.

Once we are finished with breakfast, Eli is ready for another bottle. I place my plate in the dishwasher.

"Let me feed her. You just relax," I tell him as I place the bottle in the warmer and take her from his arms.

She did a great job, sitting on his lap, propped up by his stomach, while we ate. I may know a bit about babies, but this is still a new experience for me too. I didn't realize just how hard it was to do something so simple like eat or shower with a newborn.

"You don't have to do that," he replies.

I sigh, remembering him saying that last night. "From now on, if I offer, it's because I want to."

A smirk pulls the corner of his lips up. "Noted. So sorry to offend you, ma'am."

"No need to be sarcastic," I bite back as I begin to pat Eli's back to soothe her while the bottle warms.

"Old habits die hard, babe." He chuckles.

He's breathtakingly handsome, sitting there with disheveled hair, no shirt, and a goofy grin on his face. It pisses me off that he has to be so damn attractive. Especially his stupid dimples that show themselves when he smiles. Ugh, we live in a cruel, cruel world.

I roll my eyes, which only makes him laugh harder behind me. I hate that he finds it so entertaining to annoy me, but at the same time, I love that nothing has changed between us.

The timer goes off. I grab the bottle and settle in on his couch. I realize I'm still in his T-shirt as I sit here with one leg folded under me. This is not the typical morning after with a guy. This is what married couples with kids do on the weekends. It's extremely confusing and bound to blow up in my face.

Chapter Eighteen

Walker

I try not to watch her feed my daughter and let it get to my head, thinking I could have everything I want. I just gave in to my desires, but that doesn't mean I know what the hell I'm doing. For a minute, I convinced myself that maybe, secret be damned, I could still be with her and live with the consequences, silently knowing what I know.

But I know I can't do that. An entire life of keeping that in would probably send me to an early grave, and now I have a daughter to put first.

A sharp rap at the door shatters the silence.

Jessie meets my eyes. "Are you expecting anyone?"

I shake my head as I get up. "No, I'm not. Sunday morning at this hour, I'm normally at work."

I catch her eye roll but choose to ignore it. I open the door, and Eva pushes through the door while Roman walks in with the stroller and a sleeping Addie.

"Don't get mad at me," he warns as I close the door behind him. "I'm just following my wife's lead."

Fear turns in my gut. What does Eva have up her sleeve? I turn my attention to her, but she's busy with her jaw on the floor. It takes me a second to put it together until I see the stunned look on Jessie's face, who is sitting on my couch at nine in the morning on a Sunday, feeding my daughter ... in nothing but my T-shirt.

"Eva, why are you just standing there like that? You—" Roman stops in his tracks as he walks farther into my place and spots Jessie. A big grin spreads across his face. "I told you!" he shouts.

"I can't believe it. I mean, I kind of thought maybe it was true after yesterday, but I didn't think they would give in so easily."

I step in between them. "Hold up. What the hell are you two talking about? And"—I turn to my sister—"what are you doing here?"

She folds her arms in front of her and pops out a hip. "What? I'm not allowed to visit my brother?"

I narrow my eyes at her, daring her to continue with her bullshit.

She throws her arms in the air. "Fine! I called Mom and Dad. We're going to Sunday brunch with them. I knew you'd drag your feet, telling them, so I'm helping you rip off the Band-Aid."

I clench my fists, and my nails bite into my palms.

I can't believe she did that. She has completely overstepped so far that she's in another damn zip code.

Roman just pushes his hands in the air like he had nothing to do with this.

"Eva"—my words cut through thick waves of rage—"that is—"

She holds up her hand. "I don't want to hear it. You have known you have a daughter for two weeks now. At this point, you're just hiding her. You're doing this. You know you have to. It's the right thing. Eli has grandparents, and they deserve to know, despite how cold they can be."

She checks the time on her watch. "Now, we have to leave in thirty minutes if we want to get there on time. We'll watch Eli if you two"—she smiles—"want to get ready."

Jessie continues to feed Eli while her cheeks turn pink.

"Fine. Come on, Jessie."

I've already learned that fighting with Eva is useless. She'll just keep going until she gets what she wants.

Jessie's eyes dance between mine and Eva's like ping-pong balls. "Ugh, I don't ... have anything to wear. And ... I don't think this is a brunch that I should be attending."

Eva joins her on the couch just as Eli is done sucking down the bottle.

Eva smiles down at my daughter. "Good morning, sweetie. Can Auntie Eva burp you?"

She takes Eli from Jessie and puts her over her shoulder. She begins to pat her back lightly, then shifts on the couch toward Jessie. "Just go put your clothes on from yesterday. I assume you at least have those. We can stop at your place on the way. We have the Escalade so it will fit everyone."

"Um ..." Jessie looks over at me for help.

I shrug my shoulders. I know she's looking for an out, but the selfish prick in me needs her with me. "I'm cool with you coming."

Eva's head spins. "Walker, don't be a dick. What do you mean, you're *fine* with her coming? How about ... you'd *love* for her to come?"

"Fine. I'd *love* for you to come, Jessie. Is that better, sis?" I ask sarcastically.

I don't miss the wink and smile that Roman gives Jessie, who is now biting her bottom lip as she tries to hide her own smile.

"Jessie," I continue, "come on. We'll stop at your place so you can change. I'm sure my parents would love to see you."

"Can we, um, like, address the fact that my best friend just caught me spending the night at her brother's place?" She catches Eva's eyes. "Are you okay with this?" Then she turns to me. "Whatever *this* is."

Eva's now shooting daggers at me. "Why the hell does my best friend not know what's going on between you two? Are you stringing her along? I swear to God, Walker."

I hold up my hands. "Hold on. With all due respect, Eva, I'm going to have to stop you right there. When it comes to me and Jessie, you don't know what you're talking about.

Please don't you dare pretend like you understand the depths of my feelings for her."

The panic spikes hot in my chest—a reminder of the truth I've been burying. Eva catching Jessie here is a glimpse of how fast this could all unravel, and the thought of it nearly guts me. But then Jessie shifts, her eyes darting to mine like I'm the only one who matters. And just like that, the fear dulls.

I know the secret's still there, waiting to explode, but for now? I can't stay away from her. I don't want to. If these moments are borrowed time, then I'll take every second I can get.

Jessie stands up and begins to walk toward me, pulling my shirt down as far as it can go. As soon as she steps into my room, I close the door. I follow her into the bathroom, where she grabs her clothes from yesterday, discarding my shirt. She seems to be deep in thought, barely noticing my presence.

The warmth between us from a moment ago is already fading, replaced by an ache that makes her feel a thousand miles away, even as my eyes stay locked on her.

She catches me in the mirror and turns around, standing in nothing but her black lace panties. Beautiful. Perfect. My heart flutters in my chest, making me wonder if there's something wrong with me.

The thought fades away as my body moves of its own accord to her. I take her in my arms. My lips find hers in a hungry kiss, and I put everything that I can't say into it. Her hands find my bare shoulders, and she clutches on to me and kisses me back with just as much urgency.

Before I get too carried away, I pull back and look down at her. "I just needed to feel close to you again," I tell her honestly.

"I'm right here," she replies softly.

My fingers trace her lower back, just above her thong. "But your heart felt a million miles away from me."

"My heart is trying to protect itself."

"So is mine," I whisper. "Every. Damn. Day."

A cry from the other room reminds me that there are two babies out there that are ticking time bombs. I kiss her forehead and let her go, the warmth of her presence replaced with cold air that seeps into my heart.

I dress in record time, forgoing my shower so we aren't late.

We stop at Jessie's apartment on the way and are pulling up to my parents' house around eleven.

My mother opens the door, dressed to the nines in a white suit with gold jewelry and a full face of makeup, like she's going for brunch at the country club.

She smiles, though it's controlled, like always. "Oh, my children are finally visiting. I was beginning to wonder when you two were going to grace us with your presence. How's my darling granddaughter?"

Roman carries the car seat up to the front door, where Mother peeks inside and smiles down at Addie, who is still sleeping.

"Oh dear. Is she wearing cotton to brunch?"

Eva smiles through clenched teeth. "Yes, Mother. My six-week-old does not need to be uncomfortable while we eat in your house."

Mother waves her hand. "I guess it's fine. At least we're not at the club. Everyone's grandchildren come in designer clothing, even if they're only six weeks old."

"Hi, Mrs. Harlow." Jessie steps forward and gives her a hug, giving Eva the chance to beeline it into the house.

"Oh, Jessie," she responds enthusiastically. "I'm so happy you're here. What a wonderful surprise."

My mother is a mix of contradictions. Sometimes, when her brain forgets she needs to compete with everybody around her, I feel like I get a glimpse of who she was before my parents became such socialites. I can see the genuine happiness she feels in seeing Jessie.

Though that joy doesn't last long when I step forward and kiss her on the cheek. Before she speaks, her eyes settle on the car seat in my hand.

"Walker, why do you have a baby?" Her tone turns cold.

Jessie stands next to me, a pillar of strength that keeps me from running out the door.

"Mother, this is Eli. My daughter."

Her complexion turns ghostly, and the horror in her eyes tells me exactly how she feels. I take a deep breath as I try to remember I didn't have much better of a reaction myself.

She smooths an invisible wrinkle from her sleeve as she looks over at Jessie, no doubt remembering Jessie's parents run in the same circle as hers, composure settling like armor. "Well, I suppose congratulations are in order. Though I can't say I'm impressed with your timing—or your secrecy."

That's it. Congratulations. No questions. Not even wondering who the mother is.

"What are you three doing, standing at the door?" my father jokes as he joins in the foyer. "Jessie! How wonderful to see you." He leans in and gives her a kiss on the cheek. "I just golfed with your father the other day."

She smiles brightly at the mere mention of her father. Just another reason I know I have to keep my secret buried deep inside of me.

"He did text me about golfing with some buddies," she says awkwardly, realizing my father has yet to pick up on the fact that I have a baby in my hands.

"Dear." My mother takes over as she moves her eyes toward my daughter.

Then his eyes settle on Eli, and my entire body breaks out into a cold sweat. I know what he's thinking.

There goes his career.

My father has been living vicariously through me for years now, following my career and always offering advice on how to one-up everyone around me.

"Walker"—his words come out clipped and disapproving—"can I have a moment alone with you?"

"I don't believe that's necess—" I start but Jessie jumps in front of me.

"No, it's fine. I'll take Eli. She probably needs to be changed after that long car ride."

You've got this, she mouths to me as she takes the car seat from my hand.

I allow her to walk away with my daughter as my parents stand cold and still in front of me.

"What have Decker and Maxfield said about this?" he asks, telling me exactly what his concerns are.

No questions about Eli herself. No acknowledgment that they have two granddaughters. Just the concern of what this means for my career.

"I haven't told them yet," I bite through clenched teeth that threaten to break under the pressure.

"And where is this child's mother?" my mother cuts in.

"My daughter's—*your granddaughter's*—mother is not in the picture anymore. I didn't find out about her until two weeks ago, when she showed up with Eli and told me she couldn't handle being a mother."

Mother gasps. "Oh dear. Who would do such a thing?"

Well, I suppose at least my parents never abandoned me. They have that going for them.

My father remains stoic in his posture. "And how exactly do you plan on balancing work with a baby? I've heard through the grapevine that Decker and Maxfield are on the verge of signing a major pharmaceutical case."

"Yeah, they just signed this week."

His eyes show the only hint that he's interested, opening wide as they hold mine curiously. "Well ... are congratulations in order?"

The weight in my chest is crushing. For years, I've killed myself, trying to be the son he could be proud of, and now I can see it slipping through my fingers. All he sees is failure, weakness. And, damn it, I hate how much it matters to me.

But there's something new creeping up inside of me. Anger, resentment. All these years, I've put aside my own happiness, working insane hours, missing experiences I'll never get back—all to be second best.

It didn't get me anything but self-loathing. In two weeks of having Eli, I've laughed and smiled more than the last decade.

"No, I opted out of the opportunity," I admit, not exactly the full truth, but close enough.

"Please tell me you're joking," he says, disappointment written all over his face.

"I'm sorry you're disappointed, but I couldn't handle the workload that case would bring while taking care of Eli. Now, unless you're suggesting I abandon my daughter and give her away to some stranger, I imagine you would agree there wasn't much that I could do."

He pulls his shoulders back, meeting my challenge head-on as he realizes he can't counter that without looking like a dick. "Very well. I suppose there will be other opportunities."

I nod my head. "Right."

My mother looks between my father and me like she isn't sure what to do or say next. "Let's join the others. It's not proper to hide away for too long."

That's her way of trying to put an end to this confrontation, and I appreciate it. I wouldn't have been able to handle much more of his judgment.

We walk into the family room, where they are all eating off of the hors d'oeuvre trays put out by the chef. Jessie is holding Addie while Eva holds Eli, both acting silly and goofy in an attempt to get them to smile.

The sight loosens the ache inside of me. Then Jessie's eyes meet mine, and everything feels like it's going to be okay. I have to stop myself from rubbing the part of my chest that continues to ache with affection for her.

Eva smiles up at our parents. We've always had a difficult relationship with them. Eva, being the baby girl in the family, has taken less of the brunt of their suffocating expectations. Sure, she's had pressure, but they end up coming around to whatever she wants—especially my father.

I'm not saying I've wanted him to be tougher on her, but maybe not so brutal with me.

"Isn't this great?" she asks as they watch her bouncing my daughter, who is standing on Eva's knees. "Addie has a cousin. They're only three days apart. She's so precious. I can't wait to go shopping with them. Won't that be so fun, Mother?"

If I'm not mistaken, there's a glimmer of a smile taking over her face, but it's gone before I can be sure.

"Dinner is ready," their chef announces, which pulls from the focus of the babies.

Dinner drags like an eternity. I hear the scrape of silverware, the low hum of conversation, but none of it feels real. My food might as well be cardboard—I can't taste a damn thing. I'm too busy choking on the anger twisting through me, the sadness sitting heavy in my chest. Every smile, every polite word I give is nothing but a mask, and it's slipping faster with each passing minute.

On the way back to the city, the babies sleep in their car seats in the middle row, and Jessie and I sit crammed in the third row; I barely notice how scrunched I feel as I stare out the window, watching the city lights come into view as I wonder what the hell I'm doing with my life.

I do my best to smile and thank Jessie for coming when we park outside of her apartment, but it's hard for me to disguise the storm brewing inside of me.

Eli's fingers curl tight around my thumb as she drifts to sleep, the bottle slipping from her lips. My chest cracks open at the thought of her growing up without a mother's love. A tear escapes before I can stop it—because if she ever feels even a fraction of the emptiness my parents carved into me, it'll destroy me.

Anger still courses throughout my body, even after I put a sleeping Eli into her bassinet and tiptoe out of the bedroom. I start to pace back and forth as I try to settle the tension that keeps building up inside. I should get into the shower and get some sleep. I have the entire week ahead of me. But I can't seem to settle the racing thoughts. I have no outlet for all of this built-up resentment.

Resentment at my parents for not being the parents I needed them to be, at my father for always making me feel like my best isn't good enough, and at Eli's mom for having the audacity to abandon her baby and put that kind of trauma on her.

A knock at my door stops me in my tracks. I'm still fuming as I take hard, furious steps to see who is bothering me at this time on a Sunday night.

My hand cuts the handle to the right and pulls the door open. Jessie stands there in the same clothes she wore at dinner with a bag slung over her shoulder.

I can't imagine what kind of disaster I must look like through her eyes. Hollow. Broken. Barely holding it together. My mouth opens, but nothing comes out—because before I can speak, Jessie does. She closes the distance in a heartbeat, her hands fisting my shirt as her lips crash into mine, fierce and certain, like she can kiss away every jagged piece of me I've been trying to hide.

I drag my hands under her shirt and up to her waist and kick the door shut.

"I need a shower," she whispers into my mouth.

A small smile spreads across my lips as I continue to move them along hers. "Me too. But we have to shower in the guest bathroom. Eli is sleeping."

She pulls away. "We?"

I move my lips down her neck as I walk her backward toward the bathroom.

"Yeah," I murmur against her skin, my voice rough. "We."

Her fingers dig into my shoulders as I back her into the bathroom, the door clicking shut behind us. The small space feels charged, steam already thick in my chest before the waters even on. She's looking at me like I'm the only thing tethering her to the ground, and hell if I don't feel the same way.

I reach into the shower and twist the knob. Water springs to life, but all I'm focused on is how her tongue feels against mine. My hands move along her hips, then quickly unsnap the top of her black pants.

I push them down, along with her panties. She fumbles for the buckle of my pants. We strip each other of clothing until we're standing naked in front of one another.

I grip her hip and tug her flush against me, hard and unyielding. Walking backward into the shower, I move us directly underneath the falling water and move my hand up to her cheek to deepen our kiss.

Her hands slide up my arms, squeezing my biceps, before moving along my shoulders and into my hair. I run my hands through her hair, then tip her head back and let the water cascade down.

My dick presses against her stomach, begging for attention. Instead, I push her back up against the wall and fall to my knees. I spread her lips open with my thumbs and wrap my lips around her clit. Her head falls back against the shower tiles as I flick my tongue rhythmically, then push my fingers inside of her.

It doesn't take long before she is coming all over my fingers, a mix of the shower and her release coating me. I look up at her through hooded eyes, never having felt more drugged with desire than I do now.

I stand up and steal a deep kiss. I can't wait to sink my dick inside of her until I realize something.

"Shit," I cuss as it dawns on me. "I don't have a condom."

Her chest rises and falls as the steam continues to build around us. "I'm on the pill," she breathes, "and I'm clean."

I've never had sex without a condom. Ironically, seeing as I have a child in the other room. I've never trusted another person enough to be willing to pass on one. But as her green eyes gaze into mine, I know there's no doubt in my mind that I not only trust her to do this with her, but the idea of sliding into her bare has cum dropping out of me.

I lift her up, and she wraps her legs around my waist. Then I press her back against the tiles and bring our lips together as I slam my dick inside of her in one long thrust.

The world flips on its axis as her cry echoes, vibrating through me and rooting me deeper inside her. Every inch of her clings to me like she was made for this—for me—and it nearly unravels me on the spot.

Her nails dig into my shoulders, dragging me closer, urging me not to let go. I thrust harder, water streaming down our bodies as steam fogs the glass around us, and I swear the whole damn world disappears. It's just her. Her lips on mine, her body wrapped tight around me, and the pounding of my heart as I finally let go of the control I've been choking on.

His Redemption

I murmur her name against her mouth, half curse, half prayer, because she doesn't realize she's undoing me in ways I never thought possible. And as her body clenches around me, pulling me under with her, all I can think is that I'll never come back from this.

Chapter Nineteen

Jessie

Today has been awful. The moment I got into work, everything started going wrong. From spilling my coffee on my white blouse—thank goodness I'm not in the courtroom today—to every single case that I'm working on coming back with some kind of bad news.

At nearly four o'clock, I'm ready to pull my hair out. On top of it, I'm desperately trying not to think about last night and what it meant. Walker owned my body in every sense of the word.

I hadn't known it could be like that. What happened between us in the shower felt bigger than just sex. It was like our bodies became one on a cellular level.

The moment I had been dropped off at my place last night, I knew I had to go to him. He had been crushed by his parents' reactions. I didn't even know everything that had been said, but I knew it'd cut deep. I saw it in his eyes. They had lacked the spark that I'd come to love.

I didn't think about how life-altering having sex with him would be.

A text rings from the phone sitting to the right of me on my desk. I reach for it and swipe my screen to unlock it.

It's a video of Eli lying on her mat on the floor. She's smiling up at the cat playing music above her and kicking her feet wildly with excitement. Then she starts to coo at it. She does this for a minute straight, and I smile the entire time I watch it.

Me:🖤😍🖤😍🖤 Oh my gosh!!! She is a babbling little princess. What are you doing home from work already?

I put my phone down, but he responds right away.

Walker:I'm still chugging away at work. Mrs. M is my new videographer.

I smile.

Me:Awww. I'm so glad she is working out. What a relief!

Walker:Mrs. M is amazing. But she isn't going to be good for my abs. She keeps cooking huge Italian feasts and bringing me leftovers.

An image of his abs tightening as he came in my mouth flashes through my head. I shift in my seat as a wave of desire floods me.

Me:Poor baby might have a six-pack instead of an eight. 😴

Walker:Miss Turner, I do not appreciate the sarcasm. I've already warned you once about that. My hand is itching right now, waiting to punish you.

I fan my face with my hand. The temperature in the room feels like it just went up twenty degrees. I have never once thought about that kind of sex, but the idea of Walker touching me that way is doing things to me.

I try to come up with a response, but I end up deleting every single thing I type.

Walker:Cat got your tongue, Jessie? Don't think I didn't see your reaction the first time I threatened you with a punishment. I know you want it. I've got to get back to work. I'll call you after I get Eli in bed tonight.

He's going to call me tonight? I don't know what any of this means. For the first time, I let myself consider the possibility that he may be reconsidering the idea that we can't be together.

I should be pressing him further on what he is hiding. What if it's big and I can never look at him the same?

My computer chimes with a flood of new emails, pulling me away from the start of an internal meltdown. Once five o'clock hits, I close my laptop and take it off of the docking station and slide it into my bag.

I call my dad on my walk back to my apartment.

"Hey, Jessie girl."

I smile at the ground. "Hi, Dad. How are you doing?"

He chuckles on the line. "I'm in my office, trying to get some emails out before I call it quits for the day."

"Well, you didn't have to answer my call, Dad. I don't want to bother you."

"Oh, you're never a bother, sweetie." I hear his fingers typing away as he talks. "Are you just leaving work?"

"Yeah, I needed to get out of there. I couldn't focus," I admit.

The line goes silent, the sounds of the keyboard gone. "What's wrong? Are you all right?"

"I'm fine, Dad. It's just been a long couple of weeks."

"Ah, I heard you were at the Harlows' yesterday. I suppose Walker was there to break the good news to his parents?"

I huff in annoyance. "I'm not so sure they thought it was good news."

"They'll come around. We live in a very judgmental world. Once the news is out and the gossip moves along to someone else, they'll be thrilled."

"Dad, they shouldn't care what a bunch of entitled assholes think. Eli is a gift, and she should never be thought of as anything but."

"You're right. She is. How is Walker handling it?"

"Not great. He's got a lot on his shoulders. His parents disapproving looks didn't help."

"You care about him," he says.

It takes me by surprise. "I ... I mean ... sure. I guess. I'm just trying to help him in a difficult situation."

"I always thought you two would end up together. I saw the way you two looked at each other."

It's like salt in a wound. "I don't know where you got that."

"Well, you're my daughter. I have those father Spidey senses."

"Oh gosh, Spidey senses? Dad, please."

He laughs. "It's true."

"Whatever you say." I walk through the front doors of my apartment building. "All right, Dad, you get back to work. I don't want to keep you."

"Love you, sweetie."

"Love you too, Dad."

I hang up the phone just in time to get on the elevator, which always loses service.

* * *

I settle onto my couch with a glass of wine. It's a typical Monday night for me. I make myself dinner, then go down to the gym in my building and force myself to lift some weights.

I read somewhere how important it is to keep building your muscles as you age, and it's kind of stuck.

Then I pull out my book of puzzles. It's filled with crosswords, word searches, and sudoku. I've found that it calms me down to do a couple of puzzles while I watch some of my favorite shows on repeat.

In a world filled with pain, chaos, and uncertainty, there's comfort in the familiar. Watching lighthearted shows I've already seen, knowing exactly how they'll end, is the kind of stability I crave. No surprise. No twists. Just easy laughter I can count on.

Just as I'm swiping through the shows on the screen, my phone rings.

It's a video call—from Walker.

I sit up straight, realizing my hair is still a little damp from my shower. I didn't feel like blow-drying it all the way. Now I regret the decision.

This is the kind of unpredictability in my life that I shouldn't like, but damn if it doesn't make my heart fill with false hope. Hope for something more.

Before the call ends, I slide my finger across the screen.

The moment his face pops up and he spots me, he breaks out into a wide grin—with those damn dimples.

"Hey, you." His voice comes out low and rough.

I'm twenty-seven years old. I shouldn't feel like I'm a teenager again. But here I am, giddy and my heart filled with joy as I slink back into the couch with my wine.

"Hello to you," I respond like a fool as my cheeks heat.

No one else has been able to do this to me. I'm normally such a loud, outspoken person. I'm the crazy one who never gets embarrassed. Yet put me on the receiving end of one of this man's smiles, and I turn into goo.

"Don't you look adorable?" he says lazily.

I notice he's on his couch with no shirt.

What is with him walking around all the time with no shirt and his gray sweatpants? It's like he's read a mountain of romance novels and knows that they're kryptonite.

I run a hand through my hair self-consciously. "I'm a mess. I just showered. My hair is still wet, and I don't have any makeup on."

The hard lines of his face transform, his jaw tightening. "Don't do that to me. Putting a visual in my head of you in the shower. Not after the other night."

I bite my lip as my own face must betray my thoughts. "I thought about it all day today."

I can't believe I admitted that. But I need him to know what that moment meant to me.

He groans as he sinks further down onto his couch. "Baby, I've been craving you every second since that moment."

"Craving me?" I ask on a heavy breath.

"Mmhmm," he says as he rests a hand underneath his head, his biceps now slightly flexed and looking all too good. "I nearly locked the door and jacked off in my office."

A carefree laugh falls from my lips. "You're insane! There's no way you would have done that."

"Oh, you underestimate the power of my attraction to you." He smiles slightly, but there's something deeper there, like he's completely serious.

I swallow down the growing desire inside of me. "How was your day? Did Mrs. M fill your belly again?"

He laughs. "She went easy on me this time and had a

chicken salad waiting for me. I keep telling her I don't need her to provide food for me."

"Oh, please. I'm sure you love being spoiled."

He runs a hand through his wild hair. For a fleeting moment, I see the twenty-one-year-old that I fell in love with. "You caught me. I'm kind of loving it. But I'm increasing her weekly pay by five hundred."

Ugh, I resent how nice of a guy he is. It was so much easier when I could hate him from afar, imagining that he was nothing but a slimy corporate lawyer who cared only about himself.

This has really messed up the image I desperately needed to have of him in order to protect my heart.

"What's going on in that head of yours?" he asks as his voice turns serious.

I shift uncomfortably. It's like he can nearly read my thoughts. "Nothing," I lie.

He sighs. "I know it feels messy right now, but what I feel for you isn't complicated at all. That part's simple. But if that's not enough for you, I understand. I don't want to make you feel uncomfortable."

He's putting the ball in my court. If I want to put a stop to this, no hard feelings. The logical part of my brain is trying to step in and save me from this mess. But the hopeless, romantic part isn't letting me get a full sentence in. Because this is the man of my dreams, and if there's even the slightest possibility that we can find a way to be together, shouldn't I take the chance on him?

I'm tired of letting fear make my choices. I want to fight for this—for us. Even if it's messy, even if it's uncertain, I don't want to walk away without trying. So, instead of letting my bold, fierce personality take a back seat to fear, I decide I'm going to take charge.

"The only thing making me uncomfortable right now is you lying there without a shirt on and another pair of sexy sweatpants that hang low on your waist. I can't stop picturing what's beneath them."

Pride fills my chest as I watch the shock take over his face at how blunt my words were. This is the Jessie everyone else gets. The one he used to get. It's about time she comes out to play.

"You can't say things like that"—he swallows—"and not ..."

I turn my head to the side as I watch him squirm, at a loss for words. "And not ... what? You don't think I'd say that without making sure we both got the release we desperately needed?"

"Fuck, are you serious right now? Where is this coming from?"

A lighthearted laugh escapes me. "Maybe I'm done acting like a fragile, doe-eyed girl with you. I'm letting the real me break free. The one who snuck into your room to take what she wanted."

"And what does this Jessie want right now?" His tone is quiet but weighted, deep enough to wrap around me.

I run my fingers underneath the neck of my T-shirt as my body heats at all the possibilities coming to mind. His teeth scrape over his bottom lip as he patiently waits, watching intently.

"I want to watch you"—my voice wavers—"touch yourself."

His brow lifts, surprise flashing across his face before his mouth curves into something darker, hungrier. The screen rocks back and forth for a second as he leans forward, then falls back on the couch and lies on his side.

Sweatpants. I knew it. Hanging low. Not gray. Black this time.

He must have placed his phone on the coffee table. The view of his body is causing my panties to dampen.

Next thing I know, he is resting his head on his hand. It feels like he's a model and I'm about to paint his portrait. I'd buy that shit.

He uses his other hand to hook his thumb into his waistband and inches his sweatpants down a couple of inches. He stops, teasing me with a small smirk on his face.

"Don't I get to see you too?" he asks.

"I thought we were doing what I wanted," I tease back.

"Baby, I'll give you what you want. I just want to see you. All of you. You don't have to do anything."

I lean forward, placing my glass of wine down on the coffee table, then prop up my phone against my coasters. As soon as I scoot back on my couch, I realize just how comfortable I am with him.

I wouldn't do this with a man I had only slept with once. I may be outspoken and brave, but I still have to work up to trust my partner. But despite all that's happened between us, I trust him.

"This is all you get right now," I reply as I settle into the cushions.

Instead of looking disappointed, he appears mesmerized, like this is all he needed in the first place.

He pushes his sweatpants all the way down to his thighs, and his thick cock bounces free. I nearly lose my breath as I watch his hand wrap around his dick and give it one slow, long tug.

Holy. Shit. This is better than any porn I have ever seen.

The veins in his hand pop as he grips himself tighter and runs along his length. When he gets to the tip, he rubs a thumb along the top, which glistens with his pre-cum.

"Tell me you like this. Tell me you want more," he demands.

I swallow, trying to remember words and how to use them. I nod my head.

"Talk to me, baby," his deep voice continues. "Tell me."

Heat courses through my body, begging for some kind of relief. My own hand itches to slide into my pajamas.

"I want more," I reply.

"Good girl," he replies.

He goes back to stroking himself. I watch with a steady, quiet gaze, taking in every muscle and vein with reverence. His jaw tightens while he looks down at himself, dick hard as a rock in his hand.

"I wish I were there," I choke out, not able to hold back just how desperate I am to be with him.

His pleading eyes are too irresistible for me not to give him what I know he wants.

"Would you wrap those soft lips around my cock and take me all the way to the back of your throat again? I fucking love watching you gag on me."

There he goes again with those dirty words that have a direct line to my pussy. I feel myself clench with desire.

Instead of answering, I shift onto my back and lift my shirt over my head and toss it to the side, my shorts and panties joining it next.

His deep groan tells me he likes what he sees. I match his position, on my side with a hand supporting my head.

"Tell me …" I look back at him as he glides his hand along his shaft, a little slower this time. "What do you want me to do?"

"Fill your hand with your breast, baby. Play with it for me."

I obey his command, loving the feeling of him watching me while I do. I pinch my nipple, which travels straight to my core, and a soft whimper falls from my lips.

"Fuck yeah. If I were there, I'd bite down on that perfect pink nipple with my teeth. Just enough to cause you pain, and then I'd soothe it with my tongue. Would you like that, Jessie?"

"Yes," I breathe as I move back to massage my breast.

"Tell me what else you'd want me to do."

I don't even have to think about it. "Your tongue on my clit."

"I'd lick that clit so good for you. Then I'd make you suck on my finger, getting it good and wet so I could slide it into your ass. I promise it would make everything feel so much better."

I've never done that before, but he makes it sound so enticing.

"Would you let me do that for you?" he continues.

"Yes," I gasp, needing more.

"Fuck, I'm close. I wanna come with you. Move that hand down to your clit. Show me how you touch yourself."

I let go of my breast and bring my hand all the way down to my pussy, letting my fingers slide through my folds.

"There you go," he whispers. "Get those fingers nice and wet first."

The instant my fingers graze over my clit, a shiver of relief rushes through me, but it's gone too fast, just a fleeting taste. The ache only sharpens as I circle back, building heat with every stroke. I keep moving, slow and steady, the pressure climbing, while he watches, fist working his cock in time with the rhythm of my hand.

"I'm close," I pant as I go quicker, chasing the sweet relief.

"Me too," he says on a heavy breath. "I'm barely hanging on. Come with me."

He groans and grunts as he pumps thick white shots of cum all over his stomach. The visual is too hot for me to hang on for a moment longer. I follow him into oblivion as my own orgasm takes over, and I spasm repeatedly, soaking my fingers and thighs with my own release.

We lie flat on the couch, breaths coming jagged and uneven. After a beat of silence, we know we have to say goodbye. It's getting late, and we made a mess on ourselves.

Just when I think he can't do anything else tonight that will take me by surprise, he proves me wrong.

"Good night, beautiful," he says softly. "I'll dream of you tonight."

Chapter Twenty

Walker

I sit at a table in a low-key bar in Manhattan as I wait for the guys to show up. My buddy Colton asked for a happy hour to get the guys together. I originally declined until Eva told me to get my butt out with the guys and that she would stop over and hang with Eli and Addie until I got home.

I was still hesitant this morning while I was on the phone with her. Mrs. M, not subtle in her eavesdropping, told me I should do it. She said not letting myself take breaks from work or parenting wasn't good for me and that Eli needed a father who was happy and healthy.

I'm doing my best to take advice from the people that I trust, so even though I was skeptical, I agreed.

Lincoln is the first one to show up. His wife, Kylie, is at home with their baby boy, who is about to turn one soon.

Roman walks in moments later.

We order our drinks as we wait for the rest of the gang to show up. There are six of us. We all went to college together here in NYC. Lincoln is the CEO of a major airline company, Roman owns several high-end hotels across the globe, Colton is a doctor in oncology, and then Sawyer and Dean own a massive tech company.

"Why does it feel like it's been years since the six of us have gotten a drink together?" Lincoln asks as he takes a sip of his whiskey.

Roman laughs. "Because there's always one of us missing. Life, man—it only gets crazier."

"Speaking of," Lincoln replies, "how is Addie doing?"

Roman steals a glance my way first, no doubt wondering if I'm going to step in and tell Lincoln about Eli. I will. I'm just waiting for everyone to get here.

Sawyer and Dean come in next, the most casually dressed out of the five of us. Typically, tech guys don't have to worry about playing the part.

"It's about damn time I saw your face." Sawyer clips Roman on the back. "You look good for an old man."

Roman scoffs. "I can't wait until you fall in love and have kids. I've got an endless list of jokes that I'm patiently waiting to use."

Sawyer winces. "Hate to break it to you, brother, but that ain't gonna happen."

Colton appears behind Sawyer. "What's not gonna happen?" he asks.

The group breaks out into a chorus of laughter.

"Sawyer is apparently immune to love." Lincoln smiles.

Colton shakes his head with an amused look. "I feel ya, man. Just keep your head down and focus on work."

Sawyer nods. "Damn straight."

"Enough about this fool's emotional issues," Dean quips as he gestures to Sawyer. "I need a drink."

Time passes along as we enjoy our drinks and catch each other up on work. Roman and Lincoln update us on how their wives and kids are. For all the kidding Sawyer and Colton do about never falling in love, they are genuinely happy for Roman and Lincoln.

Roman's eyes settle on me with a thoughtful look. "Walker," he inserts, "anything new with you?"

His eyebrows rise, as if to silently tell me that now is the time. I take a breath and push my shoulders back to try and relieve some of the building tension.

"Uhhh," I start as I look around at curious eyes, "there has been one little surprise that's taken up a lot of my time."

"You've got my attention," Colton says. "The only thing that takes up your time is work."

I chuckle at the irony. "Yeah, it used to be that way. Now, it's something a little different."

"Don't leave us hanging," Sawyer replies.

"I have a daughter," I say on an exhale, relieved to just get the words out.

I trust these guys with my life, but I still brace for the same reaction as my parents. *Are they going to tell me I've ruined my career too?*

"A daughter ..." Lincoln states as if maybe he didn't hear me correctly.

My head moves up and down as I look down into my whiskey. I tell them the details, and some of them even remember Amelia.

"Wow," Colton says. "How are you handling all of this? And where is ... Eli, is it?"

"Yeah, Eli. She's with Eva right now."

Roman nods when everyone's eyes meet his, letting them know he knew about this.

"At first, I was pretty fucking scared."

I chuckle as I realize my mistake. "I'm *still* scared. But it's different now. I'm less concerned about how it will affect my life and more about how all of this will affect hers."

Lincoln slaps my back a couple of times. "I'm damn proud of you, man. That's a hell of a situation to be thrown into, and it sounds like you've handled it like a true man."

Roman nods his head. "He has. He's been great with Eli. He's an amazing dad. We should all be proud of him."

Lincoln grabs a drink and lifts it up. "To Walker," he announces.

Everyone clinks their drinks together. Meanwhile, I'm trying my best to keep in the tears that want to break free. These guys have no idea what it means to me to have their unwavering support. It's true what they say about family; it's not always blood. These guys are my family.

Dean orders the table another round of whiskey on him as the conversation thankfully turns back to lighthearted fun.

"Colton, how's work going? You are rarely the one setting these little happy hours up. Everything all right at the hospital?"

His eyes are droopy and tired, which can be normal for a doctor, but they also hold something deeper in them. He's going through something. I don't know what it is, but I can see it.

He smiles, but it's not as wide as usual. "Just needed a break. You know, long hours and all."

I don't buy it. He always works long hours. In fact, he thrives on it. He has been chasing this addiction for years, trying to save every single one of his patients. I've worried it would one day catch up with him.

Instead of calling him on it in front of everyone, in such a public space, I try to steer the conversation for the next hour to lighter grounds. Right now, I'm thinking he needs to laugh and forget for a little bit.

Roman and I call it quits early so we can get back to Eva and the girls. All of the guys insist on having some kind of get-together this weekend so they can meet Eli. Not only did I worry about them being supportive, but I also had no idea how quickly they would want to be part of this new version of my life.

Roman insists we use his driver so we can get back to the girls faster.

When we walk through the door, Addie and Eli look freshly bathed, and they're in their pajamas, resting in the dip of Eva's arms while she reads a book.

Before I can ask how the night went, Jessie comes walking out from the kitchen with two bottles in her hand. My heart and body both take notice.

"Hi." She smiles at me while she continues to walk the bottles over to Eva.

She hands Eva a bottle, then takes my daughter into her arms and sits down next to Eva and begins to feed her the bottle.

The image of it—like the scene from the other morning—sticks with me, tangling everything in my head. I don't know how to separate the simplicity of casually dating from the reality that she's woven so tightly into the most intimate parts of my life. She's not just someone I'm seeing. She's already part of the moments that matter most.

"I called Jessie to come hang with me while you guys were out," Eva clarifies, like it matters to me the reason she's here. I'm just happy to see her. "I just want to give Addie this bottle, and then we need to head out."

"How was the night out?" Jessie asks as Roman and I take a seat in the chairs diagonal from them.

"Good," I reply. "It was really nice to see the guys."

Eva and Jessie give each other a knowing look.

"Did you tell them about Eli?" Eva asks.

Roman smiles. "He told them. I can tell he was nervous.

Not sure why. He should know by now that we've always got his back."

"Good for you," Eva says. "I know it was hard for you to do that. All of this will get easier. If I haven't said it already, I'm so proud of how you've taken all of this on. You jumped into this role as Eli's father so seamlessly, and you're doing a phenomenal job. She's so lucky to have you."

"Thanks, sis," I choke out, filled with emotion.

Addie sucks her bottle down like a champ, beating Eli by a landslide. Eva gets a burp out of her immediately. Then they get her strapped into the car seat and head downstairs to the driver, leaving me and Jessie alone.

Eli finishes her bottle, and Jessie giggles. "Dude, she is conked out. Look at the milk coma this girl is in right now."

Eli's bottom lip is hanging open, her precious eyelids shut, and she's not making the tiniest movement, even as Jessie nudges her arm slightly.

I smile. "Last time she did that, she nearly slept through the night."

"Oh, maybe you'll get lucky tonight." She wiggles her eyebrows.

My body goes rigid at the possibility. I look her up and down. "I hope so."

She swallows. "I can go put her in her bassinet."

Heat surges through me at the thought of her here, close enough to touch. The memory of her last night—writhing beneath her own hand—burns bright in my mind, making the need to claim her almost unbearable.

The moment she walks out of my room, I push myself out of the chair and stalk right up to her. Her eyes open wide, surprised for a fleeting second, before I see the desire etched inside of them.

I walk forward, but she takes a step back.

"Jessie," my deep voice says, "do you think you are in control again?"

Another step forward, but she does the same thing. "I'm always in control," she whispers.

"That's cute," I reply with a smirk as I keep walking forward, leading her directly into the guest bedroom. "But I think you want me to take control."

I place the monitor on the dresser, then give her my full attention. "Tell me, Jessie"—I bring a finger to her chin and make her meet my eyes—"do you want me to take control tonight?"

"Wh-what do you mean?" she stutters.

I crane my head to the side. "Do you want to see what happens when I take all of the control away from you?"

Her breath hitches, and her lips part, the blush on her chest giving away the effect this is having on her. She wants it. And I want to give it to her. I want to bring her to new highs she's never experienced before.

"Do you mean?" she whispers softly.

I wrap an arm around her waist and bring her body flush against mine. "I mean, I want to mark that pretty little ass of yours while I pound into your pussy. I want the control. I want to make you come so hard on my cock that you see fucking stars."

"Yes," she says on an inhale.

My dick twitches with excitement. "Good girl. I want you to undress yourself for me. Nice and slow."

I crawl onto the bed and brace myself against the headboard, my eyes locked on her. "Start at the end of the bed. I want you right in front of me."

She obeys, tugging her black tank top over her head before letting it fall to the floor. Her red lace bra makes my cock twitch, her breasts spilling out of the top just enough to tease, leaving me desperate for more.

Next, she unhooks the button of her shorts. My dick is straining through my trousers, begging for freedom. I unbuckle my belt, and we both unzip at the same time. She shimmies out of her shorts while I reach into my boxer briefs and pull out my throbbing cock.

"Crawl to me," I order, pumping myself slowly, never breaking her gaze.

She places her hands on the end of the bed, followed by her knees. Her teeth latch on to her bottom lip, and she crawls along the bed until her face is only a foot away from my cock.

She watches as my fist glides over my length. The hunger in her hooded eyes tells me she likes it.

"You like watching, Jessie?" My voice roughens, replaced by a deeper, darker tone. "Is that why you came so hard last night? Couldn't help being a bad girl while you watched?"

Her tongue comes out and licks her lips as her eyes never leave my dick.

"Suck me, baby," I demand. "I know you want to. Show me just how much you love to gag on me."

Her delicate hand replaces mine. She moves it up and down twice, then leans forward and takes me into her mouth. It's just as good as the first time, the second time—fuck, I'll never get over it. Her mouth on my cock is pure heaven.

I let her work her way up and down, getting it nice and slippery so her mouth can really move quickly along me. There's so much more I want to do, but it'll all end right here if I let her keep going.

I place my hand on her cheek and lift her off me, swiping the spit off her bottom lip. "Back on all fours, baby."

I move her to the corner of the bed and push up onto my knees.

"Fuck, Jessie," I growl, feeling the control already beginning to slip as I see her ass cheeks pop out of her barely there red lace panties. She's pure temptation. "You're so sexy—too sexy. I'm about to show you what that does to me."

I let my fingers glide gently along her right shoulder to her shoulder blades. Her skin breaks out into goose bumps. My fingers continue down her spine, then over her right cheek, where I lay my hand flat and squeeze. It takes Herculean strength not to slap her precious ass right here, matching her skin to the color of her panties.

No, first I want to build this up for her. I want her desperate for it. Begging me to punish her.

I move the thumb of my other hand inside her panties. "Fuck, baby. You're soaking wet."

My thumb is already drenched in her desire. I dip it further down to her clit and start rubbing circles while I squeeze her right cheek, itching to mark it.

Her breaths are starting to accelerate as I continue to work her clit. Then I move two fingers back to her pussy and push them forward, roughly moving them inside of her.

"Oh God," she gasps. "Yes."

I smile, then run my hand from her cheek up to her back and to her neck before I descend to her other cheek and offer it another squeeze—harder this time.

My fingers continue to move inside of her, pressing down on her G-spot over and over. She's so wet that she's dripping down my hand. I want to lick it off, but I don't want to stop pleasuring her.

Such a sweet dilemma.

She turns her head and looks into my eyes with such desperation. "Walker," she cries, "more. Please. More."

I squeeze her cheek enough to hurt, and she gasps, holding my gaze.

"What do you want?" I ask as I continue to fuck her with my fingers.

"Punish me, like you promised," she begs.

That's it. That's all I needed. I remove my hand and bring it back a couple of feet before landing my first smack on her left cheek, not letting up with my fingers.

"Oh fuck!" she says on a shout.

"Did you like that, baby?" I ask as I soothe it. "Do you want more?"

"So much more," she whines.

My dick is so close to her pussy, waiting impatiently for his turn. Soon, but first, I need to light up her ass.

I move my hand back and slap her skin with more strength this time. Her pussy clutches my fingers tighter with each slap until she's a crying, panting mess, and I can't hold back any longer.

Her cheek is nice and red, just how I like it.

I remove my fingers, place my hands on both of her cheeks, and spread her apart. Then I line up my dick at her entrance and slam into her, holding nothing back.

We moan together. This is only the second time I've been able to sink myself inside of her, but somehow, it's even better. I feel like I'm flying.

I grip her cheeks and pull out, thrusting back inside with no mercy. She needs to use her own arms to keep herself in place. Then I just let go. I fuck her harder than I've ever fucked anyone in my life.

"Oh my God, Walker," she shouts. "Holy. Shit. I'm ... ahhhh ... I'm gonna come soon."

I growl, "You hold that fucking orgasm in until I tell you, baby."

With her cheeks spread apart, her back entrance is right in front of me and so damn pink and perfect. I glide my thumb down between us and get it nice and wet, then bring it back up. I circle around her entrance, teasing the idea.

She turns her head back around. "Fucking do it. Shove your thumb up my ass."

This woman. This woman is going to kill me, talking to me like that. Even when I try for total control, she sneaks her own in there, and I love it.

I love that she is always challenging me.

My thumb dips into her ass just an inch, and I circle it around, trying to stretch her out a bit. One of these days, I'm going to fuck her here. I look back up to her face for her reaction, and her jaw is dropped. She looks completely surprised at the sensations.

I push it all the way in, and she moans loud, all while my dick continues fucking her mercilessly.

The visual of my thumb going in and out of her ass while my dick dips into her pussy is too much. I feel the beginning of my own release creeping up.

"Ahhh," I grunt as I do my best to hold it off, "come for me. Now, baby."

The second I feel her walls spasm against me, I pull my dick out of her and let my release coat her ass with each stroke of my cock. The way it hits her cheeks, red from my hands, is the best work of art I've ever witnessed.

I collapse on top of her, squishing her body down to the mattress. She laughs, not bothered by the weight of my body on hers.

She cranes her neck over her shoulder. The smile on her face does me in. I lean down and kiss her lips, claiming her with the same hunger I just buried inside her.

Chapter Twenty-One

Jessie

Eva invited me over for some drinks while the guys have their monthly poker night. Lincoln's wife, Kylie, is here too, with their son, Max. We are sitting outside on the terrace with Max playing on the rug with his blocks while Eli and Addie are asleep in the nursery.

Eva set up a separate crib for Eli. This is apparently their test to see if they can sleep in the same room. The monitor is attached to Eva's hip, which she keeps checking on every couple of minutes.

I smile, thinking about how Walker does the same.

I haven't really had a chance to even say hi to Walker yet. I've been outside with Kylie ever since he came in with Eli. I'm not sure what I'm supposed to do in this kind of environment.

I spent three nights at his place this week. The other two nights, we video-called for hours. No sex on the calls. Just talking about our days.

We laughed about how he'd walked into work with a burp cloth still on his shoulder without even realizing it. Apparently, no one noticed, and his assistant, Bradly, ripped it off him the second he walked into his office.

I don't understand why he won't tell the other partners at the firm about Eli. It's starting to bother me that he wants to keep her a secret.

He's had her for three weeks now. It's all working out with the nanny, and he's managing his caseload. I don't understand what the big deal is. I want to say something to him, but I'm afraid. I don't even know what the hell we are doing right now.

That's another topic that keeps sounding in my head, telling me I need to ask him before this gets too far.

It's gone beyond sleeping with each other a couple of times. We are now actively planning on seeing each other, talking every night, sharing our deepest secrets. That's not casual.

"So, how are things going with my brother?" Eva asks with a smirk behind her wineglass.

Kylie's eyes bug out, and she nearly chokes on her sip of wine. "I'm sorry ... what?"

Eva looks at me curiously. "Turns out, Jessie and my brother have a little thing for each other."

I study the contents in my glass. "Yeah, it's not like that."

"Well"—Kylie leans forward—"what *is* it like?"

My chest rises and falls with my deep breath. "Honestly, I'm not sure yet."

Eva sits up tall. "Do you need me to beat him up? I've done it before."

I chuckle. "No, Eva. I appreciate the offer, but I don't need you to beat him up. We've just got this weird history, and we haven't talked about what all of this means now. He's got a lot going on right now."

"And you're not going to elaborate on what this history is with my brother?" Eva raises an eyebrow.

"Will you hate me if I tell you I'm not ready to talk about it?"

She offers a small smile. "I could never hate you."

"Ditto." I smile back at her.

"What's he like in bed?" Kylie whispers. "He seems like he'd know his way around a—"

"Whoa!" Eva throws up her hands. "I'm sorry. Too weird. Nope. I cannot hear about how good my brother is in bed. I don't need the images."

Kylie and I both laugh. I get it. Though I might need to pull Kylie aside to finish because Walker absolutely knows his way around a pussy. Like ... *blow your mind and leave you speechless* kind of good.

After an hour and a half of picking on snacks and gossiping while the guys play, Roman opens the door of the terrace.

"You ladies interested in playing?" He smiles at Eva.

Eva jumps up excitedly. "Me! Me!"

I know she loves playing poker. I, on the other hand, don't play often, but I'm always up for anything.

Kylie looks at me and shrugs. "I managed to get Max to fall asleep in the guest room. I might as well. Though I must warn you, I'm not very good."

"That makes two of us." I smile and wink.

"Perfect." Roman claps his hands and rubs them together.

You'd think he was excited to take our money, but after we walk back to the table, he shocks me.

"All right, I'm putting in the money for the ladies. Go easy on them." Then he looks at Eva. "Well, maybe not her. She's too good."

I find an empty seat next to Sawyer, who I've known to be a ladies' man, just like Walker, who is now watching me from across the table. The soft uptick of his mouth when he looks at me has my heart fluttering.

"All right"—Sawyer shuffles the cards as he looks around the table—"does everyone know how to play Texas Hold'em?"

Lincoln pinches Kylie's side. "Let's just say, this one here is lucky she's playing with Roman's money."

She gasps. "Hey, I know how to play. And I might just surprise everyone and walk away with everything."

Lincoln winks at her, and she smiles, then bats her eyes at him. They are so cute together.

"Deal the cards, Sawyer. Don't talk to us like we don't know how to play because we're women," Eva scolds.

Speak for yourself, girl.

He's spot-on with his assumption that I don't know how to play—at least very well.

The cards are dealt, and we are now on the fifth card that just got flipped over. I'm sitting on three sixes. Half the table has folded, leaving it down to Walker, Sawyer, Eva, and me.

I'd feel a heck of a lot better if I had three of a higher number. And I really don't know the odds of people getting better hands.

I throw my cards down in defeat. "I fold."

When Sawyer eventually shows his full house, I feel justified in my decision. We play for another hour before I lose all of my money. Well, Roman's money.

But it's been filled with laughs and jokes that have had me almost in tears. Sawyer has been his usual flirty, touchy-feely self next to me. Not that he knows at all that there's anything going on between me and Walker.

Walker, on the other hand, is stiff and serious as he watches Sawyer lean closer to me.

"Don't worry; you can play with me," he whispers.

I try not to roll my eyes at what I'm sure is a sexual innuendo. "I bet you'd like that," I joke but grab my wineglass. "I'm gonna go refill my glass."

Kylie, who was out before me, jumps up. "Oh, oh, me too!"

"Okay."

She tiptoes over to me like she's on some secret mission. We are at the island, resting against the edge as I refill both of our glasses.

"Now you can tell me about Walker."

My head falls back as I laugh uninhibitedly at her eagerness to know the details. "Have you been holding that in all night, just waiting for a time to get me alone?"

She shrugs like she isn't embarrassed. "Hell yes!" She looks over at Walker, who happens to be watching us.

I can tell by the look of amusement on his face that he knows we're talking about him.

"Come on. You've got to tell me."

I smile at Walker, then direct my attention back to Kylie. "Fine. He's incredible in bed."

"I knew it!" she exclaims. "I bet that man has a mouth on him."

I nearly choke on my wine, covering my mouth as laughter bursts out of me. "Kylie!" I hiss, my cheeks burning.

She only grins wider, clearly pleased she's struck gold. "What? Don't play innocent with me. I can see it all over your face." She points between me and Walker, lowering her voice even though it's obvious he's close enough to catch every word. "The man practically oozes sex. I just knew he'd deliver."

Out of the corner of my eye, I catch Walker leaning back in his chair, arms crossed over his chest, that damn smirk tugging at his mouth like he's enjoying every second of this interrogation.

"God, you're impossible," I mutter to Kylie, feeling like I've known her forever.

"Impossible and right," she singsongs, clinking her glass against mine.

When I finally dare to glance at Walker, his gaze pins me in place, hot and unyielding. The look in his eyes makes one thing crystal clear: later, when we're alone, I'll be paying for every word Kylie just dragged out of me.

When it's down to Eva and Sawyer, everyone else starts to gather around the island to munch on the food. Walker makes his way to my side, then rests his hand on my hip and leans forward to whisper into my ear.

"You talking about me?" he asks, his cockiness evident in his tone.

I peer over my shoulder to look him in the eyes. "Maybe. Maybe not."

"Don't worry. I'll get it out of you tonight," he whispers.

I turn around to face him and cross my arms over my chest. "I'll tell you," I reply, and his eyebrows lift in surprise. "If you admit you were jealous, watching Sawyer flirt with me."

He scratches the back of his head. "I mean, Sawyer flirts with everybody. It didn't really—"

I push him in the chest. "You're so full of it. I saw you pouting in your chair."

He grabs my hand before I can bring it back and pulls me forward. "Watch yourself, or I'll remind you how easily I can take that sass right out of you."

"Promise?" I say with a wink.

He shakes his head. "You're something else."

A cheer from behind us pulls our attention from each other. Eva is pointing and laughing in Sawyer's face, and he looks like he is less than thrilled at her gloating.

Roman comes to her side. "Babe, let's take it down a notch."

Eva scowls. "He's the one who assumed we didn't know how to play because we were girls."

While everyone is busy joking around about Sawyer losing to Eva, Walker walks up to me. "I'm going to get Eli moved to her car seat. Come home with me?"

I should say no. We are moving fast. I need to pump the brakes and take a little breather. But I ignore that part of my brain because the truth is, every time he looks at me like that, resistance doesn't stand a chance. So, instead, I find myself nodding my head in agreement.

He walks back to the bedroom to get Eli. I walk over to Eva, where she is cleaning up the chips.

"I think I'm gonna head out. Thanks for having me."

She chuckles to herself as she places the chips into their slots. "If you and my brother think you're being subtle, you're wrong."

I open my mouth to respond, but then I'm pulled in the direction of the other side of the room, where Walker is holding a screaming Eli.

"Oh, I don't think she liked being woken up," Eva sighs.

Walker looks flustered as he tries to grab the stroller and diaper bag. I give Eva a peck on the cheek and run over to help Walker, no longer worried about what it looks like.

I swing the diaper bag over my shoulder and place the car seat in the stroller while he tries to soothe a screaming Eli.

He waves a distracted goodbye to everyone as we shuffle out of the door and ride the elevator down. Once we're out on the street, we get Eli placed in the stroller. I hold the pacifier in her mouth while Walker begins to push the stroller. The movement soothes her just enough until we make it the couple of blocks to his place.

The moment we get into his penthouse, we work as a team to get her bottle ready and her changed for bed. While Walker feeds her and rocks her to sleep in his room, I walk into the kitchen to find something to eat.

I have a sweet tooth that's calling. After several minutes of rummaging the pantry for cookies, chocolate—anything—I come up short. This man needs to get some sugar in here.

The only thing I find are maraschino cherries in his fridge. I prop myself up on the island and pop the jar open. If it wasn't weird, I swear I'd drink the juice out of the jar.

I don't hear him walk out of the room. His presence startles me when I see a shadow creep up next to me.

"Ahh!" I jump, and cherry juice hits my chest and runs down my shirt. "You scared the crap out of me."

A lazy smirk appears on his face. "What are you doing over here?"

He stands directly in front of me, in between my dangling legs. The warmth of his hands on my knees spark an immediate fire low in my belly.

"I was eating the only sweet thing you had in this place," I say as I chew the rest of my cherry. "But now I'm covered in sticky cherry juice, thanks to you."

His eyes are dark and thoughtful as they take in the mess running down my chest. His right hand ascends to my inner thigh.

"I can think of another sweet thing in my house," his deep voice replies as his fingers graze over my pussy through my jean shorts. "And it's a hell of a lot tastier than those cherries."

"I'm all sticky and gross," I breathe as I glance down at my white shirt, now covered in red juice.

He reaches for the bottom of my shirt and lifts it over my head. "There," he says, "that's better. I can help clean you up."

His tongue glides across my chest, lapping up a section of it like it's his favorite dessert. He hums his approval, then moves to the center of my chest. His tongue goes between my cleavage and licks all the way up to my neck, where he bites down with his teeth.

"Tastes so sweet," he whispers.

My body is trembling with excitement.

"But," he continues as he descends down my stomach, "there's one spot that is sweeter."

He unbuttons my shorts, and I lift my ass off of the counter to help him shimmy them down, along with my panties. Then he places one of my feet up on the counter so I'm open and exposed to him.

His warm breath hits my clit and sends waves of anticipation down my spine. My jaw hangs low as I wait eagerly for the first swipe of his tongue, but he just hovers above me.

"One last thing," he says in a commanding voice. "Just remember that no one will eat this pussy like me. Especially not Sawyer."

Then he winks and gives me exactly what I want, his tongue from my ass all the way up to my clit. I know that's his admission that he was jealous and it makes me smile and nearly cry at how good it feels to be worshipped by him.

He pushes my leg up to my chest, giving him better access to me—*all* of me. Then he starts swirling his tongue around my back entrance, and I gasp.

I love the look in his eyes as he does it. It's a sinister one that tells me he knows that I like it.

He then replaces his tongue with his finger and moves his mouth back to my clit, where he does exactly what I like—sucking on it, followed by fast flicks. I am like a wild animal as I thrash around the counter, clutching at his hair, as if that's going to do anything but suffocate the guy.

But I can't help it. This is what he does to me. He owns every single piece of me like nobody has ever done before.

I come all over his face on a high that I'm not sure I'll ever come down from.

When he pulls up and I see my wetness all over his face, my pussy clenches with pleasure. He doesn't even wipe it off. He goes straight to his pants, where he unbuckles his jeans and pulls out his cock.

I try to contain the tsunami of emotions that floods inside me, but it's no use. I'm gone for this man, and there's no coming back.

Chapter Twenty-Two

Walker

I wake up feeling unsettled. Something isn't right, though I can't name it. Sunlight streams through the window, painting my room in soft gold, but unease clings to me, heavy and insistent. Then it dawns on me. I jolt out of bed when I realize Eli never woke me up, but she's not in her bassinet.

My stomach churns as panic rises in my throat until I remember Jessie spent the night. She slept, tucked under my arm.

Everything in my life that had once felt like it was falling apart felt like it was coming together.

I walk out of the bedroom and instantly catch a whiff of something amazing. Then my whole world turns on its axis as I watch Jessie, wearing my college shirt, with my daughter in a sling resting on her chest, while she cooks breakfast.

Her hair is up in a messy bun. She shimmies around the kitchen, and I notice her earbuds are in.

She doesn't notice me at first, her hips swaying as she flips something in the pan, quietly mouthing the words to whatever song she's listening to. Eli makes a little squeak from the sling, and Jessie grins down at her before swaying side to side.

I pause at the entrance of the kitchen, taking in how natural it looks for Jessie as she hums under her breath, one hand steadying Eli without a second thought. My chest aches with a warmth I have never felt, like this is what mornings were always supposed to be.

When she finally turns around and sees me, she pulls one earbud out with a mischievous smile.

"Caught me," she says, cheeks pink. "I promise Eli doesn't hate my singing as much as you probably will."

I walk into the kitchen with a lazy smile, running my hand through Eli's baby hairs. "Were you singing? I was too busy focusing on the dancing and wondering if you're wearing any panties under my shirt."

She huffs a breath of frustration, though I see the hint of a smirk as she turns back to the stove. The smell hits me again, and my stomach rumbles with excitement.

"What are you making?" I peer over her shoulder.

"French toast. I had such a craving. I had the ingredients sent to your door. What kind of person doesn't have cinnamon?"

"People who clearly need someone like you," I murmur, pressing a kiss to her messy bun before reaching for a mug and filling it with coffee.

I place my coffee cup down and set the kitchen table. As a New Yorker, I'm used to breakfast on the go. These quiet mornings with Eli, and now Jessie, are becoming the best part of my day.

I take Eli from Jessie and secure her in a bouncy seat on the floor in between our chairs. Jessie sits at the end of the table with me diagonal from her, Eli in the middle.

"I don't remember the last time I had French toast," I admit as I smell the aromas. "I'm looking forward to this. Thank you."

She winks. "Just returning the favor."

"You don't need to do this, but I appreciate you getting up with her. I'm sorry I missed it. Was she crying long?"

"No, I woke up before her. I wanted to let you sleep in, so I just told myself to get up early."

"You set an alarm? I didn't even hear it. It must have been soft."

She laughs. "No, I just told my body before I fell asleep that I wanted to get up early."

I nearly choke on my coffee. "You told your body? That is not a thing."

"Yes, it is," she says over her big bite of toast. "I do it all the time on the weekends. If I want to sleep in, I just tell my body it's time to get some good rest and not worry about getting up early."

I stare at her for a beat, waiting for her to tell me she's joking. But she is completely serious.

"Normal people set alarms, Jessie. You're out here living like a Marvel character."

She covers her mouth as a boisterous laugh breaks free while she chews. "A Marvel character? It's not that big of a deal. Anyone can train their body."

I shake my head. "You're something else."

She takes a sip of her coffee. "So, what's on the agenda for you today?"

I look down at Eli, who is currently content in her seat. "What do you do with an almost eight-week-old? I suppose just hang out here."

Her face softens. "You can still go out. Why don't we do something fun?"

"Like what?"

"Oh gosh, Walker. Do you not remember what fun is? You used to have a lot of it back in the day." She taps her chin as she tries to consider our options.

My cell phone buzzes in my pocket. I reach into it and pull it out to find a text message from my assistant.

Bradly: Emergency! Mr. Walthorn has been accused of breach of contract by several suppliers. They are threatening to go public and ruin the deal unless rectified immediately. I'm running into the office now. Meet you there!

My head drops low, and a heavy weight presses down on my chest. Just seconds ago, I was planning a day with Jessie and Eli, and now I'm ditching them to go into the office for a scumbag who can't keep his word and screws over his vendors.

Jessie's face drops. It's as if she knows what's about to happen before the words leave my mouth.

"Work," she says faintly.

I nod my head. "I need to go into the office."

She chews a bite of her French toast slowly. "For how long?"

I pull at the tension mounting behind my head. "I don't know. Could be awhile. I'm sorry. I really wanted to spend the day with you." I sigh and look down at my phone. "I need to see if Eva can take Eli."

"I'll take her."

"No, I'm not asking you to do that."

"It's fine," she replies, though not with a lot of conviction. "I'm here, and we were planning on hanging out anyway. I'll spend the day with her."

I feel like if she could finish that sentence, it would be, *Because you won't.*

My mind is being pulled in a million different directions. I want to spend my free time with my daughter. I don't want to miss these moments of her growing up. But I also do have a career. One that is needed in order to give Eli the life that she deserves.

But is the life she deserves one with more dad time and less money? A less demanding job doesn't mean you go broke. You have a ton invested in stocks.

The thought nudges inside my brain and won't leave. Even after I thank Jessie and get ready to go into the office. But it's a ridiculous thought. I'm not going to walk away from what I've worked so hard for. I'm a partner at one of the largest firms in the city of New York.

Who the hell walks away from that?

Bradly and I spend five hours looking through all of the contracts our client signed and what the claims against him are. It'll cost him nearly three hundred thousand to square up with all of the costs he screwed his suppliers out of. But that's nothing compared to losing this deal with his competitor.

It's in his best interest to pay the money and get this deal made before any whiff of this gets out.

After I make the call to him, he bitches and moans for another hour, but I finally convince him to pay the damn money. All of this could've been settled by him not being a prick and honoring his contract, but here we are.

He's stealing my weekend away from me, and he couldn't care less. All he cares about is the money he's losing. He wants my sympathy for having to cough up three hundred thousand dollars today, but he isn't going to get it.

When I open the door to my place, I find Jessie lying on the ground with Eli next to her. Eli is babbling on the floor as Jessie holds up a musical toy above her head. Jessie smiles and talks to Eli, encouraging her as she works to make sounds.

"That's right, Eli," she says with a smile. "You are such a good talker."

I take a step closer, and Jessie turns her head.

"Oh, hi," she says, her soft smile for me not as bright as it was for my daughter. "How did it go?"

She stands up and picks Eli up, and she places Eli in her swing.

I undo my tie and toss my briefcase onto the ground with a thud. "Crisis averted."

"That's why they pay you the big bucks."

I get the feeling there's sarcasm and resentment in that comment. I know she thinks I sold my soul for the money.

"Are you hungry for dinner?" I ask as I lean down and kiss Eli's forehead.

She watches me intently. I wish I knew what she was thinking. I want to know all of her thoughts and feelings.

"I should get back to my place. I'm tired, and I have some errands to run. Groceries to buy."

Guilt gnaws at me. She put everything off so she could watch my daughter.

"I'm sorry, Jessie. I really wanted to spend the afternoon with you. I hate that it ended up this way."

She shrugs. "Work comes first."

Ouch. I guess I know how she feels about what happened.

She grabs her purse and offers a small kiss to my cheek. "See you later, Walker."

I stare at the door long after it clicks shut, guilt clawing at my chest. Jessie shows up for me, for Eli, in ways I don't deserve. And yet the ongoing thing she doesn't know—the secret I've buried deep—hangs between us like a ticking time bomb. I don't doubt my love for her anymore. That's been solidified. I doubt her ability to handle what could destroy her if she knew the truth.

Chapter Twenty-Three

Jessie

The man is so infuriating. He looked miserable when he came home from work last weekend. I've kept my mouth shut this entire week because I know he's stressed out, trying to manage everything.

I know he wants to spend time with Eli. But I know he is still committed to his work. It's impossible for me to watch him, knowing this isn't what he wanted. Maybe I'm wrong though. People change. They evolve.

Could I be wrong for holding it against him that he wants something different from what he said he did when he was twenty?

One thing I know for certain: my heart already belongs to him and Eli. When I'm with them, it feels like I finally fit, like everything inside of me is whole. And that terrifies me. Because if I open my mouth and tell him, if I let him see just how much I've fallen, I risk shattering all of it.

What if loving them out loud is the very thing that makes me lose them?

So, instead of doing the thing I know I should—sit Walker down and demand clarity, force him to talk about what we're doing and this secret he guards so tightly—I do the opposite.

Honestly, how bad could it be? It's not like he murdered someone or has some dark criminal past. More likely, it's something stupid, like he slept with someone I couldn't stand. Annoying, sure, but not life-ruining.

I push the conversation off again, pretending it can wait.

I head over to his place after work. A Friday night, where I plan to slip into the comfort of his arms and lose myself in a quiet night with him and Eli. For now, it feels easier than facing the truth.

The moment I open the door, Mrs. M is holding Eli in the air, naked, as Walker stands there, covered in what definitely looks like Eli's poop. It's all over his once-crisp white work shirt. He looks stunned while Mrs. M appears to be holding in a laugh.

I curl my lips in so he doesn't see me holding back a smile. "What happened here?"

His eyes soften when they meet mine. "I got home at the end of her bath. On the way to the changing table, she decided to let one loose on me."

Mrs. M looks at him with adoration. I can tell she has a soft spot for Walker. "Back in the day, if this happened to my husband, he'd be whining like a baby. You're a good man."

"Here." I run over to the changing table and grab some wipes to help clean Eli up just enough for another bath.

"Walker, go throw your clothes in the washer and take a shower. We'll take care of Eli."

"You sure?" he asks.

"You smell," I tell him. "Get out of here."

He chuckles to himself and walks off. I grab another fresh wipe and drag it along Eli, then toss it in the garbage.

"Okay, I think that's about as good as we can do," I tell Mrs. M. "I can give her a bath. You go home."

"Oh, I can't leave you two in the middle of this chaos. Let me help you at least get set up for another bath. Then I'll get going."

I take Eli from her as we both go to the guest bathroom, where the baby tub is sitting inside the bathtub. She pulls out the baby wash while I hold Eli, who is babbling to us, in my arms.

"You're good for him, you know," she says as she turns on the water.

"I'm sorry?" I ask, not sure what she's referring to.

She smiles mischievously. "Walker. You are just what he needs. I can tell. He's lucky to have you."

"Oh, um, we're not really …" I stumble over my words. "It's just … that …" I sigh in defeat. "It's complicated."

Mrs. M tilts her head with a knowing smile. "Sometimes, complicated things just need a little time to work themselves out. The right things usually do."

Her words linger long after she turns back to the bath, settling over me, leaving me with a sense of hope.

After the water temperature is set and she's laid out fresh towels, she dusts herself off. "Well, I better be getting home to my husband. There are chicken cutlets in the oven."

"You're the best." I smile back at her as I place Eli down in the baby tub.

I squirt some baby wash on the hand towel and start with her hair, then make my way down her body, all the way down to her little toes.

This girl just melts my heart. I can't believe how much I love her.

Mrs. M's words still ring in my head. I just hope she's right. This is a complicated situation. I'm just not sure it'll work itself out.

Later in the evening, Walker and I are snuggling on the couch, watching a show. I'm curled up in this arms, our legs tangled together. His hands mindlessly rub my body while his eyes focus on the show. I press myself further into his body as my eagerness to feel closer to him takes hold of me.

"Thanks for helping with Eli tonight," his groggy voice says.

I smile into his shirt. "How could I not? You looked so helpless, standing there, covered in baby poop."

He squeezes me tight as his chest rumbles with a laugh. "Helpless? I think it was more like shock."

I laugh with him. "Either way, it was cute."

"Cute? I don't think I agree with what qualifies as cute to you."

I look up at him as my lips spread wide. "*You* looked cute. The poop? Not so much."

Something shifts in the room, in the way he looks at me.

His smile fades, and he swallows. "You're so beautiful that, sometimes, it hurts me right here when I look at you." His hand rubs over his heart.

The confession makes my heart race, like a wild animal trying to escape. Words fail me as we look into each other's eyes, the world falling away until it feels like nothing exists but him and me.

His thumb brushes over my cheek. He places his fingers behind my neck, then pulls me in for a kiss. His mouth covers mine hungrily, the kiss sending the pit of my stomach into a wild swirl.

He pulls his mouth from mine and gazes at me. "Follow me," he says with quiet emphasis.

I follow him into the guest bedroom, where he leads me to the center of the bed. Before I lie down, he strips me down slowly, then pushes me back onto the pillows. He's not in a hurry, like any of the times before. Instead, he takes his time ridding himself of his own clothes.

I can't help but take in the eyeful of Walker, standing on the side of the bed, completely naked—his dick hard, the tip dripping with a bead of his cum.

He crawls onto the bed, taking a long swipe at my pussy on his way up before claiming my mouth. I shiver at the sweet tenderness of his kiss. I bury my hands in the thick of his hair.

He breaks the kiss, then positions his dick between my lips and pushes himself inside of me inch by devastatingly slow inch. His eyes meet mine as he continues until he bottoms out, filling me with all of him.

For a moment, he just stares into my eyes as his chest rises and falls rapidly. Then he starts to move unhurriedly in and out, like he wants to draw out every bit of this and savor it. Each time he pushes inside, he hits the spot that brings me closer and closer to the edge.

Our lips barely brush over one another. His thick cock stretches me beyond what I'm used to, but the sting is filled with a pleasure so perfect that my eyes begin to water.

I try to blink the tears away, embarrassed by the emotion. But Walker kisses the corners of my eyes while he moves inside of me like he knows what this is doing to me. It's a small act, but it feels profound in its meaning.

Together, our breathing quickens until I can't hold back any longer. My orgasm crashes through me, every nerve sparking, every thought consumed by him. It's not just pleasure; it's everything we've survived, everything he makes me feel, breaking me open and stitching me back together, all at once.

Chapter Twenty-Four

Walker

I need to tell her or end it now. I've already royally fucked up by letting it get this far. I don't know how I thought there would be anything casual between Jessie and me. Because she is the air to my lungs. Being without her is like suffocating. But this secret is like pollution to our world. It's constantly sneaking around and threatening to destroy us.

Eli is now nine weeks old. Jessie has been in my life regularly for over a month, and everything I thought I knew about myself and my future has been blown to smithereens. As I try to put the pieces back in place, I find they no longer fit where they once did.

She's coming over tonight after work. I have to decide by this weekend. It's an impossible decision.

Bradly appears in my office with a strange look on his face.

"What's going on, Bradly?" I ask from my chair behind my desk.

He closes the door and walks in closer, taking a seat in front of me. "Just overheard Pierce talking to some associates in the break room."

I roll my eyes. I've successfully dodged him the last couple of weeks. I refuse to go into the break room where he frequents. Call it being a sore loser, but the thought of hearing about the case makes my head hurt. Or how he'll definitely become a majority partner after this case if he wins. I'm sure all he wants to do is continue to rub the possibility in my face.

"Being a prick, I'm sure," I add.

He smiles and nods. "Always. He was talking about you. Saying he's noticed you've been leaving work at five p.m. for weeks now. Thinks you're no longer putting in the time you should as a partner at the firm."

My jaw muscles bunch and twitch with restrained fury. "The man has some nerve, letting my name fall from his dry, crusty lips."

"Are you going to talk to him about it?"

My voice drops low, my words clipped. "I'll deal with him. Thanks for letting me know."

"No problem, boss."

Bradly gets up and leaves me to stew in my office, my mind churning with all the ways I'd like to wipe that smug look off Pierce's face. The man thrives on playing dirty, and humility has never crossed his path.

Instead of leaving the office with excitement to see Jessie and Eli, I have the weight of Pierce's words hanging over me. They crush down on me like my father's look of disappointment, knowing I let the opportunity slip through my hands.

When I walk into my place, I am short and quiet with Mrs. M. She tells me about Eli's day and then pats my shoulder and offers a smile. She can sense I've had a bad day.

"Go cuddle your daughter," she says on her way out. "It'll make everything better."

Once the door is closed, I rid myself of my jacket and tie, then walk over to Eli, who appears to be happy in her swing. I turn off the music and motion, then unbuckle her, scooping her up into my arms. Her head rests just under my chin, and I take in the smell of her innocence.

Innocence the world hasn't trampled over yet. I squeeze her a little tighter at the thought of her losing it one day.

An hour later, while Eli and I are snuggling on the couch, Jessie walks in the door. She still has a key from the first week she stayed with me to help. I like knowing she feels so comfortable that she still uses it.

Yet another reason why I know the clock is ticking on my decision.

Her bright smile, the one that used to light me up inside, now cuts both ways. I want to hold on to it forever, but all I can think about is how many more of those smiles I'll get before the truth rips it away.

"Aw, look at you two," she says adoringly, then leans down and kisses me on the lips, then gives a sleeping Eli a kiss on her cheek. "How was your day?"

"Fine," I reply as I stand up and gently place Eli back in her swing.

"Oof." Jessie wraps her arms around my chest. "That doesn't sound so good. Wanna talk about it?"

"Not really." I rub her arms and kiss her lips. "I just want to enjoy a glass of wine and some dinner with you."

Her lips linger on mine, and then her tongue slips inside and mingles with mine for a second, just enough to tease. "That can be done. I'll go open a bottle."

She pulls away. The absence of her body leaves me with a cold feeling of abandonment, the same one my parents left that I've been chasing to replace for years.

When will it ever be my turn to feel completely loved for who I am? Not defined by my success or my bank account. I know it's not Jessie's fault that we're in this predicament, but it still hurts nonetheless.

I pull out the dinner that Mrs. M left in the oven. Steak and potatoes with a salad in the fridge.

"Okay, here we go." Jessie hands me a glass of wine, filled to the rim.

I look down at the glass, then back at her. "You trying to get me drunk?"

"Nah, I don't need you drunk to get what I want from you," she says with a wink.

I laugh, and for the first time since Bradly walked into my office, I can breathe a little easier. "I can't argue with that."

We place our glasses on the dinner table and get our plates ready. Mrs. M seems to always cook for two. I never told her I'd be feeding another adult each night. It's strange, her picking up on something I never told her.

"How was your day?" I ask as I cut into the juicy steak.

She ponders over my question as she chews. "In comparison to how bad it could be, it was pretty good."

I turn my head to the side as I study her. "Do you often have awful days?"

"It's hit or miss. Depends on if my cases are going as planned. If they're not, if I have to hand a child back to an abusive parent because of the legal system"—her eyes turn down—"those days are the worst."

"Jessie," I say more sharply than I meant to, "you know that's not your fault. Do you hear me? Not even a little. That's on the system, not on you."

She shrugs her shoulders, not seeming convinced by my words. "Doesn't make it any easier."

I nod my head in understanding. "You're incredible—you know that? These kids are lucky to have someone like you fighting for them."

A twinge of jealousy hits me in the gut. She's doing exactly what she wanted to do. Me? I'm a traitor to the highest degree. I wanted to fight power and corruption; instead, I'm adding to it. Acknowledging the truth leaves a bitter taste in my mouth—the taste of shame.

It remains with me throughout the rest of dinner and while I put Eli to sleep.

I walk back into the family room, where Jessie is now cuddled up on the couch with a blanket and the remote. I fall down next to her, then rest my hand behind my head as my legs sprawl out.

I feel her eyes on me while I watch the show she has on in the background.

"Can we talk about it now?" she asks hesitantly.

I look over at her. "Talk about what?"

"What happened at work today. Whatever has you acting so weird tonight."

I let out a long sigh, the weight of the day pressing heavier on me. This isn't the conversation I wanted to have tonight, but there's no escaping it now.

"It's just a partner at my firm, the one who got the pharmaceutical case; he was talking to colleagues of mine about how I haven't been a very good partner, leaving early the last couple of weeks. My assistant overheard him."

She looks at me without much of an expression. "He sounds like a prick."

I nod my head. "Yep. That's Pierce for you. A prick."

"So," she continues, "who cares what he says? As long as Decker and Maxfield understand, then it doesn't matter."

My eyes shift down to my lap, where I pick off an imaginary piece of lint from my sweatpants. "I haven't told them about Eli yet."

The stillness in the room feels sharp, Jessie's quiet eyes saying everything I'm too much of a coward to admit.

"Are you ashamed of her?" Her voice is etched with shock.

I snap my head up at her. "Of course I'm not ashamed of Eli. I love Eli."

"So, why have you been hiding her from them? These are supposed to be your mentors. Shouldn't they know something that impacts you and your work schedule so dramatically?"

"Yes. I'm planning on telling them. It's just been chaotic. I'm trying to get my head out from under water."

A cynical laugh escapes from her. "Really? Are you sure you're not worried about whether or not they'll think you're as valuable as you were before you had such a big commitment outside of work?"

Her words are so spot-on that it nearly pulls a gasp from me. She always knows exactly what's going on inside of my head. It's alarming at times.

"Is it so wrong if I am?" I ask defensively.

"I mean, if that's who you want to be. If where you want to spend your time is a place that sees your daughter as a roadblock to more money."

"That's not fair, Jessie."

"No, Walker. You know what's not fair? You walking around, hiding shit from people you claim to care about."

The double meaning to that statement is clear. It's exactly what I knew was coming by jumping into this without a plan, without a decision.

"You hide Eli from the people who should know her, and you hide the truth from me. Do you realize what that says, Walker? That we're both just things you keep locked away until it's convenient."

"That's not what I'm doing, Jessie. I'm just ... I'm trying to hold it all together. You don't understand. If I tell you, if I lay it all out, I might lose everything."

Tears begin to fall down her cheeks. She does her best to wipe them away, but they continue to come down. I reach over to smooth them away, but she shoves my arm out of the way.

"You're already losing me. I can't do this anymore, not when you keep half of yourself locked away. Until you're ready to be honest with me about *everything*, we're done."

She jumps off of the couch and grabs her purse from the chair in the foyer. I chase after her, toward the door, as panic begins to build in my veins, adrenaline pumping through me.

"Jessie, wait, please ..."

She turns around with those tears stuck in her eyes, making my heart shatter. "No, Walker. I'm done. You don't know what the hell you want, and I won't stick around, waiting for you to figure it out."

She shuts the door in my face, leaving me standing alone as I try to figure out what just happened. How did it all spiral out of control so quickly? One minute, we were getting ready to watch a show, and the next, I've lost the most important woman in my life. The woman I love.

My head falls back as I try to stop the tears that threaten to come. I should have never let it get this far. I let myself pretend there was a possibility I could have it all. The woman I love, a beautiful daughter, and a successful career. Now I'm on the verge of losing everything, all because I'm too much of a coward to take what I want.

Chapter Twenty-Five

Jessie

I hate him. I hate that he has this power over me. I hate myself for not being smart enough to say no from the beginning. Mostly, I hate how much I love him despite all that has happened. My heart feels smashed to pieces so small that there's no use in even trying to put it back together.

I want to call him and scream at him. Beg him to stop being so afraid of what everyone else thinks about how he should live his life and just live it for himself. But I know that will fall on deaf ears. He's proven himself to be too weak to stand up for what he believes in, and I'm the collateral damage.

Anger seeps deep down into my bones, hardening me from inside out. I feel the old, protective Jessie coming back. The one who will use humor and insults as a defense mechanism to guard herself.

My muscles are tense from the lack of sleep I got last night. Thankfully, it's Friday. I just need to get through today, and then I can bury myself under the covers and hide away from the world.

I feel my phone buzz in my purse that I tossed on the ground this morning when I got here. I reach in and pull it out to see who's calling. A wave of relief washes over me when I see my dad's name flashing across the screen. This is exactly who I needed to talk to.

"Hi, Dad," I answer with a sense of comfort.

"Hi, sweetie. Guess what," he says cheerfully.

"What?" I reply.

"I'm in the city for some business. Want to meet me for lunch?"

My shoulders fall, losing some of their tension. "Yes. I'd love to have lunch."

"Great. Let's meet at your favorite spot. Noon work?"

"Perfect. I'll see you soon."

I shuffle through my paperwork for the next hour as my mind continues to spiral with the memory of last night. There's a part of me that's angry with myself for pushing him away—angry that I took away the happiness I'd felt over the last couple of months.

When I finally get to the restaurant, I spot my dad sitting at our favorite corner booth. He knows the owner and somehow always gets our booth, no matter how late of notice he gives them. Just seeing his face has my eyes watering. He's the one soft place for me to land, and right now, I need him more than I can ever remember needing him before.

I take my seat across from him and place my purse next to me. He smiles brightly at me.

"There she is." He places the menu down. "I was thinking I might get the—" Then he stops mid-sentence when his eyes meet mine. "What's wrong?"

My bottom lip quivers. I try to fight off the tears, but one betrays me and cascades down my cheek. I wipe it away and blink rapidly. "It's nothing." I shrug my shoulders and look out the window.

His silence fills the space between us, dragging on until I have to look back at him.

He raises his eyebrows. "It's not nothing. You're upset. Talk to me, honey. Tell me what's bothering you."

The waiter interrupts us to get our drink order. Once he's gone, Dad goes back to studying me, waiting for me to talk.

"Just ... boy drama. Nothing you can do about it," I answer, rubbing my hands over my legs nervously.

"Well, I don't know about that. I may be old, but I can still throw a good punch if I need to."

My chest shakes lightly as I let out a laugh that tastes more like defeat than humor. "I don't need you to beat anybody up for me."

"That's true. You're tough. You could do it yourself." He winks.

I roll my eyes. "I don't think that's a good idea."

"Is this about Walker?" he asks point-blank, no beating

around the bush. "You've been spending a lot of time with him and his daughter."

He knows me too well. I should've known he would figure it out. I've been very open with him about the time I've been spending with Walker and Eli.

Just thinking about Eli opens the floodgates.

"I love them," I admit out loud for the first time.

He reaches across the table and grabs my hand. The warmth of his hand offers a touch of solace. But he doesn't press me to talk; instead, he just offers quiet companionship.

Then the words just spill out of me. "We were more than just friends. At some point during all of this, we became more. I shouldn't have let it happen. It's my fault. He had warned me from the beginning that we couldn't be together."

That seems to surprise him. "Why?"

A bitter laugh bubbles out of me. "I don't know." I throw my hands in the air in frustration. "He won't tell me. He's the most stubborn, annoying man on the planet. I mean, what on earth can it be that he can't even tell me what it is? This isn't high school. Just be a man and tell me."

"Huh." He scratches his chin. "That is odd. Not like Walker at all."

Even my dad can see this isn't like him. But I'm angry. And right now, I just want him to tell me Walker is an asshole who doesn't deserve me. They may not be the words that will get me through the situation, but they would get me through the day.

Dad isn't like that though. He doesn't speak lies to placate anybody. He tells it like it is. It's one of the reasons I know I can always trust him.

"Maybe the Walker we think we know isn't the one who exists today."

The waiter comes over and takes our order, temporarily distracting us from our conversation. Dad orders for both of us as I try to compose myself and wipe away the evidence of my sorrows.

Once he's gone, Dad adjusts his silverware while he appears to think. "Life isn't always easy. Sometimes, the pressures of the outside world can weigh down on you until you barely recognize yourself anymore."

"Why does it sound like you're condoning his behavior?" I ask defensively.

His eyes look pained. "I just can't help but feel like he's battling something inside of him, something his father drilled into him that's hard to shake. It doesn't excuse the mistakes, and God knows I don't want to see you hurt. But a part of me wonders if what you see in him is real, if maybe he's trying to crawl out from under all of the weight. I'm torn, Jessie—between wanting to protect your heart and not ignoring the possibility that the man you've fallen for is still fighting to be better."

His words cut into the deep wounds inside of me that are tired. Tired of fighting for something that feels like a battle where my heart is the casualty.

"I can't wait around any longer for his honesty, for his truth."

"You're right. You deserve better than that. No matter what happens, I know you will be okay. Because from the time you were little, you held a strength inside of you that I've envied. No matter what, you stay true to yourself. I'm so damn proud of the woman you've become. Never let anyone dim the light inside of you. It makes the world a better place."

"Thanks, Dad," I reply through blurry vision. "Ugh, enough about this. What's new with you?"

"I got to see your brother last night," he tells me after he takes a sip of his drink.

"How's he doing?" I ask, feigning my interest.

Ethan and I are like oil and vinegar. We just don't go well together.

He always cared about his image, treating me like an inconvenient little sister who got in the way of his attention. For years, I figured it was just a weird sibling-rivalry thing and we'd outgrow it and become close as adults. Maybe once we matured. But it appears Ethan as a mature adult isn't much different from the one I grew up with.

Don't get me wrong; I love him in the *he's your brother so you have to* kind of way.

"He's had a hard go at life in the last six months. Was passed on for a big promotion and Melissa broke up with him."

A twinge of guilt eats at me for not feeling surprised at all. "That's ... too bad."

Dad chuckles. "Now, I know you two have had your differences. But he's getting there. Working through his own struggles. We had a long talk last night. A deep one."

"I didn't know he was capable," I say with my straw in my mouth.

"All I'm saying is, go easy on him. Life is teaching him some tough lessons at the moment. I don't like to see either of my kids struggle."

"Yeah, I know. You're a great dad. We're both lucky to have you."

He reaches over and squeezes my hand.

"Well"—he sits up straight—"let's talk about something else. I sense that right now, you need a distraction."

I smile reluctantly. "You can say that again."

He proceeds to talk nonstop for the rest of lunch, making fun of the people in their social circle and telling jokes that I've heard a hundred times. But it's exactly what I needed to get me through the day.

As soon as I'm home from work, I change into a cozy set of pajamas and pop open a bottle of wine. I turn on the TV, but I can't distract myself from the soul-crushing pain that sits heavy in my chest. I try to play a game on my phone, clean, scroll through social media, until I toss my phone on the ground and sink into my couch cushions.

I can picture Walker and Eli snuggling with each other at his place right now. If I hadn't gone off last night, I would be with them right now. Everything inside of me wants to run over there and beg for him to take me back.

But I can't. I won't.

Instead, I let my head fall forward and cry. My tears wet the couch. Each one is a release of the loneliness taking hold of me and threatening to take me under.

Chapter Twenty-Six

Walker

I need to get out of my place. Each spot I move to holds a memory of Jessie that reminds me of what I had ... and what I lost. Her words play on repeat in my head, a cruel soundtrack that keeps telling me what a coward I am. For letting her leave without falling to my knees and begging her to stay. For ever being the man who could make her shed a tear of sadness.

Eli cries in my arms, and I know I can't stay here a second longer. I pack up a diaper bag and place her in the stroller, hoping she settles enough on the walk to take a nap.

As I walk the streets of the city, my mind struggles to take in my surroundings. It's like all it can do is spin in a circle of lost hopes and dreams while the world around me continues as if nothing is wrong.

But everything is wrong.

I knock on the door and hope that she's home. It opens, and Eva's shocked expression turns to worry in an instant as her eyes look me up and down.

"You look awful," she states matter-of-factly. "Is everything okay?"

My head shakes back and forth as emotion bubbles up from a dark place where I've hidden over a decade of hurt from everyone—including myself. It's like a dam has broken, and I can no longer keep all of it hidden.

"Oh my gosh." She opens the door. "Get in here."

I push Eli into the foyer and park the stroller. Eva takes over and takes her out of the car seat, then walks us into her place, where Addie appears to be lying on a blanket on the floor, kicking her feet with excitement. She places Eli next to her cousin, then motions for me to sit on the couch, sitting right next to me and taking my hand.

I glance around their place, realizing it's Saturday. "Where's Roman?"

"He's out of town. Had to check on a hotel in Italy. Don't worry about him. Talk to me, Walker."

I rest my elbows on my thighs and take in a shaky breath. "I don't even know where to start."

Her warm hand begins to run soothing circles on my back. "Just start talking. We can fill in gaps later."

"It's Jessie." My voice cracks. "She ended it."

Eva gasps. "What? Why would she do that?"

"Honestly, I'm shocked she gave me a second chance in the first place. I sure as hell didn't deserve it."

Her head cranes to the side. "Second chance? When was the first chance?"

"Almost ten years ago."

"What?" she nearly shouts. "TEN years ago! That's ..." She stops to do the math. "We were in high school."

I nod my head. "You had just graduated. It was actually your graduation party. She snuck into my room that night."

I realize the details are a little odd to be discussing with my sister, but I'm in no frame of mind to sugarcoat it.

So, I continue, "She went down on me. Best fucking blow job of my life." She gags, and I smile. "You said you wanted the story."

"Yeah, but I don't think I needed to know her skill level on the matter."

"Sorry. I like to give credit where credit is due."

She sighs. "Just ... go on."

"Anyway, I honestly didn't know it was her. I thought it was Natalie."

Another gag from Eva. "She was the worst."

"True. But she was safe. I had already begun to have these ... feelings for Jessie even though I knew they were wrong at the time. She was too young. Natalie was just a distraction." I run a hand through my hair. "Anyway, when I found out it was Jessie, I wasn't exactly thrilled. I yelled at her. Told her we could never happen. Led her to believe I felt nothing for her. It was never the same between us after that."

She sits in silence for a moment as she takes this information in. "I guess it makes sense why she hated your guts for so long."

"Yeah, I pulled away from her after that."

"But ... if you really had feelings for her, what was the problem? She was eighteen and heading to college in the city where you lived. I get that she's younger than you, but six years is nothing. You were still in law school yourself. It doesn't make sense."

"That night ..." I start, and my body begins to tremble with the memory. I've never told a single soul about this. "I overheard something I shouldn't have. It's something I told myself I'd take to my grave because it would really hurt Jessie. I knew I couldn't be with her as long as I had this secret. It was just easier to be a dick to her to keep her at a distance."

"What the hell did you overhear?" she whispers.

My head shakes quickly. "I've never told anyone about it. It's just too ..."

"Okay," she replies softly, realizing the struggle I'm having telling her. "So, what made her end it now?"

"She found out I hadn't told my partners about Eli yet. Everything spiraled from there." My head falls into my hands.

"Why haven't you told them about Eli?"

"Because I'm a coward. A piece of shit who's worried about his image, about being the best, rather than what's important."

"Let's not do any name-calling. Be kind to yourself. Can I ask something?"

His Redemption

I lift my head and look over at her.

"Are you happy at your job?"

"I ..." My voice trails off as I have a flashback of all of my years at the firm. "I don't know. There's been some good moments. It felt good to make partner. To feel like a success."

"That's not what I asked. Are you *happy* there? Do you enjoy who you work with? Do you love the work that you do?"

"Who likes the people they work with? I mean, it's not exactly what I wanted to do when I was younger, but I'm an adult. Goals change."

She nods her head, seemingly not satisfied with the answer, but she lets it go. "So, Jessie got mad at you for not telling your company yet and ... ended it?"

I scrub a hand down my face. "She continued on about honesty—about this secret I'm holding on to. She decided she couldn't deal with half-truths. She's right. She deserves more. She deserves the world, and I can't give it to her."

"So, she knows there's a secret?" Eva asks with a hitch to her voice.

"Yeah, I told her before we started anything this time around. I was bound and determined to keep my distance, but I wasn't strong enough."

"Do you love her?"

A bitter laugh escapes me. "More than I thought was possible."

"Then you need to tell her," Eva says matter-of-factly. "There's no secret that's worth losing the love of your life. Whatever it is, I'm sure it can be figured out. You're probably just making a bigger deal about it than it actually is because you're so protective."

My eyes meet hers, and I see the confidence she feels with her advice. She thinks she knows what's right. I'm about to show her what I've hidden from the world for far too long.

"Jerry isn't Jessie's biological father."

Her lips part, but no sound follows—only the stunned silence of a truth she never imagined. My legs bounce up and down with nervous energy. I thought saying it out loud one day would feel like a release, but it's still a secret from the one who would truly be affected by it.

"W-w-w-what? How? T-t-t-that can't be ..." Eva stutters through her words. "Where did you hear that?"

"I overheard her parents at your graduation party, fighting in the garage. Jerry wanted to tell Jessie the truth. Meredith was furious. She said it would devastate Jessie and ruin their image if Jessie ever told anyone else."

"I don't know ... that's ... that would destroy Jessie."

"Yeah, it would."

"Her dad is her best friend. He's the only one in her family she feels connected to. If she knew he wasn't actually her ..." Eva doesn't finish her sentence.

We both know how hard this would be for Jessie. I don't know if she would ever truly recover from news like this.

How could I take away the one person in her life who keeps her grounded?

Every part of me wants to tell her, to free us both from this burden. But love isn't just about honesty; it's about sacrifice. If telling her means destroying her, is silence the greater mercy?

"She would be destroyed," I finish for her.

"I'm so sorry you've carried this around for so long. That must've been so hard."

Tears begin to prick the corners of my eyes. "It's been hell."

Her arms wrap around my neck, and I let my head fall onto her shoulder and begin to sob. It's a childlike cry that has no limitations, as everything I've held together for so long flows out. For the first time in our relationship, I let my sister comfort me in a way that a mother comforts her child. A comfort I've never gotten from our own mother.

When we finally pull apart, I notice Eva's tears that stain her cheeks.

"I'm sorry." I wipe my face. "I didn't mean to lose it like that."

"Please don't apologize. I think we both needed a good cry."

I chuckle at the ridiculousness of that. Of course, Eva would savor a cry like it's a treasured moment; meanwhile, I'm slightly humiliated.

"So, what do you think you're going to do?" she asks as the babies start to talk next to each other.

I almost forgot they were there, so consumed with my emotions.

"One problem at a time. I'd like to head into work and just rip off the Band-Aid and tell them."

Her eyes open wide. "Like ... right now?"

I check my watch. "Why not? They're probably all at the office anyway."

"Do you want me to watch Eli while you do it?"

"Can you?"

"Of course. I'm sure they both need to go down for naps soon anyway."

"I packed her bottles. She should take one and nap for a while."

I stand up from the couch, and she stops me as she stands.

"Hey"—she opens her arms and gives me a hug—"I'm proud of you. You're not only an amazing dad, but an incredible person with a huge heart. Never doubt that."

"Thanks," I manage, my voice rough around the edges. "I love you, sis."

"I love you too," she replies lightly.

I head out of her place and walk down the streets of Manhattan with my hands in my jean pockets, feeling a bit lighter. I don't have everything figured out, I don't have the women that I love, but I have at least one action item. Talk to my work.

All I can do is take it day by day, moment by moment.

Just as I thought, I walk into the office and see Stewart and Henry talking in Stewart's large corner office. I'm sure everyone is all hands on deck, gathering information for this new case. Money is a big motivator, and this case could pay out more than anything this firm has seen before.

A wave of nausea hits me as I realize just how sick that makes me. The company has bottomless pockets, and they're essentially writing a blank check to make sure nothing incriminating comes out against them.

I take large, deliberate steps forward and tap my knuckles on the door. Both of their heads shift toward the door.

"Ah, Walker. Good afternoon," Stewart says with a smile.

"Good afternoon," I reply. "Do you two have a moment for a word?"

"Sure," Henry mutters sharply.

I walk farther into the office as my heart begins to race. "I, uh, just wanted to make you two aware of something that has come up in my personal life. I've worked here for a long time, and I figured you would appreciate the transparency."

They remain stoic in their stance as their eyes stay fixated on me.

"Go on," Stewart replies.

"Um, a couple of months ago, I found out I have a daughter. She's three months old. It's been a bit chaotic in my life as I try to balance work and being a father."

Confusion seems to wash over both of their faces.

"Did the mother ask for joint custody?" Henry questions.

"No, sir. The mother decided she wasn't cut out for the role. She is no longer in the picture."

Their eyes dart briefly to one another, silently communicating before returning to me—both looking a shade more unsettled than I'd like.

"Is this why your pitch for the case fell so flat?" Henry's voice is like ice, each word clipped and deliberate.

He bypassed the part about me being a father, about the struggle of juggling such important roles in my life. Straight to this case. Just like my father.

It stings.

"Uh, yes." I scratch the back of my head uncomfortably. "I knew I wasn't going to be able to deliver my best while trying to navigate this new life. My available working hours have definitely shifted."

"Becoming partner at this firm often means a sacrifice is needed. Both Henry and I have families, but we did it the right way. We have wives at home to take care of our children, wives who know what kind of commitment it takes to succeed in this business. That's what a woman is for. How do you suppose you're going to be able to remain properly committed to your work while also taking on the role a woman should have?"

My nostrils flare with fury. I knew these men were cutthroat, old school. But I made excuses all of these years for why I've stuck around.

His Redemption

Suddenly, it feels impossible to ignore the alarms sounding in my head. They do not have my best interest at heart. Not only is what he said incredibly misogynistic, but it lacks any sort of understanding outside of his own small-world views.

It's like everything clicks into place. I'm not happy here. Working here has sucked so much joy from my life. It turned me into one of the men I'd always detested, growing up. No matter how I spin it, I became the very thing I'd claimed to hate.

Bile rises in my throat at the thought. "With all due respect, Stewart, my daughter means more to me than any client or case ever could. For years, I've compromised my own integrity to reach the top at your firm. Today, I've finally seen the light. I want nothing to do with you or this firm who doesn't support the people who helped build it. I will pack up my office. I will have someone get in touch regarding buying me out."

I turn around and walk toward my office with stiff dignity. It doesn't take long for me to pack up my belongings. As I place my awards and framed degrees in a box, it's impossible for me not to notice the lack of pictures of family or friends. No photos of a wife or children fill the space. Just endless hours of school and work, culminating in an epic quitting story that will surely give my friends a laugh at our next encounter.

When everything is packed up, I take a look at my office. My eyes scan what was once a badge of honor in my world. Corner office in Manhattan, hand-carved mahogany desk that cost more than most people's cars.

Anger radiates through me as I think of all the time and energy spent in here, cleaning up others' messes. I gave it everything I had, just for my people to abandon me the moment my life takes a turn and doesn't fit perfectly into their mold.

At least I know that money is not an issue for me. I never cared for a private jet or yacht to blow away my savings. Plus, my shares of the firm will certainly add up to enough to pay off my penthouse in full. Not to mention the investment I made into Sawyer and Dean's tech company a decade ago, which is now a billion-dollar monster that pays incredible dividends.

As I walk back to my sister's place, the weight of my decision plays in my head. I'm sick to my stomach at the thought of spending so many years working for such pricks—more so the idea that I'm one of those pricks.

I can't even talk to the one person who called me on it. She knew I was swimming in a pool of creatures that I'd claimed to despise. I defended my actions for so long, telling myself it was part of growing up, that I didn't even recognize the dark world that surrounded me. A world where everyone is only out for themselves and will stomp on you the moment they smell a hint of weakness.

I need to see her. This isn't fair.

Why does her mother's mistake have to dictate a lifetime of suffering for the two of us? Maybe it doesn't have to. Maybe there's a version of the truth that doesn't destroy us but frees us instead.

I call Eva to see how long she can watch Eli. Roman's out of town, and the guilt of even asking hits hard.

His Redemption

But when I tell her I quit and that I need to see Jessie, she groans and tells me, "Then stop talking about it and go to her already."

She has no idea what I'm about to do—or maybe she does. My pulse won't steady, my thoughts race. I shove down the guilt and walk down the street toward Jessie's place. One way or another, everything is going to change tonight.

Chapter Twenty-Seven

Jessie

I'm deep into binge-watching my comfort show. After crying myself to sleep late last night, I woke up with no motivation to do anything but wallow in self-pity. I'm giving myself the weekend to feel however I want to feel. After tomorrow, I'm pulling myself together and moving forward with no regrets.

For now, comfy pajamas, reruns of my favorite show, and ice cream are my therapy. And crying. Tons of crying. My eyes feel like they're swollen from a crazy case of allergies.

I'm proud of myself though. I reached for my phone so many times last night to call him, but I was able to talk myself out of it each time. Because no matter how bad my heart hurts now, I know it will only be ten times worse if I continue down this path with no signs of him owning up to his mistakes.

At the end of the day, this is his fault. It was his decision to keep some ridiculous secret like we were teenagers.

An aggressive pounding at my door makes me nearly jump off my couch. Its loud and desperate sound has my heart racing, and I wonder if something terrible has happened. I left my phone in my bedroom to keep away the temptation to text him, but now I'm panicking.

I peek through the peephole. All I see is a man with his hands resting on my doorframe, head hung low. But I'd recognize him at any angle.

I can tell by his demeanor that something is wrong.

Oh my God. What if something is wrong with Eli?

The chain of my lock rattles as I slide it free and turn the knob. I tug the heavy door open. His head lifts, and I see pain in his eyes. His hair is disheveled—evidence that he's been pulling at it.

I swallow down my fear and the instant pain of regret that stabs me right in the gut as I realize I walked away from this man. This man who, no matter how hard I try, I will never erase from my heart.

"Jessie," his deep voice states, sounding tired.

My leg rises to take a step closer to him, but I have to remind myself to stay back. "Walker," I whisper. "What's wrong?"

"I quit." He lets out a long breath.

It feels like my brain is short-circuiting. I stare at him wordlessly, trying to understand what he's saying. He can't mean …

"Can I come in?" he asks.

I nod my head and open my door. He walks past me and moves straight to my family room, where he begins to pace back and forth, back to pulling at his hair.

My feet take slow steps toward him, stopping at the edge of the room.

"You quit?" I ask, wondering if I imagined hearing those words.

He stops moving and stands still a couple of feet from me. My arms just want to take him in and comfort him, but I realize I still need to protect myself.

"I told them." His eyes turn down. "You were right. I should've told them about Eli from the beginning."

I watch him intently as he pulls at the back of his neck, clearly struggling to find the right words.

"They ..." His head shakes back and forth. "They weren't thrilled. More concerned about my hours and how I would maintain such a grueling schedule if Eli's mother wasn't present. It was pretty clear to me they had no interest in supporting me through the process. So, I fucking quit."

I'm not exactly surprised. Those firms are ruthless. It's cut or be cut. Nothing about them screams, *We're here to help out our own, no matter what.*

He laughs nervously to himself. "I'll take that look on your face to mean you aren't exactly shocked."

I open my mouth, then close it, trying to find the right thing to say. "I'm sorry. They really should support their employees. It's sad they can't see the amazing thing that you are doing for your daughter."

"Yeah, well, we're all a bunch of assholes. Deep down, I knew that."

I raise my eyebrows. "You're including yourself in that?"

"How can I not? I've been one of them for over a decade. I'm no better than any of them."

His inner distress is not something that I ever wanted to see, even with all the conflicting emotions I feel toward him at the moment. His eyes are glossy, like he's been crying. I wonder if he can see the sadness in mine.

I reach for his hand and take it into mine. "You know you're different from them. You always were and always will be."

He shakes his head. "I don't deserve to get off the hook like that."

"I don't really care what you think you deserve," I bite back. "And I'm proud of you for standing up to them. Do you regret it?"

A muscle quivers in his jaw. "No, I don't. I'm angry. So damn angry. At myself for being a sellout for so long, at them for proving me wrong, at the world for being so unfair."

Yeah, join the club. Anger still simmers in my bones, but the person I should be directing it to is standing in front of me, looking like he just lost a puppy.

His hand drops from mine, and then he takes a step closer and places it on my cheek. My eyes close of their own accord as I let the heat of his skin soothe the loneliness I've felt the last two days.

"You've been crying," he whispers in a troubled voice.

I open my eyes and look up at him and nod my head. There's no use denying it. I'm a wreck without him. It's like all the colors drained out of my world the night I walked away from him, leaving nothing but the quiet ache of what used to be.

A glazed look of despair spreads across his face. "There are so many things I'd do differently in my life ... but I can't find myself to regret them because they brought me Eli. But you ... if only I could have protected you better."

I shudder inwardly. Another cryptic message that does nothing but keep me out in the rain.

"Walker ..."

"I know. I know I owe you the truth. I've owed it to you for years."

My breath catches in my lungs. Is he going to tell me? Will we finally be able to move forward after all? Hope floats in my chest until I see just how tortured he looks.

"It can't be that bad, Walker. Whatever it is, just tell me."

He takes my hand and walks us over to my couch. I follow his lead and take a seat next to him. With my hand still in his, he rubs familiar circles over my skin.

"Before I tell you this, I just need you to know one thing." He takes a deep, shaky breath and releases it.

I start to wonder if this is something bigger than I could possibly imagine. He looks like he might be sick.

He continues, "I've been in love with you before I really think I knew what love was. Before we were both old enough to comprehend the depths of love, I loved you. And now, I'm more in love with you than I thought possible."

The man I'm hopelessly in love with just admitted his love for me. I should be soaring through the sky with a joy that is unmatched. But his admission feels like it's etched with goodbye.

"The night you came to me in my bedroom"—his voice is distant, like he's brought back to that point in time—"I had just overheard your parents arguing in our garage."

My body stiffens. My parents. This is about my family. I can sense that my world is about to crash. I know it's coming. I feel it.

His eyes hold mine. He doesn't want to continue. This is it, and he's beginning to second-guess whether or not he should tell me. But now I *need* to know.

"Just say it," I whisper and clutch his hand.

"They were arguing because your dad wanted to tell you the truth. Something your mom thought was best to keep from you." He takes one final drag of a breath. "Your dad ... he's not your biological father."

My body is assaulted in a raw and primitive moment of grief so powerful that it threatens to destroy me. Dad. My dad. My rock. Not my father. The truth doesn't just break me; it hollows me out from the inside, leaving nothing but the echo of everything I thought I knew.

I should scream, cry, throw something. I should yell at Walker and beg him to take it back. But I'm too shook to do anything but sit in silence while my brain does a flashback of every single moment of my life, wondering what else was a lie. Was anything in my life real?

All the years I've spent thinking my dad was the only one who got me, the only one in my family who I connected with. And he isn't even my father.

Walker leans his head forward. "Jessie"—his voice cracks—"I'm so sorry. I know what your dad means to you. I never wanted to be the one to have to tell you this."

I can't even look at him. I pull my hand from his and rub my arms up and down, trying to soothe the shivers that have taken over.

Walker says my name again, quieter this time. "Jessie ..."

I shake my head, my throat too tight to speak. My mind is swirling with memories—Dad teaching me how to drive, the way he answers the phone for me, his gentle hugs, our jokes. None of it makes sense anymore. Every memory feels like a lie, wrapped in something that used to feel safe.

The air feels too hot. I stand up from the couch and begin to wave my hands in front of my face as I try to regain some kind of composure, but the gesture is futile.

"I need to ..." My voice breaks. I swallow hard, forcing the words out. "I need to go home."

He rises from the couch and stands in front of me. "Jessie, maybe you should wait until ..."

"I have to!" I shout, my tone sharp but trembling underneath. "I can't sit here and pretend I can make any sense of this. I need answers. And I need them now."

He nods. "You shouldn't drive right now. Let me take you."

"No." I wrap my arms around myself, taking a shaky step back. "You've done enough."

That comes out harsher than I meant, but I can't take it back. I'm unraveling, and he's standing there, watching me fall apart with those eyes that say he'd fix it all if he could. But he can't. No one can.

"I know you were just trying to help," I whisper after a long pause. "But I can't talk to you right now. I need to talk to them. I need to hear it from my family."

He opens his mouth to protest again, but I shake my head, cutting him off.

"Please, Walker. Just ... go."

The plea in my voice seems to stop him cold. He takes a step back and nods his head.

I turn away as he walks by me, desperate to hide the tears that begin to fall down my cheeks. It's not until I hear the door click shut that I fall to the ground and let out a gut-wrenching sob. My hand comes up to my chest as I try to breathe through the pain and tears.

It's not until my body lets out every bit of tears it had that I can stand up. I grab my purse on wobbly legs. Every breath feels wrong. All I know is I have to get home and talk to my parents.

Chapter Twenty-Eight

Walker

I pace back and forth in my living room as I try to decide whether I'm going to drive to Jessie's parents' house. I could drop Eli off at Eva's. I could just sit in the street and monitor, wait for her to get back to her car, and then at least I'd know she was okay.

Then I look down at Eli's sleeping face on my chest. I can't wake her up and leave her. I've been gone all day. Besides, this is something I can't fix. It's for Jessie and her parents to work out.

The look on her face when I told her will haunt my dreams for the rest of my life. I just took her world and crushed it into a million pieces. I could see the betrayal that cut deep to the bone, and it wasn't just directed at her parents.

I was also on the receiving end of it. She said it herself. I'd done enough.

She didn't want anything to do with me. Not the person who'd hidden this from her for so long, who then decided to destroy her world by bringing the secret to light.

My phone buzzes on the cushion next to me. It's been going off all day. It appears Eva told Roman what happened with Jessie, who decided to tell the rest of the gang since he's out of town.

They've been texting me all day. I haven't responded.

The silence in my apartment is unbearable. Every tick of the clock grates against my nerves, a reminder that time is moving on without her in it. The air feels heavy, like even it can't stand to sit with me in this mess I've made. My chest aches with the kind of emptiness that no amount of logic can fix, just a hollow echo where her voice should be.

I keep seeing her face when I told her. The shock, the devastation, the way she looked at me like I was a stranger. I've faced down billion-dollar lawsuits without flinching, but this—*this*—has me coming apart at the seams. There's no defense, no argument strong enough to undo what I did.

There's a sudden knock at my door.

"I know you're in there," Colton's voice booms from the hallway. "Open up."

My head falls back on the couch before I stand up and place Eli in her swing. I buckle her in, press the start button, and play the music.

I twist the knob and open the door. Colton stands in front of me in his gym clothes, black shorts and cutoff black shirt.

"What are you doing here?" I ask.

He steps into my place. I close the door and follow him in.

He glances down at Eli in the swing, then turns to me. "I'm here to help."

I suppress the sigh that wants to break free. "There's nothing you can do. Nothing will help. Just ... I just want to be alone."

He shrugs. "Too bad. Go change into some gym clothes. We're going to the gym in the building."

My head juts forward, eyes narrowing. "Um, I can't go to the gym. What about Eli?"

"We're taking her with us. We can put her in the car seat. If she gets upset, I'll hold her. You need to get some of this adrenaline out of you. It'll help you. Trust me."

It sounds like he's talking from experience. Although I still feel like I should protest, the idea of running and lifting appealing, just to rid my body of the adrenaline coursing through my veins. I might actually get some sleep tonight if I do.

"Fine," I groan and stomp into my bedroom.

As I pull my shirt over my head, I hear Colton in the other room. "Do we need to pack a bottle or something for her?"

I throw on my gym shirt, then shorts and walk back out of the room. "No, she just ate. I'll just grab the diaper bag."

After I throw on my tennis shoes and move Eli to the stroller, we head out the door and into the elevator. She is squirming and scrunching, but as the stroller moves, it seems to settle her back down. I don't think she'll last long, nor do I see Colton really holding her, but fuck it. I'd rather not argue with him. I don't have the energy for that.

The gym is empty, not surprising since it's five o'clock on a Saturday. I park the stroller in the center of the room.

Colton pats my back and motions for me to follow him. We each step onto a treadmill.

"Let's do some sprints," he says.

We both hit the number four and walk for a couple of minutes to warm up. He doesn't try to talk, and I wonder if he's figuring out in his head what he wants to say.

"All right, here we go." He interrupts my thoughts. "We'll work our way up. Sprint at eight for sixty seconds. On the count of three. One. Two. Three."

The first round doesn't get my heart rate up that much. He makes us do another four rounds with a minute walk in between. Then he pushes us up to a ten four times before moving to twelve. By the time we're done, I'm pouring sweat and gasping to catch my breath.

I press Stop and lean my hands on the rails of the treadmill in an effort to recover.

"Nice work. How do you feel?" he asks.

"It's ... been ... a minute ... since I've worked out," I respond in breaths as I motion to Eli still sleeping in the middle of the room.

He smiles. "Yeah, you've been a little busy."

I follow him over to the bench, where he starts to rack the barbell with weights.

"Are you settling into fatherhood now?"

I place my hands on my hips. "I still don't know what I'm doing half the time. It feels like I'm on an island with no one to talk to."

"If you ever need advice, I'm only a phone call away."

I turn my head to the side with confusion.

"I'm a doctor. I may be in oncology now, but I made my rounds during residency. I saw a lot of infants."

"Ah." I nod in response. "I honestly never even thought of that. I'll keep it in mind. I'm sure I'll be a basket case when she gets sick for the first time."

"It's scary when it's little ones. They can't tell you what's wrong. You can feel helpless in the beginning."

We take turns doing sets of six presses. My arms and chest scream at me all throughout the process in the best way. It's exactly what I need.

Just as we move over to the dumbbells, Eli starts to whimper softly in the stroller. I turn to move toward her, but he puts his hand up.

"Not so fast. I said I'll hold her. You give me three sets of ten hammer curls."

His directness makes me laugh.

"Yes, sir."

I start to pull each dumbbell up, one arm at a time, inhaling and exhaling with each movement. Colton joins me with Eli propped up on his arm, her back leaning against his chest so she's sitting up and looking out at me.

Her eyes move from left to right, like she's trying to take in the room in front of her. I smile at them through the mirror as I continue.

"You look like a natural," I tell him.

He begins to walk back and forth behind me while I struggle through my reps, pushing through the burn. "Don't think this means I'm a reliable babysitter." He smiles. "My schedule is unpredictable."

"Wouldn't think of it," I reply. "You're not even a reliable friend."

He feigns offense. "Excuse me. I am here, making sure your ass doesn't sink down a hole of self-pity."

"Don't worry about that. There's no self-pity going on here. More like self-hatred."

That makes him stop in his tracks. "Want to talk about it?"

"Not even a little bit."

I finish up my reps, and he tells me to switch to an upright row. I should tell him I can pick my own workout, but it's nice not to have to think for once. So, instead of being stubborn and arguing, I pick another weight and do his suggestion.

He narrows his eyes. "Tough shit. We're talking about it. Have you heard from her?"

"No."

He stops in place. "Have you reached out to her?"

"No."

"Well, aren't you the talker? Why not?"

I huff out my exhale more dramatically than usual, hoping he gets the point. "Because she doesn't want anything to do with me."

"Did she tell you that?"

"Not those exact words."

"Ah, so you're projecting your worst fears to protect yourself."

"Just because she didn't use those exact words doesn't mean everything is fine. You weren't there. You didn't see the betrayal in her eyes. She blames me for keeping it a secret for so long. She told me I'd done enough, then asked me to leave."

He just watches me as I finish out my reps. I place the weights back down on the rack.

"It's a shitty situation you were put in. Roman gave us all the rundown. You did what you thought was right for Jessie. She'll come around and see it. I'm sure she just needs time."

I know better than to get my hopes up, thinking there's a possibility that she might forgive me. I wipe my forehead with the back of my shirt.

"Come on." Colton nods his head. "Let's get back to your place. Get a shower and have a drink. No more talking about Jessie. We'll just hang out."

I don't argue with that. Wallowing in my own sadness was not working like I thought it would. At least Colton can be here to make sure I don't do anything stupid, like drive to Jessie's parents' house and insert myself where I don't belong.

Chapter Twenty-Nine

Jessie

I sit in my car and grip the steering wheel like it's a lifeline. I've been sitting in my parents' driveway for thirty minutes, trying to work up the nerve to go in. I couldn't even cry if I wanted to. I'm pretty sure my body can't produce any more tears.

The entire drive out here was a blur of emotions. My body still trembles with adrenaline. There's no way this can be true. It would change everything I thought I knew about who I am. The one person who gets me, who I modeled myself to be like, is not even who I thought he was.

All this time, it was a lie.

I force myself to move. The car door slams, too loud in the quiet neighborhood, and for a second, I just stand there, my breaths coming too quickly. My legs feel like they belong to someone else as I walk to the door. I press the bell and wait, my heart pounding in my throat.

Footsteps. Then the familiar sound of the lock turning.

My dad—no, not my dad—opens the door in his golf attire, like it's any other Saturday. The faint smell of sunscreen and aftershave hits me, and I wonder if he and Mom spent the day at the club, laughing, pretending everything was normal.

The sight of him twists my stomach. The man who raised me. The man who tucked me in at night and told me monsters weren't real.

"Jessie? You okay, sweetheart?"

I swallow hard, my voice catching before I can stop it. "No. Not even close."

I step inside, not willing to kick off my shoes, despite knowing my mother would prefer it. I need the possibility of a fast escape.

"What's wrong? Is it Walker?" he asks in his soothing voice.

I laugh bitterly. "I guess you can say that's part of it. Is Mother here? I need to speak with both of you."

He appears slightly on edge. "Sure, sweetie. Why don't you go make yourself comfortable in the family room? I'll go get her."

I wait for what feels like an eternity before they both join me. They sit on the couch directly across from me.

"Hello, dear. This is quite a surprise," Mother says cautiously.

I fold my hands on my lap, cross my legs, then uncross them. I can't stay still. My hands move to my hair and tuck it behind my ears several times.

"I'm sure it is," I reply coldly.

They both sit in silence and watch me fidget in my seat. Dad's eyes look me up and down, then close. He knows I know. I see the defeat in his posture.

"I know," I blurt, aware of the tremor in my voice.

Mother is clueless. Her puzzled look quickly becomes one of irritation as she waits for me to continue.

"How did you find out?" he asks.

His quiet admission tears at my insides.

"So, it's true?"

Mother's eyes squint as she looks between us. "Find out what? What on earth is going on?"

Dad sighs. "Meredith, she knows."

Her eyes blaze with sudden shock. She corrects her posture, like she's on the defense now, then turns her head back to me. "How could you possibly …" She trails off.

I imagine this is a secret that only the two of them know. She never thought it would see the light of day.

"Walker overheard you two arguing at my graduation party." My eyes meet Dad's as tears begin to fall. "You're really not my dad?"

He makes a choked sound, and then his face falls into his hands. I've never seen him cry before. It just makes me cry harder, makes the weight on my chest feel heavier.

"It's not what you think …" Mother starts, but Dad pulls his head up and cranes his neck.

"Enough, Meredith. No more excuses. We lied to her. Don't try to defend it."

"I'm not going to sit here and look like the devil while you cry and play victim. That's not fair to me. If the truth is out, I get to speak."

"What are you two talking about?" I wipe my cheeks.

Mother takes a deep breath. "We thought it was for the best. I promise it wasn't meant to deceive you. I was doing what I thought was right for you—what was right for our family."

"How is lying to me what's best for me?"

She looks over at my dad, who is slumped on the couch. "After Ethan was born, your father and I struggled in our marriage. He was working a lot. I was angry. Lonely. When he approached me and asked for a separation, I couldn't bear the idea. I needed a break. Some friends took me on a trip to clear my head. I ended up having too much to drink and slept with someone."

I go still—too still. It's as if my body has forgotten how to move, how to breathe.

"By the time I found out, he was long gone, and your father and I had discussed the idea of trying again. We didn't want you to feel left out, like Ethan had two parents and you didn't fit in." Her armor begins to crack as thick tears begin to stream down her face. "I promise I never made the decision lightly."

"All these years, you made the decision to protect me?"

She must hear the doubt in my voice. I watch her wipe away her tears, and then she looks up at the ceiling as she tries to regain control. "Oh, I don't know. I suppose years down the line, I held some unresolved resentment about the entire situation. I worried a lot about if the truth got out. Would you hate me? Hate us? Would you not look at him as your father anymore? Then maybe some more selfish concerns. I worried about what others would think about us."

For a moment, I can't even hear her. The room feels too small, like the air's been sucked out of it. My pulse is pounding so loud that it drowns everything else out.

Protect me? That's what she's calling this?

My laugh cracks on the way out, sharp and humorless. "You didn't protect me. You built my entire life around a lie and expected me to thank you for it." My voice trembles, but I don't stop. "You didn't want me to feel left out? What about now? Because that's exactly what I am—on the outside of a family that was never really mine."

Dad's head jerks up, his eyes red-rimmed and desperate. "Jessie, don't say that. You are mine. You'll always be mine."

"Am I?" I whisper, my throat raw. "Or did you just pretend so it would be easier?"

He stands, and I can see the pain written all over his face. "No. I raised you. I loved you. That's never been pretend."

But it's too late. The words can't reach me.

I stand up and put my hands up in defense. "Then you should've trusted me to love you anyway."

With that, I run to the front door like I'm suffocating and the only thing that will save me is the air outside. The moment I take my first inhale of the hot, muggy summer air, my hands grip my knees, and I cry out loud as the pain sears through me.

Before they can chase me, I sprint to my car and get inside, then hit the gas. The entire drive home, I'm in a daze as I try to navigate my feelings. Seeing them cry, their pain—it made me so angry. They are not the victims in this; I am.

The moment I get back to my place, I know I'm too wired to go to sleep. I park my car and decide to walk along the streets alone. It's not the smartest thing in the world, but I also know the streets of the city like the back of my hand. I stay on the busy ones. It's Saturday night, so I don't have to worry about them being busy at eleven, they always are.

I try to focus on just my steps instead of the turmoil inside of me. Everyone walking down the street next to me acts as if life is full of the most amazing possibilities. I used to feel like that.

Now I know the truth—life is full of lies.

Then I look up and realize I'm standing in front of his building. I don't even think twice before I open the door and run to the elevator. I know the code to bring it up to the penthouse.

I know it's late. I'm sure he's sleeping. But I need him. I need him more than I've ever needed anyone.

Chapter Thirty

Walker

So much for thinking the workout would relieve enough tension to give me a good night's sleep. I lie awake on the couch as I click through the channels, looking for something—anything—that might distract me from the hollowness I feel inside.

Then it happens. I hear a faint knock at my door. At first, I think I'm hearing things, and then it comes again. It's soft, but I know I'm not hearing things.

I peek through the peephole, and my heart nearly sinks to my stomach. I fumble with the locks and pull the door open. She's standing in front of me, hugging herself, her eyes telling me how lost and alone she feels.

"Jessie." My greeting is a husky whisper.

She bites her bottom lip as tears spill over, her whole body trembling. I don't think; I just move. My arms wrap around her, pulling her in until there's no space left between us. She collapses against me, her fingers clutching my shirt like she's afraid I'll disappear. When her head drops to my chest, a raw, broken sob tears free—the kind that sounds like it's been buried for years.

I rub soothing circles on her back. "It's okay. I'm right here," I whisper, though we both know that's not true.

Nothing about this situation is okay. It's messy; it's filled with years of lies and deceit. But all I know to do is comfort her the best way I know how.

When it feels like her cries have slowed, I walk us into my place and close the door. "Come on. Let's go sit down."

With her hand in mine, I lead her over to the couch. We both take a seat, and I pull her into my arms. She rests her head against me once again.

"Do you want to talk about it?" I ask gently.

Her hand comes up to my chest. My first instinct is to place mine over it, to keep her there. I don't know if it's to comfort her or myself.

She doesn't answer my question, and I don't push. The silence stretches, but it's not the kind that feels heavy; it's the kind that feels like breathing after being underwater too long.

After a while, I brush a strand of hair from her face, my fingers lingering against her skin longer than they should.

"You should get some sleep," I murmur.

Her eyes lift to mine, red-rimmed and tired. "Can I stay here?"

I nod, my throat too tight to speak.

I grab her a blanket and a pillow, but when she settles on the couch, I hesitate before turning away.

"Jessie," I start, but I have no idea what comes next. What apology could fix what she's been through? What promise could she even believe right now? So, I just say the truth. "I'm glad you came."

She doesn't look up, but I catch the faintest nod before her eyes flutter closed.

And I stand here, watching her breathe. I know I should walk away, but instead, I sit on the floor beside her, close enough that if she reaches out in her sleep, I'll be there. Even if I don't know what that means anymore.

* * *

"Morning," a soft, familiar voice says in the distance.

I turn over and realize my back is killing me. Why am I so cold? Why the hell is this bed so damn hard?

I open my eyes, and it takes a couple of blinks for me to figure out that I'm on the floor. Then it dawns on me. Jessie. I slept next to her.

After tossing and turning for hours in pain, I must've fallen asleep in the early hours of the morning.

I look up and see Jessie with a cup of coffee in one hand and Eli in the other. All the pain in the world means nothing when I see the two people I love the most with each other.

"Morning," I reply in my rough and sleepy voice.

She laughs lightly. "Why do I feel like it wasn't such a great night of sleep for you?"

I groan, then wipe my face with my hands. "I'm getting old. This shouldn't hurt so much."

I turn to the side and slowly lift myself off the ground, then scoot to the couch as I try to work out the kinks in my back and shoulders.

"You didn't have to sleep on the ground."

Eli starts babbling in her arms, which makes both of us look at her.

"I missed her," Jessie says as she peers down at my daughter.

When her eyes meet mine, I respond, "We both missed you."

She closes her eyes and takes a deep breath. "I'm ready to talk. Whenever you are."

"Whatever you need, Jessie, I'm here. Let me just go to the bathroom."

I move quickly across the room, afraid that if I stop, she might change her mind. Still, part of me slows at the last second, wanting to memorize this—the sound of her voice, the softness in her eyes, the fragile thread of hope that maybe, just maybe, this isn't the end of us.

When I'm back, she is sitting at the kitchen table with her coffee. Eli is in her bouncy seat on the floor next to her. A fresh cup of coffee sits in the empty chair beside her.

I take a seat, her presence enough to soothe the fear in me

just a bit. After I take a sip, I place the mug down and shift in my seat so I'm facing her.

"You look better this morning," I tell her.

She smiles. "Does that mean I looked like shit last night?"

"No," I reply quickly. "I mean ... you look rested."

"I'm kidding," she says with a trace of laughter. "I did sleep well. Thank you. I do feel better this morning."

"Good," I reply carefully.

I don't want to rush her even though I'm dying to ask her what this means. Her showing up here, spending the night, snuggling in my arms.

"I went to see my parents yesterday. Or my mom and ..." she starts, then trails off for a moment. "I don't even know what to call him."

A stab of guilt hits me. "Jessie, I'm so sorry."

She holds up a hand. "I spent a lot of time thinking about all of this on my drive. I should have never gotten so angry at you. It wasn't fair."

"Of course you should have. You have every right to feel however you want about all of this."

She shakes her head. "No. I get it. You were put in the middle of my parents' mistake. I don't know what I would have done if I had been faced with that kind of decision for all those years."

"Probably the right thing. You're a much better person than I am. How did it go with your parents?"

Her shoulders tense. "Awful. They confirmed it." She looks away from me and blinks rapidly. "I'm sorry." She laughs and fans her face. "I keep crying."

"I don't mind tears. I've done my fair share of crying in the last couple of days."

Her face falls. "You've cried?"

I pull at my neck, slightly embarrassed. I know men are supposed to be the tough ones who don't cry, and admitting that to her isn't exactly very manly, but I can't help it.

"I did. When you lose the woman you love, you realize strength doesn't mean a damn thing anymore."

Her eyes soften toward me, but I don't want to push aside what matters.

"How are you doing with it all?"

"Oh God. I don't know. They told me the story. But even if I could find a way to understand the situation, it doesn't make it any easier."

She tells me everything that was said. About her dad wanting to leave, her mother feeling broken and needing an escape. All of it.

"It's not exactly what I expected," she admits as she stares down at her coffee. "I had my mother pegged as the reason it all happened. Now ... I don't know. I mean, I get it. You have a newborn baby, and your husband is never there. Then he wants to separate. That could break anybody. For the first time, I looked at her differently. Through all the pain and anger I felt for both of them, I felt a glimmer of understanding."

I'm shocked. That's not how I saw any of it going down either. "It just goes to show that everyone's carrying something—a past, a reason they turn bitter toward the world. It doesn't excuse what they do, but it explains it. We all have our scars, and maybe some of us learn how to grow through them faster than others. But for some people ... it just takes longer to find their way out."

She looks up at me, fear written all over her face. "But what if I can never find a way to forgive them? Do I just lose both of them?"

I grab her hand and hold it on the table right in between us. "You'll find a way through the pain and anger. I know you will. You're the strongest person I know. And I know your parents; they'll be right there, waiting for you when you're ready. You take all the time that you need."

"You really think so?"

I give her hand a squeeze. "I know so."

"Thank you for listening and for just ... being here for me."

My gaze finds hers, steady and certain. "I wouldn't be anywhere else." I think for a second before I continue, "What would help right now? Anything. Tell me."

She sighs as she seems to ponder it before she responds, "People. I just need to be around people. Noise. Distraction."

"Done," I reply. I let go of her hand and grab my phone.

"What are you doing?" she asks warily.

"I'm creating noise and distraction for you," I say with a wink.

Chapter Thirty-One

Jessie

This man is insane. I don't know how he pulled this off, but here we are, in a suite at the Yankees game with ... everyone. Eva, Roman, Colton, Sawyer, Lincoln, Kylie, Dean and all of the babies.

Kylie, Eva, and I are sitting on the carpet inside the suite as we play with the babies, who are sprawled across a large blanket. Kylie's brother, Ben, is outside of the suite in the seats with the guys. He is only fourteen years old, but a wise kid for his age. He and Kylie have been through so much together, and it's so nice to see such a happy ending for both of them.

I look down at Eli, who's looking over at her cousin, Addie. She begins to babble and blow bubbles at her, and I can't help but smile with affection at them together.

"Hey," Eva says, pulling my attention. "How are you doing?"

"I'm hanging in there. Still a bit in shock, I guess."

Kylie and Eva both nod their heads in understanding.

"I can't imagine," Kylie replies. "I'm so sorry you're going through this. Just know we're here for you whenever you need us."

"Thanks." I smile.

"You'll get through this," Eva says matter-of-factly. "It's going to hurt for a while, but one day, the ache won't feel so sharp. Sometimes, the things that break us open are the same ones that let the light in."

We both look over at Walker, who's laughing at something one of the guys must've said. He still manages to get my blood pumping without doing anything but be himself.

"He was a wreck when he came to me the other day," Eva confesses.

"Was he?" I ask, my heart beginning to race.

She meets my stare. "Like I've never seen him before. I've never seen him cry. It broke my heart. He's been tortured with this for years. He never wanted to hurt you."

"I wanted to blame him at first. To label him as someone who would lie and hurt me. But he didn't ask for any of this. He just ... got caught in the fallout." My throat tightens, and I force a shaky breath. "He's made mistakes, sure. But this—what happened—it wasn't his to fix."

"Does that mean you two ..." Eva starts, the hope in her voice evident.

I answer honestly, "I'm not in the headspace right now to do anything but heal. It'll take time. I love him. I do. I always will. I just hope he'll be patient with me as I try to process everything."

Kylie smiles. "I get the feeling that man will do anything for you."

I wrap that hope around my heart for comfort—something I desperately need right now. I just need to take life day by day.

Eli begins to fuss, and I take that as her cue to be fed and take a nap. I know Walker will get mad since he's always making sure I'm not helping out of obligation, but I love my time with Eli.

I get her bottle ready and sit in a chair in the corner where we have her travel crib set up. As I feed her, my heart fills with so much love that it feels like it might burst. I love her so much, and I love her father.

Is this what my dad feels for me, even if I'm not really his?

I can't focus on that right now. I peer down at the sweetheart in my arms. Something tells me this isn't the end for the three of us. That there's more in store for me and Walker.

I set Eli's empty bottle aside and wipe away a stray droplet from her chin before laying her gently in the crib. She sighs, content, and my chest squeezes with love so fierce that it's almost painful.

The noise from the stadium drifts in the suite's open door—cheers, the crack of a bat, laughter. Life moving on.

I stand, suddenly needing air. Maybe a drink. Maybe … him.

When I step outside of the room, the afternoon sun hits my face, warm and grounding. The guys are all lined up along the front row of the suite, beers in hand, teasing each other over whose losing money on a bet. Walker's at the end, his cap pulled low, a quiet smile curving his mouth as he listens.

For a second, I just watch him. The man who's carried so much guilt but who still managed to show up for me, for Eli. Then I make my way over, heart pounding in a steady, uncertain rhythm.

He looks over at me as I stand beside him, surprise flicking across his face before it softens into something I can't quite name.

"Hey," I say, reaching for one of the drinks on the ledge.

He wraps an arm around my shoulders. "Hey, you. I was just about to come in and check on Eli. Does Eva have her?"

"No." I take a sip of the beer. "I fed her. She's sleeping in her crib."

"Jessie, you didn't have to—" he starts, but I cut him off.

"What did I tell you about this shit, Walker?"

He chuckles and adjusts his hat with his other hand. "Right. Sorry. My bad."

"Thanks for doing this." I look up at his dark, watchful eyes. "You didn't have to go all out for me."

"I didn't do it to go all out. I did it because seeing you smile again ... that's all I want. I'd rent out the whole damn stadium if it meant you'd look at me like this."

My heart stutters, and I swallow past the lump in my throat. The noise of the crowd fades until it's just his voice and the steady thrum of my pulse in my ears.

"Walker," I whisper, shaking my head, "you can't say things like that to me. I'm still trying to find my footing, and if you keep talking like that ... I'll forget I'm supposed to need time."

Something shifts in his expression—soft, sad, determined.

He leans forward, voice barely carrying above the hum of the stadium. "Then take all the time you need, Jess. I'll wait. A lifetime, eternity—whatever it takes. I'm not going anywhere."

He doesn't realize how much I needed to hear that. Just to know I don't have to rush through this cloud of emotions, and yet I won't lose him in the process.

The crowd roars, and we both turn our attention to the game. Eva and Kylie come out after they have the kids asleep and each find their man in the line. Walker doesn't leave my side the rest of the game, but he keeps it light.

We all laugh. We eat. We cheer.

It's everything I needed. And he did it all for me.

When the game ends, we say our goodbyes. Walker clicks Eli's car seat into place, and I lift myself up into the front seat of his SUV.

I begin to wonder if he's going to drop me off at my place. It sounds awful, but I don't want to be alone right now. Eventually, I know I need to face the noise in my head. I'm just not ready.

His Redemption

He grabs my hand that's resting on his center console. "You want to come over for dinner?"

I let out the breath I didn't know I had been holding. "I'd love to. Thank you."

I'm so grateful that he's willing to be patient with me—to give me time to untangle everything inside of me. He really is an incredible man. After years of carrying this secret, trying to protect me, taking the blame I threw at him, and letting me push him away when I didn't understand ... he still showed up. He always does. And now, he's here again—arms open, waiting for when I'm ready.

When we get back to his place, he turns music on in the background and pours us each a glass of wine. We sit out on his terrace while Eli takes her nap in the stroller, our food on its way.

For the first time in what feels like forever, the silence between us isn't heavy. It's easy. Comfortable. The kind that says everything words can't.

I glance over at him—this man who's carried so much guilt, who tried so hard to do right by everyone, even when it cost him. I used to see his distance as indifference. Now, I see it for what it was. Love. Protection. The kind of love that doesn't beg to be seen, but stands steady when the world falls apart.

He catches me looking and gives me that small, knowing smile that still manages to undo me. And in that moment, I know. We'll be okay. It'll take time—healing always does—but we'll get there.

Because it was never about perfection. It was about grace. About second chances. About redemption.

His redemption.

Our beginning.

THE END

Epilogue

Walker

Six Months Later

I used to think that happiness lie inside of one's own accomplishments. Each time I checked one off of my list, I waited for something inside of me to change.

Maybe now I'll feel something... anything.

But to no avail, a darkness continued to live inside of me. Now, as I stand at the counter and wait for my second cup of coffee, I realize happiness is a string of moments in your life.

Like now, as I look over at Jessie sitting next to Eli's highchair making funny faces at her. Eli smiles brightly like Jessie hung the moon, her four teeth showing just how big she is getting. Eli grabs another piece of her pancake from her tray and shovels it into her mouth.

"Do you like my pancakes?" Jessie asks in a goofy voice. "You're lucky I still got up early to make those for you after all the crying last night."

Eli chuckles like she knows exactly what she did to us last night, which just makes Jessie smile and tickle her under her chin.

I know now that this is what it means to be happy. To feel the love surrounding you in such a small, mundane moment, and yet knowing it's one you'll never forget.

These passed six months have had it's challenges. I didn't want to rush Jessie into anything. I was there to support her in whatever she needed. Through her many nights of tears and anger. Then to the conversations with her parents that followed. Many conversations.

There's still a deep wound there, one that I'm not sure will ever truly heal. But she knows they love her, even if they have made mistakes along the way.

Losing that unconditional trust in her dad was hard. She asked me one night what I thought about the fact that he still wants her to call him dad. I told her she needs to do what she is comfortable with, but that I can tell how much he loves her. I can see that he looks at her like his own just as much as he does her brother.

It's all still a work in progress, but everyone is taking steps to heal. Her parents are going to therapy together. Her mother has even reached out and apologized for all her years of putting herself first. It's odd how sometimes what you think will destroy you actually opens doors you thought were locked forever.

As for us. It happened naturally. Nights spent hanging out together. Laughing. Talking. Hanging out with Eli. A stolen kiss in the kitchen one night when she got up for a glass of water.

It progressed from there. Sex in the shower one night after Eli went to bed. Sex on the couch. In the kitchen. On the table. The floor.

Tons and tons of sex. And it's not just me initiating it. Jessie has quite the appetite when it comes to me, and I'm loving every second of it.

What started as comfort, a way to remind her she wasn't alone when her world tilted off its axis, gradually turned into more. Every kiss, every night tangled up together, was her grounding. I could feel it—the way her breathing steadied under my hands, the way she held on like I was the only solid thing left.

And God, I loved her. I'd known that long before she could even imagine. But love means patience. So I didn't push. I let her come to me.

At her pace. On her terms.

Slowly, the lines blurred. She stayed over more nights than she didn't. Her laughter filled the rooms before the sun did. Her shoes lined up next to mine at the door.

One night, she climbed into bed wearing my shirt—hair damp, face soft—and looked at me like she was finally seeing a future instead of a disaster waiting to happen. She finally believed me when I told her she was my everything.

"Walker?" she whispered.

"Yeah, baby?"

Her voice shook, but her eyes remained on mine. "I want this. You. Us. Not just the nights. All of it."

I swear my heart almost broke from relief. I asked her to move in with me... and the rest is history.

I have the ring. I've had it for months. I'm just waiting for the right time. How do I give the perfect woman the perfect proposal? Nothing feels good enough.

I grab my fresh cup and walk back to the table. I bend down and find Jessie's lips, pressing mine to them. She pulls back and smiles softly at me.

"How are you feeling this morning birthday boy?" she asks.

I tuck a piece of hair behind her ear. "I'm perfect."

It's the truth. What can be better than spending my birthday with my two favorite people?

Her eyebrows turn up. "Really? Even with all the screaming and crying last night?"

That pulls a laugh from me. "Nothing can bother me when I have all I've ever wanted."

"Dido, babe." She looks over at a smiling Eli. "I'm just glad she doesn't seem to be in pain right now. Teething sucks."

"Tell me about it," I reply as I walk around the table to take a seat. "Colton said her low grade fever is normal for teething. Hopefully the medicine is helping with some of the pain."

"How annoyed do you think Colton is with our constant questions at ridiculous hours of the night?"

I take a sip of the coffee and lean back in my chair. "He doesn't mind. I promise. Most of the time he's awake and on shift at the hospital anyways."

His Redemption

She drums her fingers on the table and looks off into the distance. I know that look.

"What's on your mind?" I lean in and tap my finger down on the table eyeing her own restless fingers.

She looks down at her hand and flattens it. "Do you think Colton has been acting weird lately?"

Her words catch me off guard. "What makes you say that?"

It's not that I disagree, I'm just surprised. I shouldn't be. Jessie is a very observant and caring person.

"It's just little things. I'll catch him staring off into space or clenching his fists when he checks his phone like something made him angry. He doesn't talk or smile as much."

"I have noticed. I don't know what's going on."

Her forehead creases. "Welll, have you asked him?"

"Why would I do that? I don't want to make him uncomfortable."

She rolls her eyes—something that hasn't stopped since we've started dating. I kind of love that I still annoy her sometimes. It's fun to watch her attitude come out. She likes to test me, see how far she can push it before I snap. I always take it out on her in the bedroom—the one place she allows me to dominate.

"Because he's your friend and you care about him. It's not always easy telling someone you need help. Maybe he's waiting for someone to take interest. To show they care enough to ask."

Huh, I never thought about it like that. I've never wanted to intrude if someone wasn't ready to tell me something. But we can be our own worst enemy at times and hold in our suffering. I did it for a decade until life forced me to confront what I was running away from.

Now, I'm living a life better than I could have even dreamed.

"Alright. Maybe I'll ask him next time I see him."

She smiles and nods her head like she's satisfied with my response.

Jessie

He has no idea what's in store for him. I'll never forget when we were sitting at the restaurant telling each other something no one else knew about the other and he told me he forgot his own birthday three years in a row. My heart broke for him. Everybody deserves to be celebrated on their birthday.

So, today is going to be filled with surprises. Starting right now since I just got Eli down for her nap. I close the door to her bedroom and tiptoe away just to make sure I don't make any sudden noises that wake her.

I find my man standing in front of the sink washing dishes. His hair is still messy from bed. Chest bare and grey sweatpants hanging low on his waist. He knows how to make the most mundane tasks look like a photoshoot for sexiest man of the year.

I sneak up behind him, wrap my arms through his, and glide my hands along his chest. I drag my lips along his spine. His back stiffens and his head peeks over his shoulder.

He moans. "What's going on here?"

"Shut off the sink and turn around," I whisper in my most seductive voice.

Without any questions asked, he obeys. His hands reach for my cheeks but I back away while I shake my head. He squints with confusion at the rejection.

Then I fall to my knees in front of him as I bite my bottom lip in an effort to hide my smirk. "If you kiss me, I'll get distracted," I tell him.

His throat bobs as he swallows. "Distracted from what?"

I reach for the waistband of his sweatpants and pull them down until his already hardened cock pops out. "From giving you a little birthday surprise."

He raises his eyebrows. Before he can respond I wrap my fingers around the base of his cock and lick the tip. He loves when I tease him in the beginning. I swirl my tongue around a couple of times making sure I give him a show.

His face looks almost pained like watching is just as torturous as it is satisfying. I wrap my lips around his tip and suck on it like it's a sucker, just focusing on his head while moving my hand up and down his shaft.

"Fuck, baby," he growls, his hands turning white as they clutch the counter. "This is the best damn birthday surprise I've ever gotten."

I smile and move his dick a little higher so I can drag my tongue from his balls all the way up to the top. "Just wait until tonight."

"What's tonight?" he asks on a sharp exhale.

"Tonight you get to sink your cock into my ass like you've always wanted," I reply then take his dick as far as it can go until I gag.

"Holy shiiiiit," he exclaims as his head falls back in ecstasy. "I fucking love my birthday."

Pride fills my chest. This is exactly what I want. For him to feel special. I'm not even close to being done with the surprises, but I'm glad he is already feeling loved today.

I focus on the current task at hand. Bobbing my head up and down, gagging each time I take him deep. My hand continues to stoke the part of his cock that I can't fit into my mouth. I can feel his dick twitch which tells me he is about to come.

I pull my head back and open my mouth then start to stroke his dick until white ropes of cum hit my tongue. He cusses and groans the entire way through until his entire body goes limp against the counter.

I swallow what I can and wipe the remaining cum that hit my chin and lick my finger.

His breathes still come rapidly even though his body seems completely satiated. "Baby, get up here now."

I stand up from my knees. He wraps his arms around me and presses his lips to my mine in a searing kiss that has my heart rate accelerating within seconds.

"Get. On. The. Counter," he demands in between kisses.

I shake my head. "That was for you. It's your birthday. You don't need to return the favor."

He slaps my ass as a growl escapes from his lips. "That was an order."

"But...I don't need you to," I start to reply.

Next thing I know I'm being grabbed at my hips and flung in the air until I'm sitting on top of the counter. Walker grabs me under my thighs and pulls me forward. I lean back on my elbows so I don't fall.

"This is for me. Not for you. I want to taste your pussy. Consider it an extension of my birthday present."

His mouth finds my clit and immediately starts sucking on it likes it's a piece of candy. I should protest, but I know my attempt would be futile. If this is what he want, I'm at his mercy.

We spend the afternoon at a playground with Eli after lunch at one of his favorite spots. Eli sits on a blanket eating a snack while we lean back on ours hands enjoying the sunshine. It's a beautiful sixty degrees on this March afternoon, a wonderful treat after the dreary winter weather.

So, he says as I see his head turn towards me from the corner of my eye. I look over at him.

"I've been thinking," he says slowly—cautiously.

My interest is piqued. "Yes?"

"I think I know where I want to take my career. It just

occurred to me the other day and it's been stuck in my mind ever since. It just feels... right."

I push off my hands and sit up straight. This is huge. I know it's been a struggle for him to take the time. He's loved his time with Eli, but he can't stay home forever. We've talked a bit about how he does love law. It's not something that he wants to turn his back on.

"That's amazing, babe." I reach out and give his arm a squeeze. "What is it?"

His eyes hold mine. "I want to open up a firm... with you."

For a beat, all the air seems to disappear from the room. My heart thunders against my ribs because this—this is the dream I whispered to the stars when I was a teen and believed we could change the world.

"A firm?" I manage, barely louder than a whisper. "Walker, are you serious?"

He nods once, his expression steady but vulnerable. "We always said we'd fight for the people who get overlooked. Kids in the system, families who can't afford representation, victims who need someone in their corner." His fingers lace with mine. "I want to build that. With you. Not somebody. Not in five years. Now."

Emotion surges up, burning hot behind my eyes. "You mean... like lawyers for good?" I say our phrase like it's a sacred truth we buried but never forgot.

A slow smile spreads across his face—soft and certain. "Exactly like that."

I let out a breath that feels like hope. "Walker, that's—" I choke out a laugh, swiping at my eyes. "That's everything I've ever wanted."

He pulls me closer until his forehead rests against mine. "It's all I've ever wanted too. I want to fight the bad in this world together—with you by my side."

"Yes," I breathe, no hesitation.

He grins, all boyish charm and unwavering determination, and kisses me like he can already see the sign on the door. "Harlow and Turner," I say out loud.

His smiles fades instantly. I don't know what I said wrong. Maybe he doesn't like the name. I'm open to other options. I open my mouth to correct myself but he places his finger on my lips to stop me.

"I was thinking," he says softly as he reaches into his pocket. "Something more like Harlow and Harlow. If you'd take my name."

He opens a box and the most gorgeous, twinkly diamond ring shines brightly back at me. My entire body feels like it's been plugged into a live wire— buzzing, trembling, overflowing all at once.

"Jessie," he says, voice low but steady, like he's pouring every ounce of love he has into my name. "From the moment I met you, I felt a shift in my life. I've never been much of a believer in fate, but you've always felt like my destiny. Life is brighter with you in it. I want to spend the rest of my days making sure you know just how loved you are. How wanted you are. Every single minute."

My heart clenches so tightly it almost hurts.

He swallows, nerves flickering across his features even though his voice stays steady. "Jessie Turner... will you do me the honor of becoming my wife? My partner in life, law, in everything?"

A broken sound escapes me— half laugh, half sob. How could I ever say anything but yes to the man I've loved and longed for through every messy, unsteady part of myself?

"Yes," I whisper, my voice shaking. "Of course, yes!"

His grin is instant— bright enough to rival the diamond he slides onto my finger with careful hands. My breath catches as the ring settles into place, like it's always belonged there. Like *I've* always belonged with him.

Walker places his hand behind my neck and bring me in for a kiss that knocks the air from my lungs. I kiss him back with everything that I have then bury my face into his neck laughing as tears continue to fall.

He pulls my face up and cups my cheeks. "I can't wait to build our future," he murmurs softly.

I press my hand to his chest, right over his racing heart. "We already are."

His smile softens as he rests his forehead against mine, and in that moment I swear I can see our entire future unfolding — a little office with our name on the door, Eli running around the waiting room with a juice box, a life full of purpose and love and second chances.

"Harlow and Harlow," he says again voice full of awe.

"Looks like we're officially a team," I breathe.

He takes the ring out of the box and glides it up my finger into place. It fits perfectly. I hold my hand in the air and we both study it in awe.

Then my phone goes off and pulls us from our little bubble of joy. It's a message from Eva.

> Eva: We're all set over here.

Oh, god. I laugh to myself.

"What's so funny?" he asks.

I look over at him. "I planned this whole thing for your birthday."

He forehead scrunches. "Birthday thing? You already did enough for my birthday. And now..." he holds my hand up again. "You've given me the best present I could've ever asked for."

"No, it's a big thing. Like... all of your friends and family. I wanted to get everyone together in one place to show you that you are loved. And worthy of celebrating on your special day."

Emotion tightens his features. He presses a soft kiss to my forehead. "Thank you," he whispers.

I squeeze his hand and nod toward the picnic blanket. "Come on, birthday boy. We should probably pack up before Eli decides to share her applesauce with the ants again."

Walker laughs— the kind that makes my chest feel weightless— and together we gather our things. He folds the blanket while I scoop up Eli who claps her little hands together like she's cheering us on.

The sun hangs lower now, painting everything in gold. Walker locks up the stroller and comes to stand beside us, slipping an arm around my waist as we start walking back toward the street.

I look down at my ring glinting on my finger, then up at the man who put it there. He's watching me already, eyes soft and sure.

"It feels like I was the one who got the birthday present today," I admit as we both take in the ring resting on my finger.

He squeezes my side. "Trust me, baby. You saying yes is my present. Spending my life with you will forever be the best gift life can give me."

Then we both look at Eli and smile. Well, maybe the second best gift life has ever given because Eli is definitely number one.

As we step off of the grass and onto the sidewalk my heart feels like it's fluttering out of my chest.

We're not just surviving.

We're not just dreaming.

We're finally living.

And we're doing it side by side.

Colton's Story

Colton's story is next! Don't miss this billionaire, single mom, forbidden romance. His Confession is coming March, 2026!

Pre-order here!

Follow Me on Social Media

To have access to my bonus scenes– visit my website and subscribe to my newsletter. You will be directed to a special page on my website with ALL bonus scenes.

www.nicolebakerauthor.com

Follow me for exclusive news on releases, signings, and giveaways.

Facebook@nicolebakerauthor

Instagram @nicolebaker_author

TikTok @authornicolebaker

Also by Nicole Baker

THE BRADY SERIES

Enough

Impossible

Irresistible

Persuade

Protected

THE GIANNELLI SERIES-LOVE IN LITTLE ITALY

Where You Belong

Where We Met

Where We Fall

ISLE OF HOPE SERIES

The Last Time

The First Time

The Only Time

EMPIRE STATE OF LOVE

His Temptation

His Obsession

His Redemption

Printed in Dunstable, United Kingdom